Lay It Down

Lock Down Publications
Presents
Lay It Down
A Novel by *Jamaica*

Lock Down Publications
P.O. Box 1482
Pine Lake, Ga 30072-1482

Visit our website at www.lockdownpublications.com

Copyright 2015 by Lay It Down by Jamaica

First Edition December 2015
Printed in the United States of America
This is a work of fiction. Names, characters, places, and incidents either are products of the author's imagination or are used fictitiously. Any similarity to actual events or locales or persons, living or dead, is entirely coincidental.

Lock Down Publications
Like our page on Facebook: Lock Down Publications @www.facebook.com/lockdownpublications.ldp
Cover design and layout by: Dynasty's Cover Me
Book interior design by: Shawn Walker
Edited by: Mia Rucker

Acknowledgments

To the man above, all my blessings comes from you! Through this journey, you have NEVER left me, when I call on you, you show up, plus you're always on time. You've have kept me sane and stable, plus you continue to love me. You know my heart, but I want you to know I love you. Without you there would be NO me!

Tameia & Tamaine Jr., I love y'all so much! I pray that y'all will forgive me for not been there to see y'all grow up. I hope y'all won't hold it against me, that I chose LOYALTY over ya lives. Y'all keep me on my grind every single day, y'all the reason why I go so hard. It is not easy been away from y'all especially when I was always there. Loyalty is a must in life, and I know y'all will stand by this 'cause my blood is running through ya. I'll be home when they open up these gates, so please make me proud. I love y'all till the death of me! Take care of each other, ride or die with one another no matter the cost. All y'all have is each other! My love for y'all in beyond anything!

My grandparents, Oswald & Julia James, I am who I am today because of y'all. A job well done with raising me, I turned out pretty good, because I was raised well. I ask God every day to give me one more chance to see ya face to face. I love you two with all of me.

Leather, lady, how do I start? Every time I call home to talk to my babies you answer the phone. You make sure that they are well taken care off. I don't know where my kids would be if it wasn't for you. I owe you my life because they are my LIFE. You take away from yourself to make sure they are good. I thank God for you every day. I love you, know that!

Donna, mom, thanks for all the love and support. I truly appreciate everything that you do for me. I know our relationship is not perfect but in due time it will be. I love you! William, thanks for loving my mother, she deserves it. I love y'all.

My father, I see you still mad, but it's all good, you really forgot that I am your child, huh?

Chessan, sis, I love you no matter what! And to the rest of my siblings, y'all know where and how to find me.

Doneille, this year has been crazy for the both of us, but through all the bullshit we still standing. You have shown me that you're a rider, not because we are sisters, but because it is who you are! Two things about us Jamaican women, we're UNBREAKABLE and LOYAL. Please dry your eyes 'cause I know you crying now (lol). I love you! Oh yea when I touch down, know that we are gonna fight like the old days, shawty, in my Jeezy voice :)

Gevetta, I love you, and I know you are happy that your first child is finally home. You've been with me on this journey since day 1 and your words off encouragements lifts me up all the time, thanks.

La'Tasha Wilkins aka Flowsicka (keep grinding with the mic, you will make it), Shauna Irving, Tameka Beasley, Kemper, De'Ashley White, April Pannell, y'all keep me up, the love and support is definitely real. Some days y'all emails, mails, and phone calls gives me that extra push that I need to keep going on, no matter what, I love y'all for just being there especially when I am behind these walls, and for showing me that there is still some real bitches left out there.

Kiara Culpepper aka KeKe, my dawg, keep ya head up, I told you, you need to let that pen and paper flow! You almost at the door, keep ya head held high, duck all them haters, and stay succa free. Blood doesn't make us Family, Loyalty does! I love you!

Jeremiah Scott, let this trip show you, who is for you and who is not. Keep ya head up at all time no matter what. Figure out who you are and what you wanna do with ya self. You ain't getting now younger (lol) so chill out and grow up. I am here, always have been and always will be. The love is real, remember this.

Pierre Pennix, mane, you is mean as hell, but I refuse to let you stress me out with ya crazy self(lol). Keep ya head held high, this too shall pass, my nigga! Oh yea you might get all the ladies now, not that you don't have enough already, I am just playing, lol, cheer up.

Jolon Carthorne aka Boslyfe, what's hood yo? Mane, you show love no matter what and I salute you for that. If we would have touch base, mane oh mane, the Burg wouldn't have known what to do. Keep them toes down!

A-Town, T.Gordy, Gary Smith, keep ya heads up.

Kala Buchanan, girl, you're my HITTA 4 life. This time has made our bond unbreakable. Zamien, Arionna, Brooklyn, Amanda, Logan, Hailey, she miss y'all. I knew that light and music had got on ya nerve but you never said a word. Papers all over the room, mane I put you through hell with this book, and every time I stop writing you stay telling me to pick the pen and paper back up, thanks. I love you! Keep your head up no matter what road block that you face, you are very strong.

Dolla, you might as well delete me off the email 'cause I don't hear from you but once a month!

F. Art, you are a great person, I need you to spread the word for me now :)

Spgetti, mane, WOW! They just don't know how bless I am to have you in my life. I know I stay not listening to you (lol) but bear with me, I am hard headed bad. I love you and I need for you to get on the grind with them poems too, keep ya head up and stay in the word...No matter what, God will make a way, he always do.

Wheat, friend, when I be slacking, you come to find me talking bout "you need to take ya ass to the library and write and type, quit this damn job and write, you have babies at home to feed." Thank you for just been there as a great friend, you give me advice on how to do things, I love you.

Brandi. J (Chuck), Asia. D, Shonda. H (thanks for always coming with your own hair styles), T. Davis, Alecia. B, Lanita. P, Kiwi, Trell. C, Tamera. K, Roqel. C (Rocky), Tracey. S, Crystal. S, Man Man, Ila, Joyce. L, Diana. E, Lady Dee, Pumpkin (get @ me), Shay. B, Linda. F, Heather. B, I can't even think right now it is 2am, and I am tired. Please don't blame my heart, just charge it to lack off sleep, real talk, but anyways, y'all I love and appreciate each one of ya, real talk.

Lucy. D (You have watch me grown so much, you're always there to let me know when I am going in the wrong way, I love you for your honesty and for all the times I come talking ya ears off), Shannon. L, Beverly. M, Kim. W, when I am down and just need an extra ear to listen to my voice, y'all are there, no matter what y'all have going on! With arms wide open, y'all love me like ya very own kid! I love ya, and I hope that our bond will last 4 ever.

Antonio "Dee" Williams (smile) Keep ya head up and stay out of trouble, damn, get it together yo... Nikki Williams, mane I miss you but I know you miss me too, keep ya head up and stay prayed up. I'll never forget y'all and I know we will link up on the streets when they let us free.

Esha, Savon, Melik, D.Dee, thanks for sharing ya grandma with my babies and helping ya granny raised them. I love y'all. Tammy, welcome home and congrats with ya new bundle of joy, oh yea cut them tubes out. (lol)

Shante Sutton (Shawn), mane you go hard for me, damn, real do recognize real no matter what I see. I love you, and I need for you to stay on top of things plus ya grind! Only the REAL survive. Grind time...Let's get it.

Tara & Skip, not a day that goes by that I don't think off y'all. Watch over me, I miss and love y'all so much it is unexplainable! Gone but never forgotten.

Derrick Alston, friend, thanks for all the pics, the letters, jokes and all my lyrics. You know ya letters be 20 pages long, you killing me (lol). Friends till the end.

Angela, hey girl thanks for the love, you gonna be ok, stay strong for them babies.

Moyan Forbes, ha-ha, I told you I got you and oh yea, Loyalty and Family, right? Show me ;), as you can see my actions speaks louder than words :)... Keep that chin up boo.

You know all I listen to while penning this joint was Jeezy and Boosie, matter a fact they stay blasting in my head phones. They the realest rappers ever.

The first book I read was "Trust No Man by Ca$h". That joint went so hard it made me pick up and pen and a letter pad. That shit motivated me to the fullest, I was like damn, mane this nigga doing all this from behind a cell door, so I when I reached out to him, he didn't turn his back, or shut me down. Ca$h, thanks for giving me the chance to do something that I've fell in love with. You push me so hard with this book and for that I am grateful. You told me that you knew I could do it and you wouldn't take no for an answer. Thanks for allowing me to be apart of your team. The game is Lock Down Publications, and to my fellow authors let's show the world that we are the best and **The Game Is OURS: Lock Down Publications.** NO LIE!

Aww, mane, I've ran into some real officers over the years, they know all I need is a type writer with my name on it (LOL), but anyway I am glad that y'all don't let the badges get to ya heads or change ya: Mr. D. Jackson, Vaughan, Duncan, Spencer, Robison, Mrs. E. Jenkins from Re Entry, Ms. Spears, Ms. Holland, Ms. Cockrell from education(I am always the last one to leave, sorry), B. Williams, Mr. King from laundry, Mr. Moore, my boss Lt. St. John(I am always at that beauty salon working even on my day off, let me live), Ms. Hayeward, Lt. Rosado.

Oh yea before I forget, to my kids' sperm donor, Tamaine Davis Sr., you need to watch ya muthafuckin tongue boy. You wish I wasn't the kids mother, nigga you done lost ya mind, I see for real, but let me remind you who the hell I am. I am that babyma who put you on, I am that one who gave you your first two kids. I am the same one you called the police on, yea let me drop ya pants so they can see that you is a bitch 4 real! Nigga you even took the stand on me in court, and charge me to watch ya own kids! You wish me nothing but the worst, ha-ha you must have forgot I am Last of a Dying Breed, they don't make them like me no more. I'm **UNBREAKABLE**. Six years and you still throwing salt @ me, I don't have to tell anyone shit, 'cause they all know ya ass is a bitch! You can't see me not even when I am bleeding.

To my fans, thanks for showing me love, make sure ya leave a review or get someone to do it for you on Amazon, spread the word, and hit me up by snail mail and let me know how you feel.

My haters, ha-ha, can you see me now?

Julian 'Jamaica' James 16692084
Po Box 4000
Aliceville Alabama 35442

Jamaica

Chapter 1

I had felt nothing but torture and loss almost all of my life, and the worst torture had always come from the hands of men. My trust within had been used, tested, and dragged to the point of no return. The ones closest to me always hurt me the worst and it affected me the most.

The only way I'd have peace was if I got revenge on everyone that hurt me. I'd die trying, but I refused to die by the hands of men.

I knew that I would be tried, and I planned on proving to everyone that a scorned woman was not to be played with.

It seemed like everyone that I was supposed to have with me had been taken from me since I came out of my mamma's pussy.

There I was chilling on my front porch, enjoying the breeze, and sipping on some Patron while I watched traffic flow.

My mother had left me after my first three days of life, and my stepmom, who actually loved me, had died of cancer. My damn daddy had allowed the son of his ugly ass bitch on the side to live after he took my virginity from me by force. My brother by my stepmom had died after he'd been taking care of me. My daddy had ended up on drugs...

My thoughts were interrupted by my cell phone.

"Yo," I spoke into the phone without even looking to see who was calling.

I was listening to the caller, but I was not quite understanding what I was hearing. I pulled the phone from my ear to look at the screen, which read, "Unknown Caller."

"Me and games don't mix," I said. Then I took another sip of my Patron before I continued. "I fear no one, especially not a nigga with a dick and two balls."

The caller was silent.

"Since you know so much and you've got the heart of a lion, don't let me find you and..."

The screen on my phone lit up, letting me know the caller had disconnected after exactly one minute and forty-five seconds.

I took another sip and rubbed on one of my babies as it rested in my lap, my .40 caliber Smith and Wesson handgun. I leaned my head back against the chair as my body slouched down into it. I felt the liquor having its effect on me, but that was not gonna stop me from doing what I had planned for the night.

I'd always had things taken from me, and I'd made a promise to myself to reverse that curse. I was gonna be the taker, the woman in charge, and whoever didn't like it could see if I let them live. I lifted the bottle up, and the headlights gave me enough light to see that I had almost finished the damn bottle by myself.

"Time to roll," I told myself as I eased out of the chair. I was already dressed in all-black from head to toe.

When the car pulled up in front of the house, I tucked my .40 into the back of my pants and let my 2X t-shirt fall over it. I grabbed the bottle off the porch, without letting go of the cup in my hand, and stepped into the grass. The moon was out, but it didn't seem to be very bright at all. I walked to the curb in front of the house where the car was parked and both of my best friends were waiting for me. I opened the back door and entered the car. Young Jeezy's voice could be heard through the speakers. The driver's head was bobbing from side to side, and the passenger that I was sitting behind was rapping the words.

"Eyes wide shut, I don't see these niggas, cause deep in your heart you want to be me, nigga."

I shook my head, smiled, and closed the door. I was ready to get the night started.

"Ya young punks with ya loose ass lips, I keep an AR with them loose ass clips," the passenger continued to sing.

That was my shit, *Streets on Lock*, so I joined in. "My name ain't dick so keep it out ya mouth. It is what it is. Look, I am Da South (that's right). Big Mac, you niggas small fries. You just another nigga, I'm more like the franchise."

The volume on the radio went down as the driver turned left on Monroe St.

"1725 is the number, yo," I said as I made sure one was in the chamber of my baby.

Jeezy was still talking through the speakers. At the stop sign, Black turned left again. Dimples was humming now. Another left and we would be at our spot.

Dimples reached over and cut the music off. I pulled my face mask down slowly. I had black eyeliner under my eyes to cover the color of my skin. Black pulled over on the side of the road to fix herself up. I watched from the backseat as my bitches covered their faces with their masks and each put a bullet in the chamber of their weapons.

"Let's roll," I said from the backseat. I couldn't even feel the liquor anymore, but my adrenaline was so high that I was ready to get started. Black pulled off once they were done.

"1725," she confirmed from up front.

I closed my eyes for a second and my daughter Beauty's face flashed in front of me. I knew, no matter what happened, I was getting back home to her. I would do whatever it took. The car stopped. The almost empty bottle of Patron was on the floorboard by my feet. I picked it up and finished what I'd started. The tequila burned in my chest as it went down. I made no sound, but my face was all twisted up. Dimples and Black were both looking at me. I dropped the empty bottle on the seat and opened the door up, but they were still just looking, so I spoke up.

"Ready or what?" My words were met with silence but I was ready with or without them, and I feared nobody but God himself.

"Ready!" they both said together.

The headlights were cut off, but the engine was still running. I didn't have to worry when I opened my door because the interior lights had been taken out so that it would stay dark inside. Dimples and Black both did the same. There were no street lights on Monroe, just the lights from the porches that we passed.

"1725," I whispered as we walked down the block. We walked in a straight line, Black in front, me in the middle, and Dimples in the back.

Fa' real, fa' real, I was nervous as shit. I thought the Patron would have helped calm my nerves a little, but it hadn't. I wondered if those two were nervous too.

"You gotta make it back home to Beauty, Sweets," the voice in my head told me.

1720.

I could hear dogs barking from the house across the street. My finger was on the trigger, ready to talk. Black stopped suddenly and I bumped into her. She pointed to the house on the right.

1724.

That meant the house we wanted was on the left. We crossed the street and it was right in front of us. The porch light from the house made it easy to see. Green and yellow paint and three chairs were on the porch, along with a pink baby chair and a grill. That damn dog from up the street wouldn't stop barking and it was starting to get on my nerves. That fucking Patron had gotten my head spinning and everything was looking blurry as shit.

Damn. How the fuck we getting up in this bitch without waking the tenants up?

The headlights from a car coming down the street caused us to run for cover. We leaned our bodies against the side of the house. I was holding my baby down at my side.

"Where is the car?" Black hissed in my ear. I turned around with one finger laid across my lips, telling her to be quiet, but I had to admit that it was a good question that I also wanted to know the answer to. *Where the fuck was the car at?*

I saw the lights getting clearer and brighter, but then they cut off. I heard the motor running, but then it was gone, too. It was turned off. A car door slammed and me and Black both jumped. Then we heard a man's voice.

"What the fuck? You stay fuckin' trippin'!"

I watched as a figure came down the street.

"Ok, bitch, fuck you and that nigga. I can beat my dick."

Damn.

He stepped onto the porch and I saw my only chance to get in. I ran around to the front of the house with the .40 in front of me. He didn't even hear or see me behind him because he was way too busy arguing on the phone and jiggling the keys in his pockets. The barrel of my baby touched the back of his head and I eased the phone out of his hand as his body turned stiff.

"Make this easy on yourself," I whispered into his ear.

Black took the keys from his other hand and tried to unlock the door. Dimples was behind me, breathing all up on my back. She was so close I could smell the winter fresh mint gum in her mouth. "Who else is here?"

He was shaking like a leaf and I almost didn't expect him to answer, but he did.

"Nobody."

Black better hurry up and find the damn key. Shit, we need to get inside, I thought.

"I-I-I got everything you want," he stuttered quietly.

Finally, the door was unlocked and we stepped into the house. Dimples used the flashlight so we could see.

"Make it quick," I told him. I was dizzy as shit. I needed to get home.

"Everything is under the kitchen table."

And just like that, Black left to go search the kitchen. There was a sofa, a table, a few chairs, and some other shit in the room where we were.

A light jumped on. I heard shit moving around, and then Black's voice, "I got it."

Bout time! No more liquor for me before I hit a lick, I said to myself. I backed that nigga all the way up until he reached the sofa. My .40 was in his face and I used it to push him until he sat down. The light from the kitchen allowed me to see his face.

A tear drop was tatted under his left eye and a huge gold ring was on the pinky finger of his left hand. I watched him as he looked me up and down and shook his head. I knew he could tell I was a female because my ass was sitting out in my Dickies pants.

"Go get the car," I told Dimples. She handed over the flashlight, leaving us.

Black was pulling the bag towards the front door. The man didn't beg for his life and he didn't move when his phone rang, but I smiled at his ringtone, "Soul Survivor" by Young Jeezy featuring Akon.

"You can't get that right now," I told him as it rang out.

"I'm cool," he said, cool as fuck.

I was shocked to see that he isn't scared. I might not be either after going through so much shit myself. I felt like that other shit should have killed me, but it didn't.

"She's here," Black said to me.

"Take it out," I responded.

I picked his cell up. "Close your eyes and count to twenty before you open them up," I demanded.

"I'd rather die with my eyes open than sucka out to a bitch with them closed."

Oh yea, he's got heart, and that heart I am gonna...

Pow. Pow.

I watched calmly as pieces of his head flew everywhere and blood poured out of what used to be his face as "Soul Survivor" played in the background.

I was gonna let his ass live, but when he manned up, I had to send him on his way to the other side. No man will disrespect me as long as I live.

Fa real, fa real, let me go back. Let me see who needed to pay. I'mma start at the beginning.

Jamaica

Chapter 2

My name is Sweets. *Bad bitch*! Yep, that's me. That shit ain't even in the dictionary, but know if it was, my picture would be right beside it.

I was born and raised in the best state ever, where the city never sleeps and everyone minds their own damn business. New York is the place to be, but not for me.

Daddy was thirty years old when my momma was seventeen. She was a track runner and he was a water pump operator. Shit, that didn't keep them from making me, thank God. I was born September 6, 1986 at Kings County Hospital located in Brooklyn, New York. I was my mother's first and only child, but I was my father's second girl.

My parents nicknamed me Sweet Pea because they said I was the prettiest little girl they'd ever seen, but hell, my real name is Corona Cocaine Cash. Yea, that shit sounded crazy, but it made a statement, and it damn sho' wasn't easy to forget.

My mother left when I was only three days old, so I never knew her. My father said he came home and found me sleeping in my crib with a note attached.

Richie,
I am tired of your lies, tired of taking care of your child. I know all about the other seven children you have. You have turned my life into a living hell and I am just tired of it all, so you can get one of your other women to raise her. She don't even look like me.
Yvette

I only knew what my mother looked like, and that was from pictures. Truth be told, I didn't look like that bitch at all. I was the spitting image of my father, and for that I was very thankful. I had his honey dipped complexion with big brown eyes and shoulder length black hair. For everything else, I hated my father to the fullest.

Once my mother was gone, he found someone else to perform the motherly duties. Her name was Vesta King, and she also had a child by my father. His name was King Cash, and he was six years older than me. Vesta was beautiful inside and out. She did everything she could to make my father happy, but one thing she couldn't control was whether or not he kept his dick in his pants.

Her love for him was pure and real. No matter how many kids he had, her love for him never changed. King was her only child, but she loved me like I was her own. So when she died of cancer, I cried my heart out. I wanted to die with her. That didn't stop my father though. He kept having babies and different women kept taking care of the two of us. King was twelve when his mother passed, and I was seven. Even though she wasn't my real mother, she'd always be my mother in my heart.

One of the women that took care of us was Charlenee Carter. She was ugly, and I hated her with a passion because, when daddy was home, she would treat us like gold, but once he was gone, King and I were her doormats. She would call us ugly, retarded, wicked, and stupid.

She had a son of her own, but he didn't belong to daddy. Anyone could tell because the mother lover looked just like her, ugly. His name was Damien Fuller and he was older than us. He was seventeen, and I hated how he would look at me when I was home with him.

One night, King had gone to spend the night over at his best friend Shawn's house. Daddy and Charlenee had gone out, too, so it was only me and ugly ass Damien at home. I was doing my homework when he came into my room.

20

"You act like you all that."

"Get out of my room, ugly."

Before I knew it, he was on top of me ripping my pajamas off. I tried to fight back, but I was too small, and he was so strong. I just couldn't. I prayed that King would come through the door, but that never happened. What did happen next would have you crying, and I ain't about to start that shit. I couldn't even speak I was crying so hard. Not with emotion, but with hatred, feeling that my father allowed all this to happen to me.

When King came home the next day, he found me in my room just sitting on my bed shaking and staring into space.

"Sweet Pea, what's wrong? Why you lookin' like that? And why you smell like that?"

I kept my face still with no sign of anything, but my heart was telling a different story.

"Why the hell is blood on the sheets? Corona, I'm talkin' to you."

Then tears began to fall from my eyes.

"Come on, Corona. Tell your brother what happened."

I took a deep breath and I spoke the unspeakable. "He raped me, King. He came in here and he took my pride, my joy, and my soul."

Daddy and Charlenee were in the living room watching television and we could hear them laughing from my room. King ran out, leaving my door wide open.

"How the hell can you have this woman in here with you when her son raped my sister?" King yelled at our father.

"Boy, shut the hell up and get away from me," Richie told him.

Charlenee didn't say a word. She just sat there like a dumb, ugly bitch.

Now you see why I hate my father with a passion.

That day, it was my brother, King, who bathed me and made me soup to eat. King nurtured me back to life. He slept on the floor by my bed at night, guarding the door as I slept. Our father never even came to see if I was okay. I didn't matter to him at all. I missed Vesta so much, but I was so glad that King was there to protect me.

"I know what that ugly son-of-a-bitch took from you is gonna make you different and harsh towards men. But always remember Karma is an ugly bitch when she returns, so make him pay when that time comes."

King kept it real and raw with me, no matter what. He had to teach me because I had no one else to tell me about life. King would walk me to and from school, and help me with my homework. He even cooked and cleaned for me every day. I hated doing my hair because I had so much of it, but King enjoyed playing in it and doing it. During those times, we would talk and he would "school me," as he would say, on life. I would sit and listen and soak his words into my heart. I loved when he did my hair and I did his.

Women were God's gifts to men and King always told me they should be protected, cherished, and loved at all times. He said I should never allow myself to be treated as trash, and that it was important to learn to love myself first and to carry myself as a "lady" at all times. He also taught me to never depend on a man because they would think they owned me if I did.

He taught me how to cook, wash, and clean, everything.

"The more you practice, the better you'll become. Always try to do your best at everything that you put your mind to."

I felt safe, I felt comfortable, and I felt on top of the world when King was around.

"Education is the key in life. Learn how to master it, make it your candy so you will love it," King told me one day after I got home from school with a B on my English test. "No one in this family has finished college. I want to see you walk down that road. I want to be there for you on that special day. It would mean a lot to me."

Two days before King's nineteenth birthday, he became extremely ill and it seemed serious enough that daddy dropped us off at the hospital.

"King, you gotta bet better. Please!"

"I'm gonna try. But if I don't, I want you to take care of yourself. Be strong. Don't let anyone take advantage of you. If you have to turn your heart cold to protect yourself, then do it."

Those were my brother's last words. Come to find out, King had had cancer, and it had already spread all the way to his brain. By the time they got to him, my brother was gone. Charlenee and her ugly ass son moved out soon after King passed, so it was just me and daddy. We barely spoke to each other, and that was fine with me. I didn't know who my real mother was, I'd lost the only mother who had ever loved me, and I lost my protector and my brother, King. I had a father who wasn't into raising me, so I mostly raised myself. After King's death, it was hard for me, I wanted to quit school and do my own thing. I wanted to do what the other girls in school did. They'd skip school and hang out on the streets with their boyfriends. I wanted to be loved, and I wanted to feel it. I wanted feel love from someone else to know that I did matter. But King's voice would always sound off in my head.

"Girl, you need to get your education. Without education, you ain't nothin'."

School and church became my getaways. I worked hard in school, and I graduated one year early with a full scholarship to attend Liberty University in Lynchburg, Virginia. I wanted to move away from home, far away so I could be free from the past that tried to hold me back, and that was my chance to do it. I didn't even say goodbye to my father. I just packed up all my clothes and left. I was damn sure going to miss New York, but New York wasn't going to miss me.

Liberty University was a Christian college, but its location was crazy! The damn name of the town had a bitch scared. Lynchburg. Well, Virginia was about to be my new fucking home, and I was ready.

In August of 2004, I left Brooklyn, New York behind. I took the train, and even though the ride was eight hours long, it was fun. I knew that Vesta and King were watching over me, and just thinking of that brought a smile to my face.

Adjusting to a new environment was hard, but I had to do what I had to do, and that was what I'd always done. My roommate's name was Hannah, some shit. I don't remember her last name, but she was from Germany. I remember it tripped me out that people from all over the world were there to get an education.

College was fun and exciting in the beginning. My major was computer science, even though I didn't know what I wanted to become in life. I loved numbers and my favorite subject was Math, so my Math professor asked me to tutor some of the students, which I did.

In need of money, I decided to get a job off campus. Working while going to school was tough, but eventually, because I'd been going to school all my life, I got bored with it, and I started failing classes. Instead of just allowing myself to fail, I decided to take a break. One year in college and that was that. I used the money that I'd saved up to get my first apartment. I worked at a Kroger gas station on Timberlake Road. Shit, I loved that job. That's where my whole life changed from that good little girl to this bad ass bitch. That was where I met T.

Chapter 3
Virus

In June of 2005, I caught a virus like you wouldn't believe, a *bad* one. I had just finished eating lunch with my coworker, Dimples.

As I strolled across the parking lot to get back to the booth, I heard someone yelling.

"I ain't never seen you before."

I ignored the voice completely and put a little more swagger into my step. On some real live shit, I had a bomb ass shape. I stood right at five feet four inches tall with a killer body. I guessed that was what they were hollering at. When I got back to the booth, I thanked Pam for holding things down while I was gone.

"Have a good evening," she told me on her way out.

"And you do the same."

"Can I get twenty on pump seven and a box of Grape Dutches, please?" a male customer asked.

"Yes, you can. But do you have an ID, sir?"

He gave me his ID and I noticed that his birthday was April 21, 1986. He had just turned 18.

"When's your birthday?" he asked me as I looked his card over.

"What?" I lifted my head up, looking at him.

"Since you know when my birthday is, when is yours?"

Now don't get me wrong, this nigga was fine. He had to be one hundred ninety pounds solid, around five feet eleven inches tall with thick black hair, plus he was sharp. Light skinned men weren't even my type. I didn't really have a type back then, but hey, he was on point.

"Since I can't get your birthday, can I get your number?"

Damn this nigga don't waste any time, I see. "No," I replied.

"Why?" he took a step back and looked me in my eyes.

"You don't have a shirt on, and you should never approach a woman when you have a hat on," I told him.

He looked at me with surprise and walked away. He got his gas and left, and I kept doing my job. Shit, he was fine, but he had to have some respect at least. *Just a straight up hood nigga,* I told myself. But yo, that nigga blew my mind. A few minutes later, he was back wearing a shirt and no hat. All I could do was smile.

""You ain't from around here?" he asked me.

"No. I'm from Brooklyn, New York."

He shook his head and smiled. "My name is Traymon, but everyone calls me T."

"Okay," I said, wondering what else he wanted.

"I see your name tag says Corona."

He can read. "Yea, that's my name, but I go by Sweets." I thanked God no one was getting gas. I wanted to see where this was headed.

"I ain't tryin' to be rude, but I gotta run. Can I get your number before I go? Please?" He was still smiling.

Call me what you want to, but I gave it to him. He had just impressed me to the utmost.

"I'm gonna call you tonight," he told me.

I watched him leave and I had to admit he had it going on with what he pulled off by coming back.

I got off work at eleven o'clock that night, and since I didn't have a car, my coworker, Dimples, gave me a ride home.

Dimples was five feet six inches tall, white, with blue eyes, auburn hair and a gorgeous body. Her breasts stood up just right, with a small waist and a plump ass.

Her name was Dimples Marshall, and she was born and raised right there in Lynchburg, Virginia by both of her parents. She had dropped out of college when she turned twenty-one because she figured it wasn't for her.

"So, the sayin' is true then?" I asked her.

"What saying?"

"School is not for everyone," I told her.

"I guess you could say that, 'cause it sure ain't for me."

"That's exactly what I say."

Both of her parents were pastors at their own church, who wanted nothing but the best for her. But she wanted to be different.

"Thanks for the ride home," I told her when she pulled in front of my apartment.

"No problem. What time do you have to be at work tomorrow?"

"Seven fuckin' o'clock," I was mad just thinking about it.

"Me too, girl. Do you want me to pick you up?" she asked me.

"It's up to you, either way I'm gonna be there."

I ran my fingers through my hair.

"Girl, you crazy as shit. All I want is a yes or no," she said with a laugh.

"Yes, and thank you."

"Alright, I'll be here at 6:30, okay?"

"Okay. Thanks again for givin' me a ride home. I'll be waitin' on you in the morning," I told her as I got out of the car. And ever since that day, Dimples and I lived in a world by ourselves.

I lived in a two bedroom apartment all by my damn self. I mean, I wasn't doing it big or nothing, but it was mine. My apartment was pretty much empty. All I had was two TV's and a bed. The stove and fridge came with it and every room was carpeted, except for the kitchen and the bathroom. As I did every night, I fixed something to eat, took a shower, and then I let the TV watch me sleep. At times like that, I realized how much I missed my brother, King. When I was alone, without his presence, I felt his loss and my heart ached for his words. I never expected his sudden death. I thought he would have always been by my side. I realized that reality was damn sure real because I felt the heartache like a fresh wound. The pain would always be fresh until we were united in the next life because my brother was my keeper.

"Damn, who the hell is callin' me this time of the night?" I asked myself as I headed to the phone.

"Hello?"

"What you doin'?"

It was Traymon. I already knew his voice, from anywhere.

"Nothin'. Ready to go to bed."

"Why so early?"

"'Cause it's almost 12:30 in the morning, and I have to be back at work by seven."

We ended up talking until three o'clock anyway. He told me all about himself. He was the oldest child, his mom died two days before his high school graduation, and he had three brothers and a sister.

Unfortunately, he'd lost all four of them in a bad wreck, and he didn't know who his father was. He didn't have a steady place to call home either, because he was living from place to place with his friends. His life sounded all fucked up.

"Damn, that's crazy," Dimples said.

"I know, yo, that is crazy."

I considered Dimples a true friend because she would listen to me while I talked her ears off. We got our schedules changed so that we could work together. We even took our lunches together.

T would come to my job every day and kick it with me, and we would talk on the phone every night about everything. Over the next month or so, our friendship started looking different. I knew Traymon Davis was a virus I couldn't get rid of.

Jamaica

Chapter 4
Show Love

Dimples had moved out of her parent's house to become my roommate. We already did everything else together, so why not? I told her everything about my past and the things that had happened to me. I swear every time I would tell her something, she would cry.

After King died, I was exposed to so much by my father. He had different women over all the time. He treated them all like shit, nothing like he treated the rapist's mother! He would beat on them in front of my room and talk to them like they were nothing, and they let him. He was in complete control of them. He was their owner, and they kept coming back to him. He even started doing drugs.

I remember my first time seeing him smoking a white, hard substance. I wasn't feeling well enough to attend bible study, so after school I went straight home. A foul odor hit my nose as soon as I opened the front door. I was wondering if it was the garbage in the kitchen, but I knew I had emptied it that morning, so it couldn't be. My father was sitting in the living room on the sofa with a glass stem in his hand. I watched him as he put something that looked like a pebble on the top of the stem. Then he put the other side in his mouth and used his lighter to put flame to the pebble part. I watched him inhale and exhale a cloud of smoke that flew from his mouth, and then that scent hit me in my face. From then on, I would watch him smoke himself into another world.

I watched all the things we once owned disappear piece by piece. I walked into one of his drug transactions one night in the kitchen. A man was standing by the stove and my father was on his knees begging him for some more drugs. I turned around so fast. '

"Who is that?" the man asked.

"She is nothing. Her cherry is already busted," I heard my father reply.

Devastated, I ran to my room as the tears ran down my face. I couldn't stop thinking, *Was he getting high that night when I got raped?* I made a vow to myself that I would kill my father and Damien, the fucking rapist. I didn't tell Dimples about the vow though.

My eyes had seen enough, my body had gone through it, my heart was turning cold and my vision of men was hard. But I was a leader. I would never give a man that much control over me. I planned on doing everything in my power to make and keep me happy and if that meant "killing," I was down for the ride.

"Sweets, you are so strong. I probably would have killed myself."

"Girl, only the strong survive. Yea, I used to be weak, but being weak didn't get me anywhere, so strong is all I know."

"Girl, I love you."

"I love you too, Dimples."

We made a pact to always be there for each other, no matter what. No man or woman could ever get between us.

"Let's not forget money," she said.

"Nothing, nada, will ever come between us," I told her.

One night Traymon asked if I could do his hair.

"How you know I do hair?"

"Shit, girl, you black, plus you come from New York, and people from New York know how to do every fuckin' thing."

I couldn't help but laugh.

"So can you do my hair for me?"

"You gotta come to my apartment then."

"A'ight, what's the address?"

"122 Landover Place, apartment B-11."

"See you in a minute then," he said before hanging up the phone.

Dimples had gone to her parent's house to visit. Thanks to them our apartment was beautiful, and nowhere near as empty as it had started out. They had given us a kitchen table with matching chairs and a living room suite. They'd also bought Dimples a brand new bedroom suite. In a way, I felt like I was their child also.

I was cooking crab legs when I heard the doorbell. When I opened up the door, he was standing there. Traymon is sexy from head to toe. He was wearing a fresh white t-shirt, blue Roca Wear jeans, with some white dopemans and his hair looking wild all over his head.

"Can I come in?"

I was just standing there looking at him. I was in some boy shorts and a wife-beater, with my hair pulled up in a ponytail.

"Yea, come in. I'm in the kitchen cooking." I left him standing there, because I had food on the stove.

"Lead the way, I'm right behind you." I could hear the smile in his voice.

I could feel his eyes on my body, and I wondered if he could feel the heat coming from me.

"Are you hungry?" I asked him.

"Only if you planning on feeding me."

I let his comment fly through my ears like nothing. "Are you hungry?" I asked him again as I stirred the pot in front of me.

"Yea."

His eyes were roaming everywhere.

"You can go watch TV in the living room while I finish cookin'."

"Okay." And with that he left me there to finish up.

I finished up and fixed our plates at the table. I was dishing the crab legs out when Dimples came through the door.

"Girl, everything you cook smells so good it could wake the dead," she said as she came towards the kitchen.

"And who the hell is that?" she asked as she noticed Traymon making his way to the table.

"This is Traymon. Traymon this is Dimples, my best friend and roommate."

"Nice to meet you. I've heard nothin' but good things about you, Dimples."

"Same here," Dimples responded as she looked at me.

"You gonna eat with us?" I asked her.

"Naw, go ahead. I just ate. If you need me though, I'm in my room," she said, leaving us alone at the table.

We talked a little as we ate. His favorite colors were black and blue. He enjoyed the winter more than any other season. He loved to shoot dice and gamble.

"Damn, you sure can cook."

"Well thank you. I was taught by the best, King." A smile hopped on my face thinking about him.

When we were finished, I put the dishes away and told him to wait on me in the living room while I cleaned up the kitchen. When I was done, I went and got a comb to do his hair.

He watched TV while I freaked his braids out. Boy, he had a head full of hair. Ida had to work the next day, so I decided that I should give him a little design, nothing major, but nothing too simple either. Let's just say it was sweet. It was around eleven when I finished his hair. I had a very long day of work ahead of me and was mad that I had to be there at seven in the morning.

"Can I spend the night?"

It caught me off guard. My body couldn't move. I wanted to tell him no, but I couldn't. I thought about not having a place to stay.

"Yea, but you have to sleep on the sofa 'cause my bed is mines only."

He laughed at me before saying, "Okay."

I walked into Dimples' room, where she was on her phone, talking.

"Girl, he gonna spend the night."

"What?" She didn't even cover up the phone, she just held it in the same spot.

"Yea, but he's sleepin' on the sofa." *What am I doing?* I was questioning my own actions.

"Okay, bitch, but you is crazy," she told me, and started laughing.

"I love you," I told her.

"I love you bunches," she replied, and jumped back into her conversation on the phone.

I closed the door and went to give Traymon the blanket that I had pulled from the hallway closet.

"Have a good night," I told him when I handed it over.

"You, too."

Am I going crazy? I kept asking myself.

I went into my room and left my door open a little so I could hear. Was I scared? Hell naw. He was harmless. I didn't even remember my dream, but six o'clock came quick. I got up, looked in the living room, and saw he was still there, sleeping peacefully, like a baby without any problems. I must say, he looked damn good.

I jumped into the shower, handled my business, and was done by 6:15. I woke Dimples up so she could get ready because we had to leave by 6:35 if we were going to make it to work on time. When Dimples went outside to warm up the car, I woke Traymon.

"Look, you can sleep till you ready to get up and leave, but it's too early to go now."

"Okay."

Sweets, what are you doing? "Just close the door behind you," I told him as I dusted the voice out of my head.

"A'ight, have a good day."

That made me smile on the way out the door. "I hope you have a great one," I told him, and left.

When I got into the car, Dimples had the nerve to say, "How you know he won't steal what we have?"

I had to laugh at her ass before I responded. "Girl, you act like we rich."

"We ain't rich yet, but we will be one day," she said, and then she turned the music up. Young Jeezy had become our rapper, and listening to him on the way to work motivated us.

Do ya thug thang gone get 'em up
Represent ya side nigga hit 'em up
Disrespect we gone take it there
We thirty deep lil nigga we ain't fighting fair
You better holla at ya partners
Before we catch them outside and hit they ass wit dem choppers
The .45 make my pants sag
Catch me bouncing through the club wit my black flag
You don't like it do something nigga
Where I'm from if we don't like it we do something nigga
And you know we gone ride homes
Stomp a nigga ass out until they turn the lights on
That nigga Jeezy is a Beast with them words!

Traymon was on my mind all day that day and I couldn't wait to get off at 2:00. When we 'went on break, we talked about him.

"Be careful, Sweets. Don't rush into anything."

"Dimples, thanks for just bein' here for me."

"That's what friends are for."

I was glad that I had met her. Her actions showed me nothing but love. She never judged me or anything.

· When we finally got off work, I couldn't wait to get home. I wondered why Traymon hadn't come to see me that day. I listened to Dimples complain about her feet hurting when we got into the car. I always listened to her talk the way she listened to me when I needed those extra ears to hear me. She ran the register sometimes on the floor. It all depended on who we were working for that day. I could tell that it was starting to get to her by the tone in her voice. I couldn't really complain because I sat on my ass all the time. The paycheck wasn't shit no matter which way I looked at it.

Dimples had a really good heart. She stayed positive, but I could tell that deep down inside of her, she was sad. I watched her facial expressions change whenever I talked about my parents. It was like she had been through what I had gone through, but she never talked about it.

"Don't worry, things will get better."

"Dimples, I really hope so," I said, looking out the window.

As I turned my key in the door, we could hear music playing.

"Sweets, did you leave the TV on?"

I heard Dimples talking, but I couldn't answer because what I saw when I opened the door had me stuck. On top of the table there was a vase with some red flowers in it.

"Roses?" big mouth Dimples had to say.

I went straight to my room because that was where the music was coming from. Let's just say that I wasn't day-dreaming. Traymon was posted up in my bed watching music videos.

"What is wrong with him? Girl, you can't tell me you didn't give him some last night," Dimples' crazy ass had to say before she went into her room.

All I could do was just look at him. He never once took his face from the TV.

"What the hell happened between last night and today?" I asked him.

He didn't answer, so I took off my shoes and I went to put them in the closet. But when I opened the door, my heart stopped.

Breathe, Sweets.

That nigga had moved all his clothes, shoes, hats, and jackets into my damn closet. Fuck the closet, he had moved into my apartment!

"I ain't leavin'. You're my girl now, and I'm living with you."

All I could do was look at him. My mouth didn't work, but my mind was racing, like, *Damn, who is this nigga?*

Before I could say anything, he spoke again. "I'm gonna make you my wife."

I was speechless. How was I supposed to live with this nigga, not knowing if he was mentally challenged or what? I guess you could say he showed me that he was truly a virus that I couldn't get rid of.

Chapter 5
Welcome

"Traymon, look, living here, you're gonna have to respect both Dimples and myself."

"I do respect you."

I know he heard me say Dimples too. "Yeah, you do, but when we ain't here, I don't want your friends over here. And, no smokin' either, 'cause I know damn well you smoke weed. Do all that shit somewhere else."

"I can do that," he said.

"Oh, and one more thing..."

"What's that?"

"We are not havin' sex."

His face or his body language didn't change he just answered. "I'll Wait as long as you want, baby."

His reply caused me to look at him and smile. I felt like he was the one deep down in my heart and his words made him perfect for me.

Traymon was working at the pipe company with his grandfather back then. Grandpa A, as Traymon called him, was a deacon, and he was so black that he looked damn near purple, but he was an awesome man.

Living with Traymon and Dimples was both good and bad because they would bump heads every now and then. Traymon would work from 6am to 6pm, with Thursdays and Fridays as his days off. The paycheck was a beautiful thing, and everything went a little further having three people splitting up the bills. I was damn sure saving up for a rainy day.

I remember one night Traymon wanted to fuck so bad that he held my ass and beat his dick off.

"Damn! We been together for almost five months and you can't give a nigga none?" he asked me one night when we were in bed.

I looked at him and told him, "I am just not ready." I wasn't ready to have sex with Traymon even though we were going on five months. I told him "no" that night, but he didn't say anything or get up, he just held me in his arms. The following day I told Dimples about it while he was at work. She explained to me that what I don't do another bitch will, especially when he is probably used to getting pussy every day, and now he wasn't getting any. She kept it real and raw with me and typically when men ain't getting none at home, they do step out and find someone to please them.

Dimples had left me thinking hard, I just wanted to make sure I was ready. When emotions got involved, pleasure and pain were both exposed.

I didn't ever want to feel pain again when it came to sex, I wanted it to be special. My struggle with having my womanhood taken was beginning to feel like it was taking control over my life, even though it had happened years ago. I endured nothing but pain back then, and I would rather have died than go through that again.

The remaining members of Traymon's family were crazy, crazy in a good way and bad way. They all loved me, and they loved the way that I talked with my New York accent. Since his mother wasn't alive, he called his second cousin, an older woman, "mother."

Bella was a good woman. When Traymon's mom died, she had just had newborn twins, and Bella is the one who raised them. She kept her door open for Traymon, but he loved everywhere else. Bella also had two kids of her own, but they were grown. The oldest of her children was off the chain and doing time in prison for shooting her own damn brother in public. With Virginia being a common wealth state, they pressed charges on her and sent her to lock up for two years.

The brother she shot was on his way to prison for shooting his uncle. I was thinking to myself, *Damn, this family is fucking crazy for real, shooting up their own people and shit.*

But I could either love them or hate them, and I chose to love them because they had a crazy way of showing their love. I knew soon, and very soon, they would consider me family. That was all I needed because I was falling in love with Traymon.

When I was with him, I felt loved! I felt safe. He let his guard down with me and his emotions would flow. He made me feel like he loved me to and from the moon. His actions and support made me fall deep for him.

We used to visit his mom's gravesite and take her flowers. We did crazy things and we had fun with each other. But, shit, all that was about to change.

We finally ended up having sex, and boy oh boy was it whack.

Yes, straight up whack. He came in one minute. I never thought that would happen to me, but it did. All I could do was lay there in pain and replay that fucking horrible night in my head. Even though I was a child when it happened, I believed I should have fought harder than what I did. I got weak from all the punches I was throwing, and when he stuffed the blanket into my mouth to silence my cries, I gave up. I felt the air leaving my body slowly. He had my hands above my head and pinned down with one of his hands. My legs were under his body, his weight held me down. He ripped my clothes apart and plunged his dick into me. I let the tears run from my eyes like a river. I felt like I got hit by a bus. The force took my breath away.

I blamed myself because I should have never stopped fighting. Even though I gave it to Traymon, I felt nasty, dirty, and used the fuck up. Damien Fuller had taken my self-esteem away from me. He had destroyed what was supposed to be a special moment. For that, the nigga had to pay with his life, and in due fucking time, he was going to.

"Damn! Did you just bust in a minute?" I asked him when he fell on top of me. He was so embarrassed, but I had to know. "Am I your first?" I asked him after I got up off the bed.

"Naw, but I know I'm your first."

"How you figure?"

"There's blood on the sheets."

Seeing the blood brought back memories of a different time and a different place, and just like before, the tears started rolling down my face.

"Baby, what's wrong?" he asked me as he reached for me.

"Nothin'," I lied, "I just want to go to sleep."

He helped me into the bed, bloody and all, he wipe my tears, and held me. He wrapped his legs around mine and started rocking me to sleep. I guess he thought I was asleep because after a while I heard him say, "I love you."

I didn't respond, but I thought, *Welcome to a heart of pain, Traymon.*

This is hard for me. I gotta let go of my past. I gotta give him a chance to love me like I'm supposed to be loved. I have to leave my old life behind. One day I'll tell him everything. One day.

Chapter 6
Really?

The next time we had sex, I could say that nigga put on a show. He wasn't King Kong, but he was a good size seven. Dimples would tell me what to do. She would let me watch porn and take notes. Yea, that bitch was a super freak.

"You gotta let him fuck you in the ass, too."

"Bitch, you done lost your motherfuckin' mind. That's an exit, not an entrance."

She shrugged her shoulders at me and rolled her eyes. "What you don't do, the next bitch will. I'm just sayin'."

"Well, I guess, but I ain't doin' it, so he can hit the door."

She busted out laughing at me, and I had to ask, "Do you do it in the ass?"

She turned around to display the seat of her jeans, and said, "Why you think my ass so fat and plump?"

"Ugh, you a nasty bitch."

"Call me what you wanna, but you can't call me horny."

I couldn't help but laugh at her. That white bitch was plum crazy.

Traymon had quit his job, but still somehow stayed with money in his pockets. I kept working because I loved my job. Also, King had told me to never depend on anyone, especially a man, because then he would feel like he owned me.

I never asked him any questions, but I was damn sure curious. His phone would ring at 3, 4, and 5 o'clock in the morning. I mean, the shit *never* stopped ringing.

"Who's callin' you like that?"

"My cousin, Yacc."

All the damn time? I thought to myself.

Yacc was wild and loose in the streets. Anyone could tell the way he carried himself was out of this world. I trusted

Traymon. I knew if I didn't have any trust in my relationship, then I didn't have anything at all, so I kept his word close to my heart. But I was starting to get the feeling that something wasn't right.

"Dimples, I think he's cheating on me."

"Why would you say that?" she asked me while I laid up in her bed venting.

"I don't know. I just got that feelin'."

"Well, whatever you find out and need help with, know that I got your back all the way."

Dimples' response didn't catch me by surprise, I knew I could count her in on anything that I had going on in my life because she knew, no matter what, I had her back also.

One night while we were sleeping, I had a dream that he was cheating on me. I woke up out of my dream and went straight for his phone. Once I had the phone, I went into Dimples' room.

"Bitch, wake up."

She sat straight the fuck up. "What time is it?" she asked, still mostly asleep.

"3:45 in the mornin'."

"What's wrong?"

I showed her the phone and she read the screen out loud. "Thirty missed calls, five new text messages, and voicemail is full. What the fuck he got goin' on?" she asked me, like I knew.

"Bitch, I don't know."

There were no outgoing messages, but there were twenty old messages. Sounds crazy, right? No number had a name attached to it, so I didn't know who was who. I went straight the fuck to the text messages. One number kept calling back to back, and then they'd text.

One text said, "Call me now. I got all the money."

Me and Dimples looked at each other.

Then another text said, "Are you coming?"

But the ones that blew my mind were: "So since you home with your bitch now you can't respond to me," and "Fuck you, don't call or text me no more."

I wasn't worried about Traymon, he was fast asleep.

"Fuck that, call the number," Dimples said.

I called the number from his phone, but no one answered.

"Bitches like to play games, Sweets. Just wait a minute and then call back."

So that's what I did. I waited for a minute or so, and then I resent the number.

"Hello?" A bitch answered the phone.

I had to catch my breath. I felt like someone had struck me with a knife in my heart.

"Who is this?"

"Ask your man, don't ask me," she said, and then she hung up.

Tears ran down my face and Dimples wrapped her arms around me to hold me. Thank God she was there.

"I feel played. He betrayed me," I said between sobs.

"Girl, you been through worse, you can get through this too."

She was right.

"I'm not goin' to work in the mornin', but I know you are, so go back to sleep," I told her.

What she said next had me bawling. "Sweets, I'm your friend, your best friend. You don't go to work, I ain't going either. You stay up, I'm up with you. Best friends help each other. It's what we do."

"Well, help me kill this nigga then," I told her, and as soon as the words left my mouth, my mind went wild. I went into the kitchen and got a butcher knife. I grabbed a pair of yellow latex gloves out from under the sink and put them on. Dimples got the dish rag off the counter and poured beach on it.

He never heard us coming. I walked directly to his side of the bed and stabbed him right in the heart.

"Push the cloth in his mouth," I told Dimples. I used the knife to slit his throat, and I watched as his life's blood ran out of the hole that I'd opened in him to soak the sheets.

"Bitch, did you just ask me to help you kill him?" Dimples asked me, bringing me back to reality.

"Yea, I have it all planned out in my head," which was true. I did.

"Think, Sweets. Use your head before you act it all out."

I left Dimples' room and went back to my own. After I put his phone back where I'd gotten it from, I crawled back into bed beside him like nothing had happened, like my whole life hadn't just changed with a phone call.

"I love you," I told him as he slept, which I truly did.

For the rest of the night, I couldn't sleep because I couldn't stop thinking, couldn't stop questioning myself. Had I done something wrong? Could I have prevented this from happening? What the hell did I do to this nigga to make him cheat on me? But God only knew, and I guess He wasn't in a speaking mood that night. Eventually, I fell asleep, despite my thoughts and questions.

When I woke up, it was around eight in the morning. T was already up. I could tell it was cold as hell outside from the frosting on the window.

He was in the living room on the X-Box and Dimples was still in bed. I got straight to the point.

"Please don't lie to me, T, just tell me the truth."

"What are you talkin' about?"

"I went through your phone and some girl texted you, so I called her."

His face was still on the TV.

So I continued, "She said, 'Ask your man.'"

He turned his face from the TV to look at me. "Look, I've always kept it real with you, so I ain't about to start lyin'. Me and my cousin Judo been in the trap. He asked me if he could use my phone so he could call this shawty."

"I'm all ears," I told him. Men nowadays seemed to be pathological liars, but hey, I couldn't prove him wrong. So I had to choose to either believe him or not. "And what the fuck is a trap?" I had to know.

"A place where you sling work."

I was completely lost, so I looked at Dimples, who had stepped into the room as he began to answer my question. But from the way her face was looking she was no better off. When T got up and went into the kitchen, we both followed him. He went into the drawer next to the stove, pulled out a zip lock bag, handed it to me, and walked away. The shit inside looked like butter, but it felt solid.

A solid chunk of butter? I thought.

"What the fuck is this?" Dimples asked him as we trailed him back into the living room, forgetting all about the girl and the texts.

"That's fifty-six grams of crack, otherwise known as work. The trap is a house that has crackheads and drug dealers, so I be slingin' work all day in the trap."

That was how I really and truly began to be intro-
duced to the street life.

Jamaica

Chapter 7
New Mission

"Look, Sweets, I don't want y'all sellin' drugs," Traymon said, referring to me and Dimples.

"Well I'm tired of working. I'm tired of wearin' the same clothes and shoes. I wanna wear shit I can't even spell or pronounce," Dimples said. It made me laugh, but she was right.

"Me too. I wanna be happy. I wanna be rich, you know, live like Jay-Z and Beyoncé," I said, looking Traymon dead in his eyes.

"Don't get me wrong, sellin' drugs can get you killed or in jail. The real money is robbing the niggas who hustle their asses off," he said.

"So where do we come in at in this?" Dimples asked.

"Since y'all new to this, no one knows y'all, so setting niggas up won't be a problem. I'll show y'all who to talk to. Ya'll get close to them, find out everything y'all can, and then me and my home-boy, Terry, will do the rest of the work."

"How much do we get paid?" Dimples asked, beating me to the question.

"Say we hit a lick," he began, but I had to cut him off.

"What's a lick?" I asked. Shit, I had to ask to find out.

"A lick is the same as sayin' you gonna rob somebody, but you cut it short and say 'I got a lick to do'."

Me and Dimples just looked at each other and shook our heads. Back then, we didn't know nothing.

"Ski means you wearing a mask to cover your face. Burner means gun. A bench is a scale, white is cocaine, hard is crack, boy is heroin, and poppers is pills. There's a lot that you'll know, just give it some time." Traymon schooled us on almost everything, especially how to get and keep a nigga on track.

"Okay, so what do we get?" I had to ask him again.

"Okay, say we hit a lick for forty stacks."

"Stacks mean thousands, right?" I wondered if he was tired of me cutting him off. Too bad if he was.

"Yeah, it does. So, forty thousand dollars divided by four means we each get ten stacks a piece."

"Free money? Hell yeah, I am down," Dimples spoke up first.

"Count me in," I said.

Since that day, we never showed our faces back at the Kroger where we worked. The money we made was beautiful. The lifestyle became addictive. I was in control of others. I played with their feelings, told them what they wanted to hear, and then sent my man their way.

It was crazy because those niggas actually fell for our words to the point where they told us their life stories, and we didn't even give a fuck.

I loved it, and I just couldn't give it up. But with money comes problems, and that was when they started for us.

After going strong for two years, only one person was in jail, and everyone was still breathing. Terry was the only one of us who went to jail, and that wasn't even for hustling. He caught a DUI that cost him a year, so we took turns sending him money. We couldn't leave the man when he was down, so we did what we could to keep him sane and comfortable along with showing him some *loyalty*.

Chapter 8
Are You Serious?

"Baby, I'm 'bout to take a shower," Traymon said to me.

As soon as he closed the bathroom door, his phone went off. I waited to see if he was going to come back out to get it, but he never did. So me being myself, I got it for him.

The screen read, "Text message from Regina." I pressed open to read the message. "I can't wait to kick it with you again, Boo. I really miss you, Traymon."

Breathe.

Relax.

No, fuck that.

My whole body went from cold to hot. I kicked the bathroom door wide open. Hell yeah, that shit really scared his ass.

He jumped as the back of the door hit the wall. He should've been scared, *real* fucking scared.

"What the fuck is you doin', you dirty dog motherfucker?"

"What the hell wrong with you?" he asked. He didn't even have his clothes off yet.

I swung on his ass, but he grabbed my hand and pushed me out of the bathroom.

"How you gonna cheat on me? What the fuck I ever do to you?" I pounded the closed bathroom door before I walked off.

I knew he was gonna follow me. I headed back to the bedroom to find his phone, and when I got my hands on it, I threw it at him.

"If you go lookin' for shit, you're gonna find what you're lookin' for," he had the nerve to yell at me.

I dropped my head for a second but picked it right back up. "Get your shit and get the fuck out."

As soon as I said that, he turned around and punched me dead in my right eye.

"Ugh," I screamed.

Dimples flew out of her room and into mine with her gun in her hand. "Yo, you heard what the fuck she said. Get your shit and get the fuck out." She had her 9mm pointed at him.

"Dimples, I can't see," I cried to her.

When I moved my hands from my face and realized there was blood everywhere, I panicked inside. I pushed my hands back to my eye.

"You got one minute!" I heard Dimples telling him.

Shoot his ass Dimples, my mind said.

"Bitch, you done lost your mind."

"I may have lost my mind, but you gonna lose your brains."

Damn right! This is my bitch forever, I thought.

I guess he grabbed his phone and left. I couldn't really tell one way or another, since I couldn't see too well. All I knew was Dimples' gun was bigger than his pride because he was most definitely gone.

"We goin'   to the emergency room."

"Dimples,   I don't care what we do. I just wanna keep my eye."

She got me to the emergency room in record time. The lady at the front desk asked me what was wrong. When I removed the cloth I was holding against my eye, she asked, "How did that happen, and when?"

"We were playin' football, and I caught it with my face, just now."

Then she wanted to ask me fifty fucking questions. All I wanted to do was get my damn eye fixed and leave. They took me to check my blood pressure and pulse. Again with questions.

"Are you pregnant?"

I hope not. "No."

"When was your last period?"

Shit, I couldn't remember. "I don't know." I started crying. I couldn't keep the tears from falling anymore. I felt Dimples squeeze my arm. I was so glad she was there to help me keep it together.

"Sweets, get it together," she said.

I was moved to a room and told to lie on the bed as they hooked me up to some machine. I hated hospitals because they reminded me of losing King, but my eye needed serious help. Eventually, a doctor came in and told us that I needed to have an x-ray, but before I could do that, I needed to have a pregnancy test done. A nurse came in to run a catheter and get a urine sample. Then I was shipped to the x-ray room where I was told that part of my eye socket was broken and that several blood vessels had burst.

This is what I get for looking through a phone? Damn.

"Am I goin' to lose my eye?" I asked the nurse, but she didn't bother to answer me. I couldn't even cry anymore. Come to find out, I had to have surgery to remove the blood from around my pupil, which was why I couldn't see.

"That nigga's lucky," I heard Dimples say.

Her words touched my heart, she cared that much. We were moved back to the room that we'd been in before the x-ray while the operating room was prepared.

"Are you scared?" Dimples asked me.

"Naw, bitch, what the fuck you think?" I didn't mean to get smart with her, it just' flew out.

She started laughing at me, and I felt some of the tension leave my body. That was one reason why I loved her so much. She knew how to hold me up when I was down.

"Miss Cash, you will be put to sleep for this procedure," the doctor said when he came back in.

"Sir, I don't care what you do, just make sure I can see again."

I heard Dimples laughing, and almost against my will I felt the corner of my mouth tilt upwards in a half-ass smile.

"Love you, Sweets. I'll be right here waitin' on you."

I didn't remember shit else.

***

"Bitch, you need to wake up is what you need to do."

I tried opening up my eyes, but only one of them worked. My right eye had a patch on it, and I wondered for a second if I looked like a pirate. Must have been that sleepy juice making me stupid. Damn drugs.

"My fuckin' head hurts, yo."

Just then, the doctor walked in. "Miss Cash, how are you feeling?"

"Okay, I guess."

"When you remove the patch to clean the area, make sure that it is done in the dark. More light will damage your pupil. No use of cell phones, drink plenty of water, and take Tylenol."

"Why can't I get no Percocet?"

"Because you're at least three weeks pregnant."

"What you say?" Dimples and I asked at the same time.

"Congrats, you're at least three weeks pregnant. Take care of yourself."

I couldn't even speak, much less shed another tear. I was in a state of shock.

A nurse came in to take over the discharge and the doctor left the room. "After you sign the release form, you're free to go."

Hell yeah, I was ready to go home. Ready to take a shower, and go to sleep. Real sleep, not that drug induced darkness. Feeling shocked, I turned to Dimples.

"This shit can't be serious?" I asked her.

"Girl, yes, it is serious."

"How can this shit happen to me like this? I'm supposed to be happy, but I am *not*. I didn't fuck myself to get pregnant. This is some real serious shit fa'real."

Jamaica

Chapter 9
Shall We?

I took a shower in the dark while Dimples hung sheets over the windows in my room.

"Girl, he came and got all his shit," Dimples said to me.

"Good. I'm glad he did." I was hurt, but my pride wouldn't allow me to say it.

"You gonna take him back?"

I wanted to punch Dimples in her damn mouth for asking me something so stupid. "No."

Dimples tried to cook us dinner. The chicken wings were burnt, but I ate them anyway. I loved Traymon, but I couldn't use love as an excuse to be with him. Not only was he cheating on me, but he had busted my eye up.

***

Dimples slept in my bed with me that night.

"Do me a favor, Dimples?"

"What's that?" she asked, sounding puzzled.

"Text him and say that every dog has its day and his is coming. And by the way, I'm three weeks pregnant."

She did that, and he never texted back. He never came by or called to apologize. It was like I never mattered at all.

It took four months for my eye to fully heal and my belly to start to show. I had even seen Traymon a couple of times at the mall with a girl and not one time did I act a fool. I'm a lady. I carry myself as a lady. So why would I act any different?

Dimples was doing a great job of keeping my mind off of him. She did almost everything for me, from taking me to doctors' appointments to rubbing my feet. She made sure I ate healthy, and took my vitamins during my pregnancy. If it wasn't for her, I don't know what would have happened to me.

Even though I gained weight, she told me how beautiful and sexy I was, even when I wasn't feeling like it.

As the months passed, I thank God we had saved our money because it came in handy.

***

"Today is the day I'm gonna be a father," Dimples shouted.

"What you say, crazy bitch?"

"Quit playing, Sweets. You know I'm this baby's daddy."

I couldn't help but laugh at her. That day I gave birth to a little girl who weighed in at seven pounds ten ounces, and was twenty-one inches long.

"She's so beautiful," Dimples announced.

Beautiful wasn't the word. She had Traymon's complexion, his eyes, lips, and even the dip in his chin, but she had my nose and hair.

"What are we gonna call you?" Dimples asked while looking at the new bundle of joy. That's when it hit me, the perfect name for my perfect child.

"We gonna name her Ex'Quisite."

"Huh, Sweets?"

"Ex'Quisite Queen Cash!" My baby smiled when I said her name.

"When do I sign the birth certificate?"

"What you say, Dimples?"

"I'm the father. They got to have my signature on the birth certificate, you know. So when do I sign it?" she had the nerve to say. We all smiled at that, even Ex'Quisite.

"Whatever, girl." How could I argue with the father?

Three days later, I was ready to go home, and so was Dimples. She had been taking showers in my room, and I knew she missed the tub. After I signed the last page of my release paperwork, I looked at Ex'Quisite's little face and asked her, "Are you ready?"

Looking at her, I couldn't help but wonder how the fuck my mother could have left me the way she did. And why? Just fucking why?

"Bitch, let's go." Thank God Dimples had interrupted my thoughts. Strapped into a pink car seat, Ex'Quisite looked like she was ready to roll.

Jamaica

Chapter 10
New Members

A whole nine months had passed and I still hadn't heard from Traymon, so I call his mother to let her know that I'd had the baby. She sounded super excited, and couldn't wait to see her. We talked for a few minutes, and I assured her that she would see the baby soon.

Dimples and I took turns taking care of Ex'Quisite. I was glad to have a friend like her to help me.

"How about I give Ex'Quisite a nickname?" Dimples asked.

"Shit, go ahead, since you the daddy and all." We both started laughing.

"How about Beauty?"

"Beauty it is, then. Ain't no need to second guess the father."

Beauty had a doctor's appointment, and Dimples, being the best daddy ever, drove us to and from.

"She's perfect," the nurse told me.

Beauty ate, slept, smiled, shitted, and pissed with no worries in the world, and I was cool with that.

"Dimples, I just want to say thank you. Thank you ain't even enough."

"Girl, go ahead with that bullshit," she responded.

"Naw, fa'real though, I owe you my life, plus more."

She started crying. Her tears ran from her eyes like a runaway river, as tears rolled down my face.

On the way home, we stopped at Hardees' to get something to eat. As soon as we pulled into the parking lot, we saw a light green magnum on 22's, and we could see a nigga beating on someone around the side of the car. From afar, it looked like it was another nigga he had down on the ground. But when we got closer, we could see that it was a female.

I was not down with that shit, and I would never be down with it.

"You got that on you?" I asked Dimples.

"Yea, glovebox," she answered without hesitation.

I was out of the car in 2.5 seconds, straight hopped the fuck out. The girl was on the ground in the fetal position, no screams or tears, just taking a nigga's beat down. I couldn't even see her face.

That nigga was so busy he didn't notice me until I shot him dead in his ass. Suddenly he was bleeding, and I watched him fall to the ground. I ran over to the girl while he was distracted by the bullet in his ass. With my gun still in one hand, I helped her up off the ground with the other.

Dimples helped me get her into the backseat. Honestly, I wanted to go back and put another bullet in his ass, or head. A man that beat on a woman was no damn good and didn't deserve no better. We got in the car and left.

Thank God we were only a minute away from home. Dimples got Beauty out of the car, and I helped the young lady that I had picked up off of the ground. She'd been beaten bloody and both of her eyes were black and swollen. She looked like a raccoon, and it seemed like her clothes were barely hanging on her.

"Take your time and walk," I said as I supported her weight and helped her to the door.

When we got inside the apartment, Dimples went to put Beauty to sleep while I started cleaning the girl up. I added a little bleach to some water that I had in a bucket. She took the pain like a real 'G'. Then I noticed that her head was still bleeding.

"Damn, what the hell?" I looked up at Dimples when she came back, after putting Beauty down. "I should've killed his ass."

I was mad at myself that I didn't.

"Look, we don't even know you, but girl, you can stay with us as long as you need to."

Envy Simone Moss was her name, but she went by Black. And yes, Black fit her perfectly. She was not an ugly or too dark black, but she was that pretty, dark chocolate black. So I understood where her alias came from.

She was twenty-two years old with no kids. She told us that her father had died in a club when she was only four years old and that her mother had raised her, but not in a loving way. She said her mother hated the ground that she walked on and never gave her a reason why. Her mom got herself hooked on drugs when Black was only twelve years old, so she basically raised herself. She used to run away from home when social service would show up. One day, her little brother wasn't fast enough, and they took him away. She never saw him again.

Her fucking piece of shit mom would send drug dealers into her room when she was sleeping so they could have their way with her to pay for her drug habit. Not knowing what to do, Black left home at sixteen and never looked back. Her first boyfriend was a pimp who beat her and treated her like shit.

One night while he was asleep, she took all of his money, left Roanoke, Virginia, and moved to Lynchburg. Living at the Salvation Army wasn't for her, and she had gotten a job working at McDonald's as she struggled to get on her feet.

For six months, she did everything, and learned how to do the things that she didn't already know how to do. She used the money that she saved to get a two bedroom apartment. A few days before Christmas, her boss called her into his office and gave her a promotion.

With that, Black became the new manager, not only of her job, but of her life. Things were finally looking up for her. On Christmas day, she met Terrence Morris, aka Cake. He seemed so perfect to her, and they started a friendship that eventually evolved into a relationship. For a whole year, things seemed to be superb. Good job, good man, good life. But things were rarely what they appeared to be.

Cake was a very well-known drug dealer in the state of Virginia, and everyone feared him because he was about his business. He was about that bread. He had three children by three different women, and the youngest child's mother was completely cuckoo. Her head didn't even attach to her body.

Two years into her relationship with him, he started putting his hands on her. Black started missing work, and eventually they fired her. Yup, they fired the damn boss. Ain't that some shit? Crazy. She stayed with him, thinking it was love. But the pain she felt began to destroy that love. She stood five feet seven inches and was as skinny as a stick, with short hair like Kelly Rowland. She had no confidence in herself and ended up staying with that man for another two years. She continued to tell the story of her life leading up to the parking lot where we had found her.

"I went to the store to do a little grocery shoppin', 'cause his last babymama was supposed to be droppin' their son off. I came back too soon. I found Cake rammin' his dick into her from the back in my livin' room, on my damn sofa. That was the last straw there for me."

My mouth was wide the fuck open.

"What did you do?" Dimples asked.

"I stood there and watched until he bust his nut, and then he turned around and saw me. That bitch went and got the kid from the room and walked right past me smilin'."

Oh hell fucking no. "And?" I asked her.

"I just looked at that hoe and smiled back. I know I was blessed to see that for myself 'cause if someone had told me, I would not have believed them."

"Then what happened?" This girl's story was crazy.

"Then he said we should go get somethin' to eat. By the time we got to Hardee's, I finally had the nerve to say somethin'."

"What did you say?" I couldn't stop asking this girl questions.

"I told him it was over, and he went cuckoo. Thank goodness y'all saved me."

"I wanted to kill him. I should've just kept pullin' the trigger. But don't worry, every single dog has its day comin'. Welcome. You're the new member of our family."

And I meant that.

Jamaica

Chapter 11
Tired Of Being Broke

I stayed home three months straight after I gave birth to Beauty, playing both mommy and daddy.

Dimples worked at an Applebee's as a hostess, and Black became a stripper, doing private parties. I couldn't just sit and allow other people to take care of me and mine. I was taught better by King.

I was ready to get out of the house after three months, so I found myself a job at a salon called Layers. I ran the entire situation down to Traymon's mother, Bella. She agreed to watch Beauty for me while I worked, and if she was busy, then Dimples and Black would take turns playing daddy.

Sometimes when I picked Beauty up from Bella's house, Traymon would be there playing with her. As the months went on, he found the courage to ask me if she could spend the night with him at the house that he shared with Regina.

It hurt me to know that he'd walked out on us when we'd needed him the most. But instead of holding his child against him, I showed him the real woman in me.

We always used Bella's house as neutral territory to pick up or drop off Beauty. That went on for three years.

***

Beauty was spending the weekend with her father and soon-to-be stepmom.

"Mane, I am so fuckin' tired of workin'," Dimples bitched as we watched TV one night.

"Shit, I'm tired of shakin' my ass," Black replied.

"Why the fuck can't we start gettin' money like we used to, Sweets? Why we can't get back on the hustle?" Dimples looked at me like I had the answers to life. We had already told Black about how we used to get down before Beauty was born. Traymon had trained us well. But I quit after having Beauty, and didn't' think that Dimples could handle it on her own.

"What you saying, girl?" I asked.

"Shit, ain't it obvious? We strugglin' like a motherfucker. I'm not sayin' we deep down, but damn, we broke, bitch."

"Even if we go back to our old ways, we still gotta keep our jobs." Don't get me wrong, I loved working at the hair salon. Doing hair had always been a passion of mine, but having some more money and planning for Beauty's future was bigger than a passion.

"Shit, that's cool with us," Dimples said while Black nodded her head in agreement.

"A lotta shit gotta change though," I told them.

"C'mon and lead the way," Black answered.

"Okay, we can't live together. We gotta split up. No one should know where we live, not even your mama. We must be in control of everything that we do. We keep our business to ourselves, stay low, and continue doin' what we started doin' best."

And just that quick, we were headed right back to making mad money, because we were damn sure tired of being broke.

Chapter 12
In Training

If you saw one of us out, please trust and believe the other two weren't far behind. Maybe not during the week, since we all had different jobs, but come Friday, Saturday, and Sunday we were like bread, peanut butter, and jelly, because we were on the same hustle together. That was what we did.

Phase 2 was our destination. Doctors, lawyers, teachers, dope boys, it didn't matter. You could name any occupation and they would be there, just like us.

I was ready to get off work and I only had thirty minutes left, so I took a bathroom break to call my bitches and let them know the plan. Dimples must've been in a meeting because she didn't answer, so I hit Black up. No matter what was going on, I knew she was gonna answer her phone.

"Yo, what you doin'?" I asked her when she picked up.

"Mane, you already know."

"Ugh. You a crazy bitch." That bitch was shaking her ass while she was on the phone with me. It didn't surprise me, that was her.

"Yeah, you already know I know," I laughed. "You still on good for tonight, Black?"

"Hell yeah, and I can't wait either. Dimples called me earlier on her break and said she isn't gettin' off till six, but she said that she had everythin' with her."

"A'ight, so I'll see y'all later."

"You got a babysitter?" she asked. For a bitch to be stripping, she sure was talking a whole hell of a lot.

"Yeah, her daddy picked her up from school already, talkin' 'bout how they goin' out of town this weekend."

"Shake that ass," I heard a male voice holler in the background.

"Bitch, I'll let you know everything later. Bye."

I couldn't help but laugh because I knew she had been steady shaking her ass the whole time. I would say one thing though, the girl could dance.

I loved my bitches, would ride or die for them, no matter if they were right or wrong, and that was just the way it was. There was no changing that. The love we had for each other was unexplainable. There was no nigga or bitch in existence who could come between us.

I cleaned up my station and told my co-workers to have a beautiful weekend. The clock said it was time for me to go. I hit the back door and headed to the black 2013 Impala that I was leasing at the moment. I only lived about ten minutes away, so I jumped on the highway, bumping TM:103 because that nigga Jeezy was the *truth*.

When I got home, I checked the mailbox, but there was no mail.

"Really," I said to myself. I was surprised there wasn't a bill in there. Beauty was with her dad so I had the house to myself. I lay my Gucci pocketbook down on the computer stand, put my phone on the charger, and checked my caller ID, no new calls.

It was almost 4:00pm, so I knew 'my nigga' behind bars would be ringing soon. I picked up the cordless and headed into my bedroom to change my clothes so I could get started cleaning the house.

I put on some boy shorts and a wife beater before I started to straighten my room up. I knew Beauty's room was off the meat rack with clothes, toys, and snack wrappers everywhere. I prepared myself for the tornado that I was about to see by putting on some music. As always, it was a whirlwind in her room. Once I finished with her room, I headed straight to the kitchen to start cooking dinner because neither Dimples nor

Black could cook, even though they stayed hungry. Then again, maybe that was why they were always ready to eat, because they couldn't cook for shit.

I took some chicken wings out of the freezer and put them in the sink in some warm water to thaw out. Then I grabbed my phone to text both my bitches and let them know that I was home, cleaning up. That way, if they called or texted me and didn't get an answer, they would know to call the house phone. They knew, nine times out of ten, if I was cleaning, the stereo was on.

It was 3:59 and my house phone was ringing. The caller ID confirmed that it was the Department of Corrections. I answered the phone as I headed back to the living room.

"You have a collect call from," the operator paused and a recording of Jay's voice came on the line saying, "Your baby." Then the operator continued, "An inmate at Dillwyn Correctional Facility. Press zero to accept the call. Press nine to hear the rate."

I pressed zero.

"Hey, baby."

"You miss, daddy?" he asked me.

"You know I do, baby. How is your day so far?"

"Same shit, different day."

Me and Jay had been kickin' it since my daughter was almost one. He had one more year to do, and I had been riding faithfully with him all the way. He wanted me to marry him, but I was not quite sure yet. I was gonna wait to see how it worked out before I changed my last name.

I cleaned the living room and the bathroom while I talked, and it didn't seem like it took very long for his fifteen minutes to run out. But I knew he would call me right back. I enjoyed hearing stories from inside the jail. He and his homeboy,

Easter, were getting paid behind bars. They knew how to hustle their asses off.

"Babe, you gonna get a surprise from me tonight."

"What is it, boo?"

Yeah, he wanted to know what it was, but I wouldn't tell him. Even though my man was behind bars, I still made him feel special.

"If I tell you then it won't be a surprise anymore."

"Boo, when I come home, I'm gonna take you to the moon and back," he declared.

"I'll be waitin' on you."

"Corona, I love you so much, girl. You don't even have an idea of how much I truly love and appreciate you, but I've got a lifetime to show you."

He was so sweet, all I could do was smile. Time flew by when I was having fun. We were lucky to get our *I love you*'s in before the system cut us off.

Now that the house was clean, I turned up my Trey Songz mix tape and headed back to the kitchen. But before I started cooking, I called my sperm donor to talk to my daughter.

"Yo, nigga," I say to him when he answered the phone.

"What's good, yo?"

"Shit, chillin'. Where's Beauty at?"

"Ex'Quisite, your mom on the phone." I could hear her in the background, probably talking shit. That was my girl. I smiled at the sound of her voice, even though she was not in my ear yet.

"Hey, baby! I miss you," I told her when she got the phone.

"Ma, I miss you too, but I'm playin' with my toys."

"You havin' fun?"

."Yea, I love you this much, Ma. Bye."

Just like that, she was gone. Damn.

I remembered when she couldn't even talk or walk. Now my baby was rapping and flying. Traymon got back on the phone, but I wasn't trying to talk to him. So I just told him my friend was beeping in and I had to go. He kept talking anyway, so I hung up on him. It wasn't my fault that nigga was deaf. Our relationship wouldn't go beyond our daughter. If it wasn't about her, then we didn't have shit to say, and nothing in common.

"Fuck."

It was almost five. The time was moving fast, which meant that I needed to move fast too. I seasoned up the wings. I guessed curry wings with white rice would have to do. Them bitches never complained.

They went crazy over my cooking. Come to think of it, I should have opened up my own damn beauty salon and a restaurant. I was so lost in my thoughts and daydreams that I didn't even hear Black come in, and she scared the fuck out of me.

"Sexy and you know it," she said to me.

"I try, you know." I shook my ass a little and we both started to laugh.

"Damn, that chicken smells good. I need to learn to cook 'cause one day I'm gonna cook for my husband," her crazy ass had the nerve to say, knowing good and damn well she could burn boiling water. I just looked at her and burst out laughing again.

I damn sure didn't see her getting married anytime soon. The only dick she claimed was hitting that at the moment was her dildo, 'Black Kong.'

"So, deadbeat got my niece, huh?"

"Yeah. Him, Beauty, and his girlfriend are goin' out of town for the weekend. I think he said North Carolina, some shit like that."

"Really?"

"I guess. As long as Beauty's good and well taken care of, fuck the rest."

"I still can't believe that nigga traded you in for that bitch."

"It's all good. I damn sure ain't losin' no sleep or weight over his bitch ass."

Every time I started talking about that shit, I got mad. Black must have noticed because she changed the subject fast.

"What's Jay doin' besides time?"

"He good, ready to come home and beat this pussy up," I told her as I grabbed my crotch. She just shook her head at me.

"For real though, he's a'ight. He got his GED, so I'm proud of him. He keeps talkin' about us gettin' married, and I just agree with him, 'cause I don't want to hurt his feelings or make his time any harder. But on some real shit, Black, I ain't goin' there anytime soon. Then he gets to talkin' crazy about me havin' another baby. Fuck that."

"You know what to do for that though, right?"

"Damn right. Birth control."

Our conversation was practically drowned out. We could hear the system beating from all the way down the street. I turned the stove down and followed Black to the front porch. Dimples was pulling up in front of the house. She had her hair and windows down, but her swag was up. Our white friend was so hood it was unbelievable. She was just a black girl trapped in a white girl's body. That girl kept her Suburban clean, but her rims even cleaner.

Everybody switching them sides who can you trust
Believe what you wanna believe what's to discuss
Young the type a nigga that throw you the whip and ride the bus
And still give the nigga my last, enough is enough
Bad bitch with me and she makes bread

Let her ride the dick like a ten speed.

We all loved us some Young Jeezy. That was his joint 'Get Right.'

Black started shaking her ass next to me. That was the only thing she had on her that wasn't small. That bitch stayed dancing, that was her life. She may as well have been getting paid to do something she was gonna be doing anyway. No wonder she was a damn stripper.

"Y'all bitches miss me? 'Cause I damn sure miss y'all," Dimples said as she climbed out of her truck.

"You know we do," Black responded.

All three of us hugged each other and repeated out motto, "Until our caskets drop, we shall stand together."

"The food's almost ready," I said. That was all it took to get them headed for the door. I went to the kitchen to get shit together so we could grub.

Dimples and Black were in the living room talking about who was going to pull the best looking nigga that night. I was always laughing at those two.

"Where my baby at?" I heard Dimples asking. Beauty loved her some Auntie Dimples and Auntie Black. They let her get away with murder, they spoiled her, and whatever she wanted she got, no questions asked.

"Black, fill Dimples in on everythin' while I get the plates together."

We didn't keep anything from each other, and we knew everything about one another. Yeah, we were friends, but we were also sisters. Blood couldn't have made us any closer. We were family, and nothing would ever change that.

"Dinner's ready, and I know y'all bitches hungry too," I yelled from the kitchen.

"Hell, yeah," Dimples said.

Black is right behind her. "Can't nobody cook like you, girl," she said. That made me smile because I knew they weren't lying. I loved the kitchen. It was my favorite room in the house.

"Hell fucking yeah. My favorite, I love curry chicken," Dimples' famished ass said. We sat down at the table and linked hands with one another. "Who gonna pray?" she asked.

"You the pastor's kid," I said to her.

"I'll pray," Black laughed.

"Don't take too long either, 'cause a bitch is hungry," Dimples said, stretching the word hungry out.

"God, thank you for today, thank you for everythin', guide and protect us, bless this food, Amen. You didn't think that was too long?" Black asked her when she was finished praying.

"You stay with the jokes."

"What time we leavin' tonight, ya'll?" I asked.

Nobody answered me because they both had their faces head deep in their plates. After about thirty seconds, Black finally said, "We leavin' at 10."

I reminded them that we weren't pulling any stunts that night. "We just checkin' shit out, a'ight?"

We ate, laughed, and talked shit about what we were stunting in that night. They slapped each other high fives when I told them that I was gonna be the one doing all the driving.

"I ain't drinking, so y'all bitches can have all the fun in the world."

"I love it when Jay don't make you mad," Black told me.

They knew me so well it wasn't even funny. When he made me mad, all I wanted to do was drink and act a fool. Dimples scraped the last of her food off of her plate and into her mouth before telling us she was headed to the shower to start getting ready. Black finished next and went to put her shit together in Beauty's room while I started cleaning the kitchen.

Time was definitely flying by. I didn't realize it was eight until I heard the house phone ringing. I knew it was Jay calling.

"Baby, I miss you."

"How much, daddy?"

"I miss you this much, like our princess say."

He kept a smile on my face most of the time. We talked about Beauty for a minute, and then he asked about my girls. So I gave him the rundown about my bitches and what I had planned for the night.

While we were on the phone, they called his name for mail. When he returned to the phone, he was excited because he'd received twenty cards, along with a money receipt for twenty-five hundred dollars. It was my job to make him feel like a king behind those walls. Our conversations always ended fast when we were having fun. We said our *I love you*'s before the call ended.

"A'ight, baby. Love you."

"I love you more," I said before I hung up the phone.

I did love him. He made me happy and he kept my attention. I thought we had a good relationship. He trusted me, and I was learning to trust him.

"I am so gone over you," Black said, mocking me.

"Shut the hell up."

"I'm done," Dimples announced. She had just come out of the shower with her hair wrapped in a towel.

"'Bout damn time," I told her.

"I'm next," Black shouted and took off running for the bathroom.

"You know what they say about the best," I shouted after her. "They save it for last."

"We sharper than a motherfuckin' razor blade," Dimples said, and I had to agree. She was wearing dark denim Robyn Jeans, a white Rag & Bone wife beater, and a pair of Gucci wedge heel sandals. For a white girl, she had a banging body. My bitch was fly.

Black was in True Religion Jeans shorts with the shirt to match and Louis Vuitton sneakers, Damier print. That bitch hated clothes, and clothes hated her. She loved showing her body off.

I grabbed the nine from my drawer and put it in the waistband of my skirt so the neighbors couldn't see it. I left the light on in Beauty's room and the TV on in mine. I grabbed Dimples' keys. We were taking her white Suburban, riding on them 26's.

I was Polo all the way down, from top to bottom, all white everything.

Dimples was up front with me because Black loved to ride in the back. She hit that big ass flat screen as soon as we got in. No bitches did it like us. We put our seatbelts on, and I hit the music. You already know who was coming out the speakers...

I'm what the streets made me, a product of my environment

Took what the streets gave me, a product of my environment

Now it's 28 inches on a brand new hummer (humma)

Telling you right now it's gone be a cold summa (yeah)

Blew the brains out the chevy call it suicide (side)

It's a way of life that's how us young niggas ride (that's right)

Trap or die gave 'em hope

They waiting on the sequel (jeah)

It's clear to see the boy Jeezy do it for the people (Aye)

That was from Young Jeezy's *Thug Motivation 101.*

I had Dimples put the strap in the glove box. We never left home without a strap. Niggas and bitches were grimey, so we stayed on top of them. We jammed the entire way to Phase 2. The place was only twenty minutes away from my house doing the speed limit, but if I was in a hurry, I could get there in ten.

Finding a parking space was always hard, so we always parked on the side of the building. Fuck getting a ticket, we didn't care. We'd just pay that shit. If shit went sour, then our ride would be nearby, instead of out back. Plus, we could see a good section of the parking lot.

"All types of cars out here tonight," Dimples said.

"Hell yeah," I agreed with her.

"Who the fuck driving that all-white 760 with white 22's on it? *That's* what we need to know." Black eyeballed the car hard.

One thing for sure, they had some bread, some extra good looking bread, and Black wanted some. Then again, we all wanted some. We could hear the music from outside. Thank goodness there wasn't a long line. Four men were behind us, so you already know they were checking us out.

"Damn, shawty in the all-white."

I didn't even budge to look back. I put some attitude in my waist and let my ass do the talking.

"Damn, she fat," I heard him exclaim. Dimples looked back and laughed at them.

Nicki was coming through the speakers, and I randomly wondered how she came up with that song *Stupid Ho.*

"Hey, Brandon," we all three said at the same time.

He was one of the security guards there, but he collected the money sometimes, too.

"Y'all tryna hurt 'em tonight," Brandon said as he looked us up and down like he liked what he saw.

"Naw, we just trying to have some fun," Dimples said to him.

Black paid our way in and we all got searched. One day, though, we weren't gonna get searched at all. I had to start working on that.

Chapter 13
Party Time

It was almost eleven and the place was super packed. All eyes were on us, as always. A couple bitches from around the way were present. They were clocking us, trying to see what they could learn. You could see the difference between them bitches and us. They fucked to get paid. We had jobs. No nigga paid our bills.

This bitch, Nichole, who I kinda knew walked up asking if I could do her hair on Thursday at the shop. I told her yea. Her baby daddy, Steve, was on my ass hard, but I didn't want him because everyone was saying he had that House In Virginia, HIV. His money was supposed to be mad long, but I just couldn't chance it. The money might have had the monkey too.

"See you Thursday then," she said.

I walked away to find my biches, but I didn't get too far because a nigga grabbed my arm.

"Damn, ma, you look sexy." He was brave to be touching me like that.

I scanned him up and down. He looked like he was in his late twenties or early thirties. He was handsome, and it looked like his smile was perfect, but his eyes told a different story, a story of fear, emptiness, and loneliness. They seemed cold, super cold. He had long dreads past his shoulders. He was in blue jeans, a white tee shirt, and some Polo loafers.

Damn!

"And you lookin' quite good yourself," was all I could come up with. He had me stuck.

"What's your name?"

"Corona, but everyone calls me Sweets."

"Oh yeah? I'm thinkin' I've got a sweet tooth right about now."

"Really? I wonder how many girls you use that line on."

"None, 'cause I never met one sweet as you before."

He didn't even know me, but he had me smiling, I couldn't even lie. He was trying his hardest.

"Who you here with tonight?"

"Me and my girls."

"Who you leavin' with?"

"The same people I came with." I knew I sounded like I had a slick mouth, but at least it was honest.

He smiled at me. Yup, his smile was perfect. "Playin' hard I see."

His name was Cedrick, but they called him Ced for short. I started scanning the club for Dimples and Black. I wanted to make sure they were good.

"Who you lookin' for?"

"My girls."

"You not scared are you?"

For what? I wanted to know, but I kept my smart mouth to myself that time. "I'm a big girl, and I can take care of myself. Remember that."

"You got me fallin' for you already," he said as he smiled at me again. Perfect.

"So quick?"

"Yes. I love your style, and you're beautiful. You look different, you seem different, and I like different. And to be honest, no other girl has grabbed my attention."

"Save me the story," I told him, and he laughed at me.

"Girl, what you doin'?" Black came out of nowhere, fucking up our conversation.

"Nothin'. Just talkin', and tryna find y'all bitches. Ced, this is Black, Black this is Ced."

They shook hands, and I saw Dimples over Black's shoulder talking to one of Ced's homeboys.

"Let's go dance," Black said, grabbing my arm and pulling me away.

"See you around," I told him. I could tell he didn't want me to leave him. His eyes, they were a story all by themselves.

When we got across the room, Black grabbed Dimples the same way she had done me, only she had a drink in her hand. Dimples bucked the cup in five seconds and put it on the table as we walked past. Truth was that bitch was an alcoholic. I turn back around and Ced was still watching me walk away. *Mane, I bet money makes him look radiant,* I thought.

We finally made our way to the dance floor. I saw Ced not too far away. A light skinned bitch tried talking to him, but he brushed her off like hair. He was busy watching me watch him.

The DJ was killing it. *Hard in the Paint* by Wacka Flocka came on and Black was going crazy. That was her shit. We all start dancing, and the next thing I knew, I feel someone on my neck. I turned around, thinking it had to be Ced, but it wasn't. Some lame ass tryna be pretty nigga wanted to get his dick hard off me.

"Get the fuck away from me."

"Fuck you, bitch," he said and moved on to the next bitch.

I let him have that, but I was gonna have the last laugh. That dusty bucket bitch bent over in front of him. Females kill me. A dance for free and you ain't hit his pockets? Not from one of us. I told my bitches that I was gonna sit down and scope the place out, but they knew me better than that. Cedrick was on my mind.

His swag was a trillion. He could have had any female in there, but he wanted me from what it looked like. I left the

dance floor, even though by then it was my shit that was playing. I sat at the table nearest the dance floor and I scanned the
room for Ced. I spotted him at the bar with the same light
skinned bitch from earlier. I watched him give her some
money, and I wondered who she was. I took my eyes off him
and watched my bitches having fun. I was so deep in thought
that I didn't hear him until he touched my back, which made
me jump in surprise.

"Can I get a dance?"

"No."

"Why not?"

"Because I don't want no problems with your girlfriend,"
I told him while I looked at her from across the way.

"Oh, so you funny too," he said, following my eyes. "She
ain't nobody special to me."

"How am I supposed to believe you?"

"Take my word for it."

"Take your word?" Men lie, women lie, only thing that
don't lie is numbers.

"My word is like my balls, real and authentic."

"How nice," I wanted to say something else so bad, but for
the second time that night, I held my tongue and let a smile
spread across my face.

"She's my nigga's baby ma. He got killed four years ago,
so I told her not to ask any nigga for shit while I am around. I
gave her some bread to have fun."

I wondered if he was telling the truth because I knew niggas would swear on their momma and still lie.

"Oh yeah? That's what's up."

"Can I get you a drink?"

"No thanks."

"You stay shuttin' me down."

"Naw, that's not it." Them bitches looked like they were having a jolly ol' time.

"Your girls havin' fun. Too much fun," he said to me as I watched them.

"Are you havin' fun?" I asked him.

"As a matter of fact, I'm having the best time of my life."

He had all the right answers. I hoped the Patron didn't have him talking. I could smell it on his breath. I got up to walk away, but he stepped in front of me.

"Can I ask you out sometime?"

"I gotta think about it, Ced."

"I'll be waitin'," he said as I walked off.

His short response gave me goosebumps. I had to give it to him. He seemed extremely determined.

Dimples stayed talking to a sexy ass nigga, and Black was on the dance floor with a nigga twice as black as she was. All I could see was his teeth, and I had to shake my head at that. Black and Blacker.

"Damn, take my ass with you," I said to the dude who bumped into me as he walked past. To my surprise, it was the dude from the dance floor who tried to get up on me.

"Bitch, you ain't all that."

He didn't know who he was fucking with.

"Nigga, fuck you and the bitch you came from."

Next thing I knew, that dude was all up in my face. I saw Ced behind him, and he had a couple of his niggas with him.

"Now apologize to the lady," I heard Ced say to him. Dude didn't move. His whole body was straight like an arrow.

"I apologize."

"Fuck you and the bitch you came from," I told him again. I didn't know what Ced said to him, but dude bounced. Ced was strapped, I could see the joint in his waistband. He must have put it in dude's back because that nigga was scared.

"I told you I'm a big girl. I can take care of myself."

"Why do that when you can have me, baby?" He wanted to leave an imprint on my heart, but he was leaving a dent in my brain for the night. I decided to leave him with a hint to see if he'd follow up on it.

"When you need your hair done, come holla at me at Layers," I told him and walked away. He was sexy, handsome for real, drop dead gorgeous, and shining brighter than a diamond, but it was time to go. That was too much for one night. That nigga I got into it with had made me nervous because I couldn't get to the strap fast enough. I wondered how Ced got his in.

My bitches weren't looking for me, but I found them at the bar, buying booze.

"Y'all ready?"

"Yeah, one more drink," Dimples told me as we watched as the bartender mix her liquor.

"We seen the little commotion over there, but your new BF had your back," Black said as Dimples received her cup.

"Yeah, he did," I responded proudly. "Who's the nigga I got into it with?" I asked as I paid for the Jamaican Lizard.

"Oh, that's Marcus. I got the rundown already," Dimples downed her drink, and we went through the back door to walk around the side of the building.

"Damn, bitch, your boy drivin' that?" Black exclaimed.

I stopped dead in my tracks.

Ced was in the driver's seat of that all white 760. The real question was: Did I hit the jackpot?

We stopped moving so he wouldn't see us. We watched him drive away before we get in the truck. Dimples got in the back this time because she was out for the night. I told Black to open up the glove box and get me the Nina because if I saw that Marcus dude again, I was gonna blast his ass. But lucky for him, I didn't see him.

Once we hit the highway, I let Ced settle on my mind. Black must have been feeling good because she had let her seat back. Dimples was talking trash in the back, thinking she was rapping.

I laugh at my bitches because they were the shit, no matter what. Instead of bumping some Jeezy, I pulled out Drake's CD, *Take Care*, and put on my jam, *Practice*. Cedrick was on my mind super hard.

It had been a long time since a man had made such an impression on me. Don't get me wrong, I loved Jay, but he was locked up and wasn't getting out any time soon. That was too damn much for one night. Whatever else happened just fucking happened.

We finally made it home around 3:30 in the morning. I woke my bitches up, and told Black to open the front door because I had to get Dimples out.

"I don't feel too good, Sweets," she moaned as I pulled her from the backseat.

"Bitch, I ain't tell you to get white girl wasted."

"I gotta throw up."

"Dimples, let's try to make it to the bathroom."

When I got her inside, I helped her out of her shoes and she staggered to the bathroom. Black went straight to my bedroom to lie down. I knew it was a wrap. I could hear Dimples pouring her guts out. I grabbed a blanket from the hallway closet and flopped my ass on the sofa. Dimples would crash in Beauty's room.

I had a long day ahead of me. I had to be up in less than three hours because it was Jay's visitation day.

Jamaica

Chapter 14
New Day

I didn't even hear Dimples when she left the bathroom, all I heard was the alarm going off in the bedroom.

"It's seven already?" I drug myself from the couch and peeked in on Dimples on my way to my room. She was still sleeping. I was tired as hell. Black started moving around in the bed when I turned the light on.

"Damn, bitch, turn that shit off."

"Wake the fuck up. Y'all comin' with me to see Jay today?"

"If you drive, we'll go."

Dimples came into the room and plopped down onto the bed.

"Y'all bitches and hangovers don't mix."

I had to get moving. I took a shower, put on my apple bottom jeans with a V-neck Polo shirt and grabbed my Air Force 1's. That was gonna have to do because time wasn't on my side. I forwarded the house phone to my cell, and told them hungover bitches it was time to go.

The ride to Dillwyn was almost two hours long. Visitation started at eight, and I'd be there by nine, not doing the speed limit. I wanted to sleep so bad, but sleep had to wait. At 8:45 my phone started ringing. Yup, it was Jay.

After I listened to the operator, I pressed 0.

"Hello."

"Hey, baby. Where you at?" he had the fucking audacity to ask.

"On my way to see you. Stop askin' questions you already know the answer to," I snapped at him.

"You woke up in a bad mood, I see."

"Naw, just tired. Ready to see you though."

"Where Dimples and Black at?"

"In the car with me. They sleep."

We talked about the previous night. I told him about the situation with Marcus and how Dimples threw up.

"Was it packed out there?"'

"Yeah. Same people, just a different night, baby." I wondered why people who were locked up always worry about what people on the outside are doing.

"Look, I'll see you in a minute. I hate talkin' and drivin'."

"A'ight, baby. Be careful."

It was almost nine, so I had time to call my daughter right quick to see how she was doing. Traymon didn't answer, but his bitch did. She told me both Beauty and Traymon were sleeping, but she'd let them know I called for Beauty.

Hearing her voice made me sick, but shit, it was reality. I had to accept her, but not yet. She was one sneaky bitch. I could just feel it.

The parking lot was always packed.

"Ya'll bitches wake the hell up."

"We gonna get somethin' to eat and do a little shoppin'," Black said with a yawn.

"Tell Jay don't drop the soap," Dimples giggled.

"Haha, bitch, you got jokes."

I hated going out there, and I hated how they searched me from head to toe, but I wanted for him to be happy. I'd been going out there for a year, faithfully. Rain, sleet, or snow, I was there. The line wasn't long that day, so going through the process wasn't too bad. I was placed at the fifth table in the fourth row. But instead of sitting down, I went to the vending machine to get us a drink. Those niggas down there were always checking me out. Even some bitches were giving me the eye.

When I got back to the table, the couple behind me was having a huge disagreement. Dude only had six months left, and his shawty said she was moving away. Crazy, right? But even though niggas were behind those walls, they had more than one bitch. You didn't know if what they were telling you was the truth. There was a thing called *jail talk*, and men were excellent at it.

Jay knew that I had more sense than that, so running that jail shit by me would have been a complete waste of time. He always said, "You think and act like a nigga so much. Where the bitch part at?" I had it in me, but I just didn't bring it out. We were living in a cold-hearted world.

His swagger was on point. He had a white tee under his blue button up shirt, and he was wearing Levi's with some black Timbs. My nigga was fresh to death, and didn't need or want for shit because I made sure he was straight.

"Damn, my baby lookin' like a bag of money. Turn around for daddy," he told me.

"Boy, you is crazy. Give me some sugar."

He put his lips on mine, grabbed my ass, and tilted my head back with the force of his kiss. That was the best part. Just touching him and having him touch me had my pussy dripping.

What I would have done for some of this dick, only God knew.

"You smell good, boo."

"Shit, girl, I could eat you right now, right here, if they would let me."

"Since that can't happen, what you want to eat?"

"You know, the regular."

I walked away to get some chicken wings. Not only was he watching me as I went, but he was watching other niggas clock me. Knowing that he had me made him happy. We spent five hours talking, eating, and laughing nonstop.

Visitation was over at three. I hated leaving him there, but I couldn't change it, only time could. We ended the visit the same way we started it, with a hug and kiss.

"Damn. I need some dick bad."

Chapter 15
Get Ready

Dimples and Black kept their conversation rolling when I got into the car. It almost seemed like they didn't even know I was there, until Dimples pulls me into it.

"Anyway, Sweets, the nigga who tried that bullshit with you last night, his name is Marcus. He's from Madison Street, and he's pushing mad weight, too. He just came home four months ago. He's got two kids with different baby mamas, and he keeps all the bread at his mother's house. She lives on Old Forest Road, and she works as a private sitter at night."

"How sure are you?" I asked.

"Well, his younger brother, Fatts, fuckin' with a girl from church, so she got the rundown for me. Plus ol' girl say the nigga stay strapped."

Church people some shit, I tell you!

"Last night his ass was slippin' and almost got smoked."

"Fuck that nigga, yo," Black said.

"Damn right. Let's see if he at the bar tonight. If he is, then Black, I want you on him. Cool?" I asked.

"I'm on it!"

"Anyway, I got this other nigga who lives on the other side of town. His name is Whyte. He's sexy as fuck, plus he got a big dick."

We all started laughing when she said that.

"Dimples, how the fuck you know his dick is big, bitch?" Black asked her. I wanted to hear that shit for sure.

"Last night, when he grabbed my ass, I grabbed his dick. Grab for grab, you know. I ain't shy, shit." We laughed real hard when she said that. When I say that bitch was crazy, that bitch was crazy.

"I am tired as hell, and don't feel like drivin' back."

Got you,'' Dimples said. "Get your ass in the back then."

"Y'all ain't get me shit to eat?"

"You know we didn't know how long your ass was gonna be inside, and your shit would have been cold anyway, so relax," Black said to me as I got in the backseat.

"We can go to the little country store and get you some hot dogs if you want, Sweets," Dimples yelled over the music she had put on as soon as she hit the driver's seat.

"Turn that shit down, my phone ringin' y'all." It was a 404 area code. *Who the fuck can this be?* When I answered, a male voice responded to me.

"Can I speak to Sweets?"

"This her. Who this?"

"I see you've forgotten my voice already."

"How did you get my number?"

"I have my ways, especially when I want somethin'."

"Who is it, bitch?" nosey ass Black hissed from the front seat.

"Hey, Cedrick, how are you doin'?"

"Good, and you?"

"I'm good, but for real, please tell me how you got my number."

"A friend of a friend of a friend."

"You went through all that for me?"

"Yeah, only for you though."

"I hear you talkin'," I wondered if he could hear the smile in my voice.

"Miss Lady, are you busy?"

"Naw, if I was, I wouldn't have answered."

"Has anyone ever told you how reckless your mouth is?"

"Naw, but you can tell me."

"You have the sassiest mouth that I have ever run across. But I like it, and I know that I can live with it."

"You ain't gotta put up with it 'cause we ain't together."

"N-O-T-Y-E-T," he said, spelling the words out.

Now at a loss for words, I really didn't know what to say. Goosebumps covered my body.

"You still there?"

"Yeah, I'm still here. Just listenin' to you."

"Good. You got any plans for tonight?"

"Me and my girls are goin' out."

"Oh, okay. Mind if I ask where?"

"We're not sure yet."

"Are you just tryin' not to let me know?"

"Probably a bar, but as I said, we ain't sure yet."

"I love that mouth of yours," he told me.

"Me too. If I do see you out tonight, I'll speak."

"Sweets, I would really like that, and now that you have my number, make sure you save it and use it."

Believe me, I planned to. "I won't lose it."

Conversation over, I hung up. Black may as well have climbed into the backseat with me because her whole body was practically already back there. I told them everything that was said. They were both quiet but smiling like crazy, until Dimples said, "Don't forget about us."

"That will never happen." Just like that, I lost my appetite. When we stopped at the country store, the only thing we got was gas. The ride home was silent. Black went back to sleep as Keyshia Cole's song *Enough of No Love* played.

I was tired as hell myself. I didn't even hear my phone ringing, so I missed my daughter's call. I didn't even wake up until I heard the car door slam when we made it back to the house. My first thoughts were of what Dimples had said earlier about not forgetting them. That had me mad. Why did she think that I would forget them like that?

She must have known it pissed me off because she apologized for saying it. I told her it was cool, I wasn't tripping.

"All that anger you got built up inside of you, you need to release that shit," she told me.

"I will as soon as Jay gets home."

"The way you lookin', I think Ced will be the one helpin' you with that."

"You got jokes, too?"

"I agree," Black added.

"Do you really think if Jay was out and you was in, he'd be holdin' you down like you holdin' him down?" Dimples asked me to make a point.

I hated that question because I knew the answer like I knew the back of my hand.

"Naw."

"You mean, hell fuckin' no," Dimples said, correcting me.

"Preach, girl." Black had to put her five cents in. I should have just been glad she didn't give me change for a dollar. They keep it real and raw with me all the time, no matter if they hurt my feelings or not. I would rather my feelings hurt than had my heart broken again.

"You need to get some dick in your life, for real," Black informed me.

"When you last had a nut? I mean a real nut, too," Dimples asked. "Since you ain't gettin' no dick, you need to get yourself a toy, 'cause four bitches on thumb street ain't cuttin' it."

Black laughed.

"Don't worry, when I do, y'all bitches will be the first to know. I gotta call Beauty, so y'all shut the fuck up with that language."

My sperm donor answered.

"What's good nigga?"

"Shit, our daughter wanted you, but she and shawty went to get their nails and shit done."

"Oh, okay."

"What you doin', Sweets?"

"Nothin'. What you doin' Traymon?"

"Missin' you, babyma."

"Boy, you crazy as hell. When Beauty gets back, tell her to call me."

"You ain't gonna let me hit that again?"

"Bye, nigga!"

Just because he was my baby-daddy, he thought that he could and should fuck me at any given time. He had the game truly fucked up. I would never, and I mean *never*, let him see or touch this pussy cat again.

"You should at least let him bang you out one more time," Dimples said, like her opinion was gonna change anything. It wasn't.

"At least let him give you some head," Black suggested. Another opinion that didn't matter.

"Y'all fuckin' crazy. Y'all can miss me with that bullshit."

Come to think of it, I should have at least got some head and recorded it. That way, if his shawty ever got out of line, I could put her ass back in place and let that bitch know, no matter what, he would always want this pussy. Even though my mind told me to get revenge on her, my heart still said *no*. I discarded the idea as soon as I had it. He was old meat, and I needed new spice and flavor in my life.

Jamaica

Chapter 16
Ready

Buffalo Wild Wings was the spot to be on Saturday nights. It was free to get in, a place where you could chill and watch games, or just hang out with your friends. Where there were sports, there were men, and where there were men, there was usually money. That meant me and my bitches were where the money was at.

We weren't dressed to impress or draw attention, just some jeans, fitted tees and sneakers. Black was the driver for the night, and she had a job to do, so she needed to be sober. But me and Dimples? Shit, we were gonna get it in. I needed a drink, too.

When we pulled up, the clock on the dashboard said it was 10:30. BWW's closed at two, and three hours was plenty of time to do what we went to do. As soon as we got inside, I asked Dimples if she grabbed the Nina.

"Have we ever left home without it?" She raised her eyebrow at me.

I just smiled at her. I loved my bitches.

Black spotted Marcus first. She walked off and left us standing where we were. Dimples, with her alcoholic ass, wanted a drink, so we moved towards the bar. Marcus and Black were over by the bathroom. She definitely had his attention. On some real shit, it looked like pussy ruled his ass. If that was the case, then we had him exactly where we wanted him. This was gonna be fun. Black had an ass like *wow*, and Marcus was on her.

"What can I get you tonight, ladies?" The waitress asked. She was pretty, but she had Assatall Syndrome, she ain't have no ass at all. Her name tag said her name was Brittney.

"Two Jamaican Lizards, please," I told her.

Dimples placed her order too. "One Jamaican Lizard and a Long Island ice dry tea."

"Okay, be right back." She disappeared to make our drinks.

I glanced over at Black to make sure she was cool. She was, so I relaxed a little. I watched as a white boy started talking to Dimples.

He was cute, but he wasn't her type, unless his money was right. Then he would have been just right for all three of us. I excused myself and sat at an empty table.

I was not seated for two minutes before I heard, "Excuse me, can I have the seat beside you?"

I knew that voice. "Yeah, you can." He sat, and I asked him, "How did you know that I'd be out here tonight?"

"An angel told me, and I followed the stars," Ced explained.

The waitress interrupted, "Your drinks," she said as she put two glasses down on the table between us.

"How nice of you to buy me a drink," he sounded like he was teasing.

"Na, they both for me," I told him, smiling. "But you can drink one if you want."

"What else can I drink?" He winked at me before turning his attention to Brittney.

"Two Patron and a RedBull, please."

Mane, he was so sexy. Damn! All-white tee, black jeans, and white dopeman's with an all-white fitted hat that said *Heat* on the front.

"Who you goin' for, the Heat or the Celtics?" he asked me.

"I love green, so the Celtics get my vote."

"Damn, that hurt. I thought you would at least like James."

"Naw, James too cocky for me. I like Rondo. He seems humble."

"Oh, okay, so we can bet each other when they play?"

"You got it!"

I looked around, and Dimples was nowhere in sight, but Black was still in the same spot with Marcus. Ced was very entertaining, and he kept me smiling, even though his team was winning.

"Don't look so sad, it's just a game," he said, winking at me.

"Yeah, if you say so."

We slipped conversation in on the commercials while watching the game. We laughed and mean mugged each other. The score was 104 to 98 Heats way.

My phone was ringing and the screen said it was Jay. It was almost time for lockdown, so I knew he wanted to tell me goodnight. I had to answer, so I told Ced that I'd be right back. By the time I got outside, it was time to press 0.

"You looked so sexy today. After that visit, I had to beat my dick."

"Well, hello to you too, darling."

"I hear music."

We talked about sports a little. He was on the Boston's team now because the Lakers weren't shit. At least he joined a winning team.

"Well, baby, have fun. I ain't gonna hold you," he said.

That was weird for him to say. We had only been on the phone for seven minutes. I was missing Ced's company, but I wanted to know why Jay wanted to hang up so quick.

"What's wrong, baby?" I asked.

"Shit, gonna play some poker real quick before they lock us down."

"Oh, okay. Well I love you, Jahmain Jones."

"I love you, too. I'll call you tomorrow."

That shit was weird. That was the first time he'd ever wanted to get off the phone early. He hung up before I could say anything else. Damn. My feelings were hurt. Maybe I was tripping because I had Ced in there waiting on me. My mind was racing. I wondered what was going on between Black and Marcus, and where the fuck was Dimples at. I had a lot going on, and I needed to get back inside.

Ced was still at the table where I left him. I glanced across the way, looking for Black, but I didn't see her. Where the fuck was Dimples?

"I'll be right back. I gotta go to the bathroom."

Ced acknowledged me with a nod.

My eyes were everywhere as I cut across the room. I needed to find them fast, so I rushed into the bathroom to call her ass.

"Damn, bitch, where the fuck you at?" I asked when Black picked up.

"At BDubs, chillin' with my friend Marcus outside."

When the hell did they go outside? I was just out there, I wondered.

"You in the car with him?"

"Yeah, I miss you too, mom."

"He wanna fuck?"

"Yeah, look in the kitchen drawer. It's under the mat."

"You ready to go?" I heard her ask Marcus.

"Okay, girl, just stall for a minute," I told her. I hung the phone up. I had to find Dimples fast, and I only had two minutes to get it together. I left the bathroom and squeezed my way back to the table where Ced was still waiting. My eyes were still on the prowl for Dimples. I finally spotted her ass on the other side. I told Ced that I had to go, and that I would call him as soon as possible.

When he asked if everything was okay, I told him every-thing was good. I tossed a hundred dollar bill on the table and told him to tip Brittney well.

He didn't have time to get a word out before I was gone. When I got to Dimples, I grabbed her arm, pulling her away from her friend. "Bitch, I'm sorry, but we got to go."

"I'll call you," Dimples said over her shoulder to dude.

As soon as we got out the front door, we saw a car leaving the parking lot. We ran to our car at full speed. I knew that was him.

I filled Dimples in on everything as I started the car. That sucka for pussy nigga was gonna need help when we were done with him. Dimples started changing her clothes and pulled her hair into a ponytail.

I could see the BMW ahead of us, and I knew Black was talking her ass off. I hung back to keep enough distance so that he didn't notice that he was being followed.

If he was headed to his mom's house, we were only twenty minutes away, and it looked like that was where he was going. I still had to change my clothes, but Dimples is ready. We didn't say shit. She put Flocka's CD in and put it on one of your motivation song.

All my niggas TTG
They trained to go shawty
Kick a door shawty
Lay down on the floor shawty, Flocka said.

"I need to get my clothes changed. Fast."

"I hope this dumb ass nigga stops at the store to get some condoms, at least," Dimples stated.

"Damn right."

That nigga did just that. Me and Dimples switched seats once we pulled over, and I started getting myself together.

Everything was black, so you know it was an all-black party going down. Black Dickies outfit, skull caps, Timbs and bandanas. The Nina was even black, and the duffle bag too. The nigga came out of the store with a six pack and a Four Loco. That had to be for my bitch.

He pulled out of the gas station and made an immediate right onto Jackson. Dimples hit the headlights and stayed back. It was a dead end ahead, and that was where he was headed, so we parked the car and kept track of his taillights. He turned into a driveway. We couldn't see the house number, but we also couldn't miss that light blue BMW he drove either.

We watched as Marcus and Black both exited the vehicle. Black knew her part of the job. We would wait five minutes before we started walking toward the house. Even with 20/20 vision, you still couldn't see us. We were as close to being invisible as we could get without being air. This was a quiet neighborhood, and it looked rich. We were ready and in position. Now all we were waiting on was for Black to text us to let us know it was okay.

Twenty minutes went by before we finally heard from her. Her text said, "Let's get it."

The front door was unlocked. *Job well done, Black.* I thanked God the place had carpet to muffle our footsteps. I guessed no one else was home. I had to give it to whoever lived there, the place was beautiful.

The mouth piece we had in our mouths made us sound like men.

Black saw us before Marcus felt the Nina at his head. She was on her back, looking up and making loud ass noises. He was on top of her, doing whatever it was he thought he was doing.

"Nigga, if you move I'm gonna blow your motherfuckin' head off," I told him. Black started screaming her ass off, not too loud though. It was pretty good acting. It was also irritating as hell.

"Shut the fuck up, bitch. Another sound and I'll mute you forever," I yelled.

Dimples told Black to get dressed. "And put your cell phone in this bag, too." Dimples sounded pretty good when she was giving orders. Maybe it was just the mouthpiece.

Marcus had a limp dick, but it was less than average. I wanted to laugh, but I was a professional, and I held my composure.

"Get your shit and leave, bitch. If you call anybody or say anythin', I'll find you and kill you," Dimples said.

And you know what? That bitch started crying *real tears.* Yo, that bitch deserved a Grammy for that night! She rushed into her clothes and ran out the door.

"Move if you want to, and watch me send you to meet your maker," I told Marcus who was still laying on the bed where he'd rolled off of Black. He looked like he didn't even give a fuck. He was riding cool, but I wanted him to know that at that moment, I was his master.

I tied his hands behind his back with a sheet off of the bed. Then Dimples passed me a rope out of the duffle bag and I used it to tie his ankles together. Black had left her panties. I picked them up off the floor and shoved them into his mouth.

"You look like a newborn baby waitin' on a bottle, helpless," I said to him.

Dimples threw her head back and laughed. This was a good time, and it was bound to get better.

"Fuck you." His defiance was muffled by the panties in his mouth, but I knew what he said. Attitude. I knew how to fix that.

I pistol whipped his ass, and blood splattered on the headboard and blankets. He starts screaming through the gag, and it sounded pretty loud, so I stuffed the panties even deeper into his mouth.

"Where the money and work at?" Dimples asked him.

He didn't answer, so she started to tear shit up.

"Ain't no need to answer, nigga. I already got you."

There were six Jordan boxes full of money, two boxes full of bags of white powder, and one pound of some sticky looking weed. I kept my gun trained on his ass. Dimples pulled everything out of the closet and started transferring it to the duffle bag. That nigga was looking like he wanted to cry. When I pushed him off the bed, Dimples helped me flip the mattress over on him before we ran for the door.

No one was outside, except Black. She was parked right in front of the house. We jumped in the car and she pulled off like nothing had even happened. We took our ski masks off at the stop sign, put our seatbelts on, and watched Black hit the highway.

We rode in silence the whole way home, which seemed to take forever because Black was doing the speed limit. Riding dirty was a life sentence, and we weren't going down that road. When we made it to the house, she parked the car in the backyard, and we went in through the back door. Mission accomplished. As soon as we got inside, we let loose and jumped for joy.

We counted the money twice to make sure our numbers were correct. We had gotten away with forty-two thousand four hundred fifty dollars, a whole brick of cocaine, and a pound of some good ass weed.

"What a fuckin' lick. Damn, I like those numbers," I exclaimed.

"Fuck havin' a nigga, especially when we can have his money," Black commented, serious as hell.

"Damn, Black, you look real good layin' on your back," Dimples said, and even I had to agree. She did that.

"The dick was a'ight, but the money, the work, and the smoke is even better. I gotta wash this pussy juice off me, y'all," Black told us as she headed to the bathroom.

"Next time, make sure you get a nut." I couldn't help but laugh my ass off at my own joke. *What a fucking night. One mission down and plenty left to go.*

We each had fourteen thousand one hundred fifty dollars, twelve ounces of coke, and I was gonna sell the whole pound of weed to my boss's baby-daddy and split the bread between us. We'd accomplished so much in just two days. Shit was looking real good.

Damn! Now that things have slowed down, Ced's back on my mind. I wondered what he was doing, and thinking, so I got my phone and texted him, "Just wanted to let you know you're on my mind heavy."

Shit, for all I knew, he was laid up. Oh well, I couldn't figure out if he was gonna be a victim, a lover, or both. All I could do was give it time.

***

It was eight in the morning when I heard the toaster going off. Dimples was making her a bread and butter sandwich. Crazy ass bitch. "We only have two hours to get ready for church. Mom and Dad will be lookin' for us today," she said when I walked into the kitchen. Sunday was the Lord's Day, and our family time. We went to church to thank the Lord for all of our blessings, went out to eat after, and then came home to chill.

Church was as great as it always was. Mr. and Mrs. John Marshall knew the word of the Lord, and they knew how to show it. They loved me and Black like we were their own kids.

We finally got home around 4:30. Jay hadn't called me all day, but Ced had texted me back.

"You had me worried last night, but I'm good now 'cause I see that I'm on your mind. I like that."

"That nigga Whyte's our next lick," Dimples informed us.

"A'ite what's the details?" That was our Black, on top of it already.

"Well, this bitch who works at the restaurant with me used to fuck with him, but he dogged her ass and forced her to have an abortion, so now she puttin° all his business on Front Street. Ol' girl says she gonna get him set the fuck up to get revenge on him 'cause he broke her heart."

"This the same nigga that grabbed your ass the other night?" I asked to make sure.

"Yeah, that's him," Dimples responded.

"Hmmm," snorts Black, "Karma is a bitch, and you always want that bitch to be beautiful."

"Damn right," I agreed completely.

"Y'all think Karma will get us?" the pastor's kid had to ask.

We all looked at each other. It was just reality. Do unto others as you would have others do unto you.

"Fuck that. When the times comes, we'll think about it, but for right now, money's on my mind and should be on y'all's," I told them, meaning every word that came out of my mouth.

"Anyway, back to business, y'all," Dimples proceeded with the info on our next victim. "This nigga Whyte got at least four baby mothers. He works for a construction company on Westbrook Avenue, and he lives in Timberlake with one of his baby-ma's. I think she's the most recent one, but he's fuckin' with this yellow bitch name La'Tasha who lives on Campbell Ave. So, he's back and forth. Plus the nigga got a white girl name Dove who drives him everywhere. The most important thin' is that this nigga keeps all the money in a storage unit on Park Ave. Mad nigga's want to get at him but he moves too fast, and he stays on the low, *no* clubbin' or bar hoppin', so it's hard to keep a GPS on him."

I had to stop and think. That nigga had to have some serious bread. He was balling hard. Just imagine who his plug was. Damn! I wondered if we could get that.

"Well, ol' girl says he's got at least seventy stacks in that bitch." Dimples was pink with excitement, and I knew she was thinking about her cut already. I did the math real quick in my head. We'd each get a little over twenty stacks if it was an even seventy. I knew that nigga had a lotta money because having that many women costs, or the dick was absolutely astounding. I was a thinker, and I thought good, long, and hard on this. But on some real shit, there was nothing to think about.

Seventy stacks.

"It's not what you do, it's who you know that can help you do it. That's the key to success or failure," I schooled them a little. You learn something new every day.

"Shit, I'll go around and find the address from his old joint. I'll follow him around for a couple of days to see what's up."

"Ain't no need for that, Dimples," I told her. "Jay's cousin A'Dasia works at the storage on Park Ave. She's gotta know this nigga. Black, get me my phone off the television stand."

Dimples was smiling like a faggot with ten bags of dicks. It was time to make a phone call.

"Hey, baby girl. What's good?" I said when she picked up.

"Shit, just chilling, cousin-in-law. How my big cousin doing?"

"He good. Can't wait to come home, you already know. How's the family doing?"

"They good, the baby's sleep, thank God!"

It was time to cut to the chase. I winked my left eye at Dimples and Black.

"I need your help real bad on something that you can't tell anyone about."

"What's good?" she asked, sounding like she was down.

"You ever heard of a nigga name Whyte?" I put her on the speakerphone so my bitches could hear too.

"Yeah, I know of him, but I don't know him like that. He comes every month to pay his bill on this storage unit he's renting where I work," she said.

All three of us were smiling like we had just seen the dentist.

"Yea." I was excited like a motherfucker, but I kept my voice cool.

"Why, what's up?"

"See, he got one of my bitches pregnant and ain't tryin' to help her. He put her out of their house and took all her shit. So now she don't know how she's gonna start over. Plus, havin' their baby on her own is hard. Everthin' is in the storage unit."

I hoped she believed me because that right there was all lies, but it had just flown out of my mouth.

"I could get in trouble or lose my job."

"Shit, I know, but I promise you I'll make sure she don't tell shit, and you already know my mouth is closed."

"A'ight, I'll text you the number tomorrow when I get to work."

"That's a bet. I got you, too," I told her.

"Tell my cousin I love him and I can't wait for him to come home."

"You already know I will," I said with a smile on my face.

Dimples and Black were dancing like two little girls in a candy store.

"A'ight, we doin' this shit tomorrow night, late night shit, like some John Creeper type shit," Dimples said when I ended the call with A'Dasia.

"Damn, I gotta ask Regina if Beauty can spend the night."

Asking my sperm donor to watch his own child was a problem. I either had to pay him or he was gonna say, "You know I'm gonna be missin' money." *Fuck it. I'll just pay her ass a couple hundred 'cause this lick is gonna be right.* Shit. Sometimes it seemed like I stayed on the damn phone.

"Yo, what y'all doin'?"

"Shit, on the way back home. What's up?"

"Nothin'. Where's your wife at?"

"You got jokes. She right here." Word on the streets was they were getting married. He claimed it wasn't that serious, but I already knew niggas and bitches lie.

"Let me talk to her real quick."

"Hold on." I heard the phone change hands and I heard him saying, "Sweets wanna talk to you."

"Hello?" Regina made it her business to let me know Beauty had a blast, and from it she was out cold in the back seat. I didn't really care what happened on their trip. As long as Beauty was straight, I was good.

So I got straight to the point of me wanting to talk to her. She was cool with keeping Beauty until Tuesday and I was to pick her up from school that day. Shit, she wanted to be wifey, then she had better act like one.

"Smooth operator," Black said as she did Michael Jackson's moonwalk.

We ate and watched football games, played some cards and talked some shit. Sunday was our day. Come to think of it, Jay hadn't called me all day. He sure was occupied, but with what? I couldn't be mad. Even though he was locked up, he still had a life to live, but I usually spoke to him twice a day at least. On my days off, we would talk from 8am until they cut the phones off, sometimes as late as 12:30am.

I missed his voice, but hey, I missed Ced's presence too. *Damn, I think I'm in big trouble. Fuck it. I'm human.* I felt torn between Jay and Ced. Even though Jay was behind bars, I could still feel his love from the phone calls, visits, and mail. With Ced, he was at my disposal, just a call away. I needed to feel hands wrap around me at night, but with my hustle, I was too busy for a man. So in a way, I was glad Jay was locked up and Ced was doing him, and not doing me. My job took up my man time and my money came before dick because I had a mouth to feed, Beauty.

Dimples and Black had crashed. They were both sleeping. I dialed Ced's number around one in the morning.

"Can I speak to Ced?" I asked when he picked up the phone, even though I knew it was him.

"He out of town."

"Oh, okay. Tell him Sweets called, please." Just when I was about to hang up the phone, he stopped me.

"Girl, stop playin' with me."

"You play too much. I thought I'd play back."

"I been waitin' on your call all day, sexy lady."

"So why didn't you just call me then?"

"I texted you, but you didn't text back, so I let it be. Ain't tryin' to cloud your space or be a stalker."

"Oh, yeah?"

"What you doin' this time of night, anyway?" he asked.

"Nothin'. Can't sleep even though I have to be at work at nine in the morning."

"Can I come get my hair done in the morning, then?"

"I'm booked in the morning, but you can come at one. I'll be done with you before three."

"Damn, you must think I'm just a two hour nigga."

"Naw, I don't know. But I gotta be off at 2:30, 'cause I gotta get my little girl from school." Yeah, I was lying to him. I didn't have to get her till Tuesday, but what was I supposed to do? He didn't need to know my business.

"You got a little girl? How old is she?"

"Yeah, she's almost four, goin' on twenty one."

"I know, kids nowadays are a rip. I have three my damn self, two girls, one boy."

"How old are they?"

"Christina is seven, Cobra is five, and Jr. is six."

"Back to back, I see."

"Yeah, maybe one day your little girl can play with Cobra?"

"One day." The conversation was becoming too much for me. I had to get off the phone. Not that I was tired, but because he was getting to me in a damn good way.

"Anyway, Ced, I'll see you tomorrow at one, and don't be late either."

"Believe me, the only time I'm late is when I'm havin' my way."

That man was a smart ass for sure. Sex was on my mind, so everything he was said sounded potentially sexual to me. "Sweet dreams."

"You too, baby girl."

I hung up the phone so fast it was crazy. Boy, oh boy, he had me hot.

Jamaica

Chapter 17
Where You Came From

As always, Black was the first one up, and the first one gone. Since it was Monday, I had to start the week off with a terrific breakfast, scrambled eggs with cheese, fried apples, honey bacon, grits, toasted bread, with a nice tall glass of orange juice.

"Girl, you gotta teach me how to throw down in the kitchen, 'cause you could break up a happy home just by seasonin' up some food," Dimples proclaimed to me.

"Bitch, you a damn fool for that one."

It was seven already, which meant that Beauty was up and getting ready for school. I wondered if Traymon and Regina took her together. Thank goodness for Dimples running her mouth. She took me out of my thoughts, and brought me back to the obvious.

"I wish I could stay with you all day, but a girl like me gotta go make an honest livin'," she muttered.

"Love you, too, crazy ass," I yelled at her as she was on her way out the door.

Damn. I've got a love/hate relationship with Mondays, I thought.

I got to work extra early because I needed to holla at Talena about the weed.

She was already there.

Talena was sitting in her office. I could tell that something was up with her because she was holding her head in her hands as she shook her head. I asked her what was up and she opened up to me like it was nothing. Sometimes an ear was all you needed.

Basically, Twan was stressed the fuck out and he was taking his problems out on her.

Word on the street, and from my own eyes, I knew Twan lived in the streets. The streets were all he knew. His older brother, Rome, raised him because their parents died. And since Rome had been locked up for four years, Twan had been holding shit down by himself. I kind of saluted the nigga because he didn't give up on life even though his father had killed his mother, and then himself, right in front of his sons. Rome taught him the street life at an early age, so he took advantage of it, and he opened up a salon in Talena's name.

"Girl, as long as the nigga ain't cheatin', don't have no rugrats on you, and ain't beatin' on you, then you good. Stress will fly by, just keep standin' by him."

"Sweets, I want him out of the game. Look what Rome's doin'! That nigga's never comin' home. He got life plus twenty for drugs."

The system was fucked the fuck up. Kill a motherfucker, and you get ten, no more than fifteen, but sell drugs if you want to, and you can watch them throw dirt on you from the bottom of a shallow grave.

"Talk to him. Explain it all to him, Talena. Let me ask you a question though."

"What's that?"

"What's he sellin'?"

"Weed."

"Well, that ain't so bad. It's that white shit that's the devil, but that green is a different story, and now that they legalizing it, he's gonna be good. He might do a little time, but nothin' big."

"We got kids to raise, Sweets. What happens if the system don't get him? His enemies will."

"Y'all just have to talk this shit out."

"It's a drought, and he's mad that he can't supply his workers, and he's takin' all his stress out on me."

116

And with that, I jumped right in. I needed to get rid of that weed, and since he needed it and I had it, we were good. I let her know I had a pound of some sticky icky shit and I was willing to help out if he wanted it. Her face showed relief, and she smiled, but the bitch had the nerve to tell me not to tell anyone her business. As if I'd love to have run my mouth into an indictment. I'd been knowing that bitch for three years and not once in three years had she heard my name in any shit. She apologized real quickly for her statement. I couldn't really blame her because she was protecting herself and her man. I let her know I had the shit nearby so she should call Twan and inform him. But before she could even pick her cell phone up off the desk, Twan himself came through the door with a bag in his hands. I could smell the aroma of breakfast food. We spoke and I exited the office, leaving them there kissing and shit. Too much of that sentimental stuff wasn't good for me.

About ten minutes later, I saw him walking towards my car. He was looking good and he seemed cool. I'd heard about him in the streets. As I sat in my car, I brushed the little devil off my shoulder that kept talking in my ear, but damn, he looked useful. Four fingers on Thumb Street were getting old for real, had me thinking crazy. He opened the door and sat in the passenger seat.

He wasted no time questioning me about my ride. But I let his ass know with a straight face about me cutting grass on Saturdays and Sundays. He was surprised I knew how to work a lawn mower, but what he didn't know he didn't need to know, and he would be shocked with what I really knew. I pulled the bag from the back seat and tossed it in his lap, eyeing him closely. He never thought I knew about that part of life and his face told it all because his mouth was wide open. I watched him open and inhale the scent from the bag, a huge smile covered his face.

"So, you want it or not?"

"Bossy, I like that."

Is he hitting on me? I wonder.

"Girl, where you get this sticky icky from?"

He had to know loose lips sink ships, and I refused to let a ship get sunk because of my lips.

I was charging twenty-five hundred for the whole thing, but he claimed he only had two stacks on him. I let his ass know next time I was gonna tax his ass to the white meat.

He was straight cheesing. Damn, his smile was pretty, too. *Calm down, girl,* I kept having to tell myself. He handed me the money, and looked me up and down. I didn't count it because there was no need to. I knew where to find his bitch if the shit wasn't straight. Nobody gets spared in this game called L.I.F.E.

We both got out of my car. He started walking towards his Denali and I headed back towards the shop.

"Yo, your nigga teachin' you real good," He said to my back.

"I ain't got one," I hollered back. I bet his mind was working overtime on that one. I went directly to my station because the rest of my co-workers had shown up while I was handling business with Twan. Now I damn sure couldn't fuck or victimize Talena's man. I might need him again.

Layers was the place to be if you were getting your hair done. Located in the heart of the city, you couldn't miss the shop. We had four stations, one for myself, Talena, Dahlia, and one for Kiana.

I had two perms, one wash and wrap, and Ced's dreads to do for the day. I could have worked over, but I passed on that. I had to check up on Beauty, too. Music was playing in the background, and everyone was talking and getting the latest do's when a flower delivery man came through the door.

He asked for me and everyone in the place looked my direction, so I stepped forward. I was nervous because I didn't know if that nigga was a fraud or what. He handed me a clipboard and told me to sign by the X. I did as he asked and he walked back out the door.

Conversation was almost back to normal when the door opened up again. My mouth flew wide open and my hands stopped moving. Thank God I had just finished washing the perm out of my customer's head because her shit would've been fucked up. The flower man was holding twenty-four pink roses, I counted them real quick. A small teddy bear was attached to the vase with a pink balloon. See, that was the reason why I was riding Jay's bid out with him. He was the best. Since I surprised him, he had to surprise me back.

The delivery man put the package on the desk. I thanked him and he exited the shop.

I put conditioner in my client's hair and then moved to the desk to check out my gift.

Damn! It had a card in a sealed envelope. I ripped it open fast.

You are beautiful on the outside, but I am dying to know what the inside looks like. I think we should get to know each other better. You better get on the Heat's team.

Cedrick...

I felt like I was gonna fall out. My head was spinning like crazy. I had to sit the fuck down. Talena must have caught the look on my face because she came rushing over.

"Girl, you look like you seen a dead body." I heard her talking to me, but I couldn't even reply. I was in the state of shock. No man had ever done something like that for me. And he wasn't even my man. *Get your shit together, girl,* I told myself silently.

I handed the card to Talena and watched for her reaction. She knew all about Jay, but she knew nothing of Ced, my new found friend.

"Somebody's got a secret admirer," she whispered in my ear.

"Our little secret," I whispered back before I returned to my client.

I had two heads done, one almost finished, and one left to come. I was spraying oil sheen on my client's head when the phone began to ring. It was A'Dasia.

"Girl, you ain't text me back," she complained as soon as I picked up.

"Damn, boo, I apologize. I'm at work," I said as I checked my text messages.

"Look, I sent you the number for the bridal shop. Be careful with it."

"Thanks, girl. And I got you." Shawty had come through for me. I was damn sure gonna come through for her. Business was good and looking better all the time. It was turning into an amazing Monday with endless tomorrows. I saw the information I needed in my phone, and I smiled. Hell yeah.

My last customer left, so I started cleaning up my station as I waited for Ced to show up. The clock on the wall showed the time in the air. I was sweeping up the last of the hair when I realized how quiet it seemed to have gotten in there. There was nothing but music in the air until Kiana opened her big ass mouth.

"Damn, he's fine like a dime."

I turned around to find Cedrick standing there, looking at me like I was his first meal in a long time.

"We got an appointment at one, right?"

"Yeah, Cedrick. You know we do."

"How are you, beautiful?"

"I'm doin' good. How you doing?"

"Fine now that I'm here." His eyes were scanning the place like an owl's, like he could see in the dark and cover a 360 degree radius with his vision. I wondered what his eyes saw.

"The roses are beautiful. Thank you so very much."

"Beautiful things for a beautiful lady."

I saw that Kiana had to stop what she was doing. It was clear that Ced had already become an idol in her eyes. Kiana was a young twenty year old slut around town. The news was that she had already had over twenty abortions, and that she'd slept with her mother's boyfriend, and his brother too. The bitch was just off the chain, but I promised on everything if that bitch ever touched mines, her ass gonna be history. So I gave her that look that said, "Bitch, he's mines." Confuse that, ho.

Dahlia, on the other hand, was the opposite. She was an older lady, but pussy didn't have an expiration date. She had four kids and had been married to the same man for ten years, but as I said, not everything that looked good was good. *Lord, is this a punishment? 'Cause this man is SEXY, sexy from head to toe.*

I washed, twisted, and dried his dreads. When I finished it was close to 3pm. He paid me, and even tipped me very well.

"You know, you don't have to do that," I told him.

"I am a grown ass man. I do what I want to do. I can take care of myself, and I can take care of you, too."

I smiled. "Thanks, but I got me covered."

Talena usually closed Layers at five, but that day she was closing an hour early since Twan had that weed to sell. Ced took a seat and started playing with his phone. He watched me watch him, and showed me that beautiful smile.

I cleaned my station again, gathered up my things, and said my goodbyes to my co-workers. I nodded at the flowers on the desk. "Would you please get those for me?" I asked Ced.

"Sure."

I held the door open for him and I noticed that bitch Kiana still had her eyes on him.

"Beautiful day isn't it?" He asked as we stepped out into the sunshine.

"It sure is, sir."

We walked to my car together. I pushed my alarm button, opened the back door of the driver's side, and placed my package on the floor with my bag.

"Thank you, Sweets. This is the best my dreads have ever looked. I see you put on in the shop the same way you put on in the club."

"Thank you."

"But you should see how I put on in the bedroom," I wanted to tell him, but I kept that little comment to myself. I knew he was thinking the same thing. *This man is beautiful. Lord, give me strength.*

"It's late. You gotta pick up your daughter, don't you?"

"Naw, her dad's got her."

"So, you free?"

"Naw, not really. Probably later, though."

"You stay givin' a nigga the left turn. Why is that?"

"No, I'm not," I said and pushed him playfully.

He grabbed my arm and pulled me into his. Now we were face to face. I could feel my legs wanting to break down, so I schooled myself. *Relax. Breathe.*

"You are even more beautiful up close. How could any man allow you to labor?" He said it in such a sexy way that I couldn't even speak to respond. It was a good thing that I couldn't. He kept going, "Ever since Friday night, I can't get you off my mind. Can't eat, can't really sleep, 'cause you seem to have all the qualities that I want in a woman. You remind me so much of my mother, that I will do anythin' to have you."

I would have sworn I saw a tear fall from his eyes. *Am I tripping?* I could smell his Polo Blue cologne, and then it happened.

He kissed my left cheek, let go of me, and walked back to his all-white Chevy Caprice. Lost in the moment, I watched as the old school drove away thumping Yo Gotti. It seemed like I stood there for an hour or more. All of a sudden, the sky opened up and rain drops began to fall. It was the water hitting my face that brought me back to reality. And for a second, I wondered how long his vehicle had been out of sight.

"You better get in the car before you get sick," Talena yelled at me from across the parking lot.

Damn, what just happened? Now I know I'm going crazy, 'cause I'm talking to myself. I got in the car and put my head on the steering wheel. Still dazed and unsure of what to do next, I just sat there.

My phone started ringing and forced me into action.

"Hello?"

"Let me know when you free, so I can take you out." His voice was driving me wild.

"Okay, Cedrick. I will."

"Drive safe, and if you need any help with that package of yours, let me know."

"Thanks, and you drive safe also. If I do need help, I'll let you know, but you already know…"

He cut me off before I could finish. "Let me guess, you're a big girl, and you can handle it yourself," he said with a little laugh. I had to smile at the sound of his laughter. Was there anything to dislike about this man?

"You're learnin'," I told him as I started my car up. I was ready to get back to the house. I couldn't help but ask, "What would have happened if my man had seen you kiss me on my cheek?"

"Then he better take it up with me instead of hurtin' you."

"Oh yeah?"

"And if you had a man that you truly loved, then you would have set me straight from the get go, boo."

The shit he was saying made mad sense. Did I really love Jay? That nigga was driving me crazy with my own damn thoughts. What the fuck? We talked the whole way home. Truth be told, he was charming, full of jokes, and down to earth. I liked it.

"I'll call you later 'cause I gotta get this package into the house, and it's still rainin'."

"Cool, and be good."

"You too, Ced."

That whole conversation had a bitch wigging the fuck out. Where did this man come from? It had been a delightful day so far. How could I complain? I called my daughter to see how her day had been, and as always, she put the icing on the cake just by being herself. To my surprise, her daddy didn't even trip. I bet he felt like father of the year, but to me, he was the sperm donor of the day. Sad but true.

I tidied up the house and then checked my stash spot. Shit was looking good. As I sat at the table and thought back on how far I'd come, I had to mentally pat myself on the back because it had been a long road. I also wondered if a day would come when Karma would hit me.

How will it return to me? Will I die by the hands of my enemies? Will the system toss me in jail and throw away the key? My mind was racing all over the place.

My thoughts were rudely interrupted by Plies' song *Goonette*. It was Dimples' ringtone. She claimed she had some business to handle so I would see her in an hour. Right then, I was at the crib getting my mind right. What was unsaid was always understood between me and my bitches.

It was already 5pm, and Jay still hadn't called. I wanted to call the damn prison to see what was up my damn self because, truth be told, that nigga was acting totally abnormal. I could see that I had to work as a spy to see what was really going on. I made sure he was right, the nigga got at least a stack a month, and that didn't include phone calls and books. I always questioned where the money was going. Deep down I felt like I could never fully *trust* a nigga again, thanks to my sperm donor. I felt like Jay was lying to me about some things, but I let him believe otherwise because I really had no proof, just doubts. In due time, if he was lying, then he would betray himself. I just wanted to make sure that nigga wasn't trying to play me. No one was safe around me but me, and that's how it was always gonna be.

"Yo, what's good, sis?" Black said as she entered the kitchen.

"Damn, yo. You creepin'? I didn't even hear you come in."

"Look like you in Times Square, just standin' lookin' at a picture of Bin Laden."

"Naw, just thinking." I wanted to tell her what was up, how my mind kept racing, but my mouth wouldn't let me. Lately, I'd been finding myself more committed to myself.

"Damn, who died? These flowers are beautiful. Let me find out that you have that nigga Jay's nose wide open?"

"Bitch, think again," I snorted. "Matter of fact, read the card."

I wanted to know what was going on in her head as she read, but she didn't even have an expression on her face.

"They smell good," was all she had time to say before the house phone started ringing. I already knew who it was.

"You have a collect call from, 'your baby'. Press zero to accept."

"Hey, sexy girl."

"Hey, how you doin', stranger?"

"Shit. Ready to come home."

Even though we seemed to be talking like normal, something about the conversation so far was weak. So, I told him how I was truly feeling. The nigga had the nerve to start going off, so I just kept quiet and listened. Fuck it. Let him talk.

"Shit, I just spoke to my ma. She and my aunt supposed to be coming this week or next week, so you don't have to come."

I didn't get along with his mother because she was always in our relationship, always had something negative to say about me, and she was just miserable. I put up with her just for his sake.

"When you find out that she comin' to see you?"

"Friday that passed, she wrote me and sent me a new number to call, but I ain't called yet."

Damn, and he's just now telling me. "Well, I ain't tryin' to come up there and mess y'all visit up, so you just let me know when it's a good time to come see you." *Now I have to ask when it's good for me to visit?*

"So you tryin' to be funny?"

"Nigga, how the fuck am I tryin' to be funny? You said what you had to say, and I said what I had to, so conversation over. So let it go."

"The caller has hung up." It was that damn operator in my ear.

All I could do was look at the phone in my hand. That nigga had the nerve to hang up on me. I couldn't believe it. I made my way back to the living room to see Black braiding Dimples' hair.

"Damn. That was fifteen minutes already?" They both asked at the same time.

"You can say so. That was his fifteen minutes. He hung up on me."

The phone rang again. *Oh. Hell. Fucking. No. He's calling back to back. He's got jokes for real, thinking he can hang up, call right back, and I'll answer the phone. Nigga's got me fucked up.* I turned the ringer off and put the phone back on its base.

"I damn sure have bigger fish to fry." My bitches smiled when I said that.

We talked about our day and our plans for the night because there was money to be made. Black braided my hair next. After that, I did hers because Dimples couldn't braid for shit. Damn. Now that I thought about it, couldn't braid, couldn't cook, no wonder she was still kicking it with Black Kong. She didn't have to do shit. That was my bitch though, for real.

Time stayed rolling when I had shit to do. I glanced at the TV. It was 11:30. I checked the caller ID on the house phone and saw that I had missed the chance to tell my princess good night, so texted her daddy's phone. "Tell Regina thanks. Kiss Beauty for me and pick her up from school tomorrow."

Jamaica

Chapter 18
Who Say What?

When we left the crib at two in the morning to go to the spot, Dimples was driving and Black was riding shotgun. I was in the backseat, and we were on that all-black party. Dimples drove around the building twice to make sure that we hadn't been followed.

We parked on Pierce Street, and I kept looking out the back to make sure we were the only ones out. We got out and traveled the rest of the way on foot. As soon as we hit Buchanan Street, we heard male voices and stopped dead in our tracks. I reached in the back of my tights and pulled my baby out, one already in the head. I'd rather have been caught by the police with it than get caught by a street nigga or bitch without it. We listened hard, and we slid behind a blue house, where we could see three figures in a car.

I kept my eyes on them while Black kept watch behind us and Dimples scanned the rest of the area. Six eyes were better than two, and that was a fact.

"Mane, fuck that bitch, Shay. That bitch ain't shit, but she do give some good head. Her baby daddy touch down in thirty days, so now she tryin' to push me to the left after she had me all up in her."

"Damn, cuz, I know you ain't fell in love with that joint?"

"Yo, that bitch pussy is the truth. She got that snicker bar pussy. I just gotta have it."

Those niggas were in our way because they could see the storage place. We had to wait until they moved before we could do anything.

"You smell that shit?" I whispered.

"Them niggas smokin' some good ass dro," Black answered, keeping her voice as low as mine. Their car windows were down, and they were just smoking and talking away, not knowing who was listening.

"So look, yo. Tomorrow night we in that bitch. A nigga pockets hungry. Ain't even a crackhead out here, and that plug is exactly what we need."

"Fuck that nigga Whyte and his crew." The driver started the car and drove away.

I was surprised. Did I really just hear what the fuck I thought I just heard? Me and my bitches looked at each other, but Dimples spoke first.

"Only thing is, we gettin' it first."

We crossed the street and looked around to see if anyone else was out. Not a motherfucking soul.

One by one we climbed over the fence. It wasn't really very high, maybe five feet, no more. The main entrance had a gate, but you needed a code and a card to enter. Nina was still in my hand, ready to go to work. Black had the bag, and Dimples had the tools. We got to unit 1426, and Dimples popped the lock in no time. We slid the door up slowly and went inside. I was surprised the shit actually looked clean. There were some construction supplies, a king sized bed leaning against one wall, and an air conditioner and some toys thrown into a cardboard box that looked like it was ready to bust on one side.

Ain't this some shit!

"What the fuck, yo?" Dimples sounded irate.

Black was right behind her with it, saying, "This shit can't be real."

"Calm down. Just think, yo. Where would you put money in here?"

Then it hit me the same way Traymon had busted my eye, quick and unexpected.

"In the damn mattress."

The mattress had a zipper on it like it was a jacket. My heart was racing in my chest, and my hands were sweating like a river inside my leather gloves. I held my breath as I pulled the zipper, and there it was.

"God Bless America."

I'd be damned if I didn't have some dead presidents looking right at me. I had to give it to the nigga Whyte though, he was pretty smart. I just happened to be smarter. There were no drugs, just money, and I mean plenty of money. At first I thought that duffle bag wasn't big enough, but by the grace of God, it was just perfect. The damn bag was so heavy that it took two of us to lift it. We pulled the door back down, and Dimples put the lock back on the latch while me and Black got the bag to the fence. Dimples caught up to us and climbed over first. Together we lifted the bag to the top of the fence and Dimples pulled it over. Team work was always the best work, and there was no I in team. Once we got to the car, I was able to relax a little, but only for a second because driving with a gun and a bag full of money... Mane, the Feds were calling our names. If I was going out, I was going out with a couple of police officers under my belt. Fuck what you heard before. One thing for certain, two things for sure, I was laying one of them devils down. Fuck keeping my hands clean.

I had to drive because I knew I wanted to see Beauty again, and that meant the wheel was in my hands. We were about four blocks away when a police car got behind us. I knew for a fact I was not speeding, but I checked anyway, exactly 35mph. Tags were good, and all my lights were working.

What the hell? "Fuck."

The light at Bass School turned red. Then that motherfucker got directly behind us.

"Yo, if shit go sour, I am squeezin' this bitch," I said while touching the Nina in my lap.

"Already. We in this together;" Black reminded me.

Finally the light turned green, but for a second, I thought it wasn't going to change at all. As I took my foot off the brake and hit the gas, the motherfucker behind me hit the lights.

"Stop breathin' so hard, Dimples." I could hear the air coming and going from her nose. I made the next right to get off the main street because I knew what I was about to do was beyond crazy. I was shooting first and driving off next.

That motherfucker did a U-turn and took off in the opposite direction with the V-8 engine roaring. I guessed he got a call.

Our hearts were pounding, minds were racing, and my finger was itching.

"I pissed on myself," Dimples said out loud.

I looked back just in time to see Black throwing up right there in the backseat.

"Bitch, I know you ain't just throw up on the money?" I asked.

"Hell naw, yo."

Mane, these bitches weak. That's all I could say. *How'd they get so damn weak?* Our trap car had to be replaced now.

We got home safe. I parked the money maker on the side of the house, and we used the backdoor to go inside. Dimples went straight to the bathroom to clean up while Black washed up in the sink.

"I know y'all bitches wasn't scared?" I laughed as I asked them

"Bitch, you act like you wasn't?" Black answered.

"Hell fuckin' naw. For what?" I lied. I had to because, truth be told, if I'd been by myself, I would've shit myself.

I grabbed a blanket from the closet and spread it out on the floor. Then I opened up the bag and dumped the money out on top of it. It was gonna take forever to count. Fuck getting the sheep, we got the shepherd himself.

One hundred thousand dollars.

Free.

Fuckin'.

Money.

"That nigga gonna kill himself when he finds out," Black said.

This was what the preacher's kid had to say, "Thank you, Lord for this blessin'."

"Amen," we all agreed.

Shit was beautiful for us. Licks like those made me wanna quit my day job, but that I couldn't do, not yet anyway. We divided the bread up between us, but I didn't ask for anything for A'Dasia. I'd pay her out of mines tomorrow.

Who say what? Who say bitches can't get money?

Dimples and Black called Allied, the cab service. They changed their clothes, and we decided to make a toast to each other before they left. Dimples grabbed some glasses and I poured some Cîroc.

"To our friendship, to our bond, everythin' we do, we will take it to our graves."

"Call or text me as soon as y'all get where y'all going," I said after we drank and they were headed out the door.

Black was the first to call, then Dimples. It was 4:30 in the morning, my bitches were good, and I needed to take a shower. Then again, a bath sounded pretty damn good, even though it was late, especially after the night we'd had. I ran my bathwater and put some Jasmine oil in the tub to help me relax. Then I undressed and eased myself into the hot water. I reached for my phone, once I got comfortable, and scrolled through my contacts to find the number I wanted. I pressed send and waited, but there was no answer, so I ended the call.

I was just about to put the phone down so that I could dip under the water when it rang in my hand.

"Hey, I hope I didn't wake you up?" I said when I answered.

Silence.

"Hello?"

More silence.

I remembered how it was when Regina answered my call. I knew how bitches liked to play. One more time and I was ready to hang it up.

"Hello?" I said again.

"Hey, beautiful." He sounded tired, but sexy. "Are you okay?"

"Yeah, I'm okay. Are you asleep?" I asked, knowing damn well he was.

"Yeah, I was, but now I'm up. You must be plannin' a trip to come see me and put me back to sleep."

"Is that what you want, Ced?"

"Hell yeah, that's what I want, Sweets."

"Well, give me the address. I'll be there in an hour."

"A'ight, let me text it to you. Call me when you get outside."

"Okay."

Damn. What had I gotten myself into? He was winning me over. Life was a journey. Was I willing to travel?

I washed my hair, scrubbed my skin like never before, and put lotion on myself from here to Africa. I put matching panties and bra on with my Victoria Secret sweat outfit with the lips on the ass. I grabbed my keys and off I went. I hadn't been to sleep, and now it was a new day. I texted Talena, letting her know I was taking the day off, and that I'd call her later because something had come up.

Chapter 19
Certified

I called as soon as I pulled up. He lived on the first floor, and he opened up the door as I was getting out of the car. White tee, white shorts, white slippers, damn, that nigga loved white.

"Damn, you smell good," he said to me when I got to the door.

"I just got out the shower. May I come in?"

"Sure, my door's open for you."

He lived in a one bedroom apartment. Not only was the place clean, but he had taste, nice taste.

"I'm goin' back to bed. Join me if you like. Better yet, make yourself comfortable."

This nigga trusts me already?

"Lead the way," I said to him. I followed him all the way to his bedroom. His bed was so damn big it could hold at least four grown ass adults. A sixty-two inch flat screen hung from one wall. I had to find out what was up with everything being white.

Music videos were playing on the TV. He climbed back into the bed like it was nothing. I lay my keys and Dior pocket bag beside the bed before I took my sweats off. I was wearing pink boy shorts with a wife beater underneath my sweats. He watched as I undressed myself and said, "You must be sleepin' on the floor?"

"If you think that I came over here to sleep on the floor, then you need to get on some medication."

"You know I'm just playin' with you, girl."

I climbed on to the bed. It was so soft and cozy, with silk sheets. That nigga had taste and class. In need of some touch, I moved my body towards his, placed my head on his arm, and we start talking. He told me where he was from, and all about his parents and his kids.

His father is a Jamaican who had been a big time drug dealer and met his American mother one day when he'd gone out of town to do business. He'd been born in the Bronx, New York, but he'd moved to West Virginia when he was seventeen, and he was his parents' only child. His mother died when he turned twenty-four, and two days later the system took his father. He lost both of his parents just like that, in the blink of an eye. He buried his mom and moved to Virginia. He'd been there for six years, blah, blah, blah, and I fell asleep while he was still talking. I remembered him wrapping his feet around mines. I woke up on my side with his arms around me.

It was 10am, and my stomach was talking. I went to the bathroom to release my bladder, wash my face, and I use my finger to brush my teeth. It was better than nothing. While I was in there, I noticed there were no woman supplies in sight. He was still asleep, so I made my way to the kitchen, and since it was a one bedroom apartment, everything was easy to find. The refrigerator was well stocked, and I found everything I need. Bacon, eggs, sausage, cheese, grits, and pancake mix in the cupboard. I got to work because you already know the kitchen was my favorite room in any house. I was making the last pancake when his hands hit my waist.

"You got the dead wakin', girl."

I'd heard that before. I smiled, but I didn't turn around.

"My stomach woke me up, so I thought I'd help myself around and surprise you."

I felt his dick on my ass, so I pushed him back a little to let him know that he was too close. *Lord, give me strength.* He let me go and went into the living room.

"You look real sexy in my kitchen. Then again, you look sexy anywhere. You are a ten."

I made him a plate and took it to him with a Pepsi.

"Come sit in here with me and eat," he said to me.

I made a plate for myself and sat on the couch next to him.

"Damn. Damn, you can cook, do hair, dress to kill, dance, I mean, damn. What else can you do?"

"You'll figure it all out in due time," I answered.

"I can't wait either."

I watched him eat and then watched as he plays the Xbox Kinect.

After I cleared my plate, I cleaned the kitchen while I talked to my sperm donor on my cell. That nigga wanted to keep Beauty for the week. He had to be on drugs because that was not how he got down. If she wanted to stay, then I was okay with it. At the end of the day, he was her father.

I let him know as soon as he picked her up from school to call me, I wanted to make sure she wanted to stay.

Just as I finished up in the kitchen, the doorbell rang and Ced asked me to get that for him. I looked at him like *are you serious* and he mouthed to me, "Just answer the door."

It was the same flower guy from the shop, so I knew it was a package for me.

Twenty four pink roses, no balloons or teddy bear this time. I signed, said thank you, and closed the door. I inhaled their scent. They smelled so good. I placed them on the table, and read the card attached.

Ced never took his eyes off the TV.

This morning when I opened my eyes and saw you next to me, I saw an angel. You are beautiful, especially when you sleep.

GED...

After I finished reading the card, I felt the butterflies in my stomach jumping around. *No* man had ever gone out of his way to do things like that for me. That made it super hard for me to resist him any longer. My feelings for him were growing by the second and I was slowly and surely losing control of them.

I knew I was cheesing, but what else could I do? When did he even get the chance to do that? I pushed his leg off the sofa and grab the other controller.

"You think you're ready?"

"Don't hurt me too bad. Remember, I'm a girl," I said, knowing damn well he was about to trash me in Madden.

"I will never, ever hurt you." His eyes were on me when he told me that.

I knew he meant exactly what he said, too. He could feel me and it made me happy.

Let's just say he whooped my ass bad in the game and left me for dead.

"You gave me a run at first, though. I gotta give you some respect for that."

That was when I moved in real close. "Thanks for the flowers, the balloon, and the teddy bear at the shop. Thank you for the flowers today. They're beautiful."

"Naw. Thank you for keepin' me safe last night, thank you for breakfast, and thank you for this..."

He closed the distance between us to lock his lips with mine and ease his tongue into my mouth. I couldn't take my lips from his, even if I wanted to. Damn. I had been faithful to Jay until that very moment, that damn moment.

I found the strength in me to pull away from his embrace. I had to be real because that was all I knew. "Look, I'm in a crazy ass relationship."

He gave me a blank look, so I knew that I had to explain it to him.

"Homeboy doin' a bid and I been ridin' with him for two years now. He's got one left. I haven't even kissed another man, or even slept outside of my own house until I met you. No one's gotten my attention but him, until you came into my life."

"Okay," he replied.

"I can't say that I don't want you. If I did, lightning would hit me right now. You..."

I cut him off. I had to let him know. "Just listen, please. I damn sure don't know what will happen a day from now, much less a year. Since you've come into my life, a lot of things have changed, and it's only been a couple of days. I don't want to rush things, or start somethin' that I can't finish because I do like you. Let's just take things slow and see what happens."

"I'm cool with that. I respect you for tellin' me. It shows a lot about you, and that makes me want you more. But I gotta make one thing clear though."

"What's that?"

"Keep it a stack with me, and I'll keep it a stack with you."

"You got a deal, Ced. I'll respect you, and I hope you return the favor."

"Already, boo. Can I finish tastin' your lips?"

"Naw," I said smiling. "You might not want to stop."

"Let me be the judge of that."

"I'll kiss you if you beat me to the bed." I booked it to the bedroom. Either way, I was gonna kiss him. I made it to the bed first, and when I kissed him, I made sure it was a healthy one. He didn't let his hands roam my body or anything, just our mouths moved. Then we slid between the sheets again. With only a few hours of sleep and full bellies, we were out in no time, and sleeping like newborn babies. I slept in his arms, just like last night.

The sound of his cell phone woke me up, and I turned over to look at the time.

2:45pm.

My movements woke Ced up. He got out of bed to get his phone, and I got up to get mines from the kitchen.

Four missed calls, one from Black, one from Dimples, one from Talena, and one from a number that I didn't recognize.

I called my bitches first, but I kept it super short. Then I called Talena back and told her that I had to take the rest of the week off because I had some business to handle. She asked me if everything was alright, and I assured her that it was. I called the number that I didn't recognize next.

"Hello? Someone called me from this number?"

"Yeah." The bitch addressed me by my first name. What the fuck was going on?

As I listened to her words about her husband being locked up with my husband, I knew Jay must have sent the message through her man, so here she was delivering it to me about why I hadn't been answering his phone calls. I thanked her and sent one back to let Jay know that he should call me. That nigga had the nerve to get someone else to call me because I wasn't answering the phone. A couple days ago, that motherfucker wasn't even calling. Ced was standing there looking at me like he could read me.

"Got somethin' you'd like to say?" I asked. I couldn't help the attitude, I was mad.

"One mistake can 'cause a nigga to lose you, and me to have you for a lifetime. Then I'm down to play, and win you forever."

"I hear you talkin'." I knew what he meant by that too.

"I got a couple plans I got to attend to, but I don"t want you out of my sight for a minute," he told me.

"I gotta see my daughter, but first I gotta take a shower, and pay my friend's storage bill. Since I didn't bring any clothes over here, that means I gotta go home."

"Well, I'm gonna take you to do all of that. Is that cool?"

"Yeah, that's fine."

"Let me get clean and fresh real quick, then we can be out. But first, can I get a hug?"

"Now you askin'?"

"You ain't mines yet, but believe me, once you are mines, I will not ask."

That word *yet* made me smile. I gave him a hug, a long one, and he left me there dazed.

While he took a shower, I straightened the house up as I waited.

It wasn't long before he was finished.

"You ready, babe?"

Babe? Hmmm... "Yeah, waitin' on you."

Let's just say that nigga looked like he was ready for an interview with GQ magazine. He must've read my mind easily because he said, "Even my socks Polo, baby."

I smiled at him for the 20th time that morning.

"We leavin' your car over here, okay?"

"Okay." I was down to ride.

He looked so damn good my pussy started throbbing while I was sitting in the passenger seat. A nigga who looked like that made you want to smoke a bitch just for looking, real talk. I gave him the address to my house, and it took about twenty minutes to get there.

Damn, 3:30 already.

I opened the door, and showed Ced in to the living room. He made me feel comfortable at his house so I returned the favor by getting him what he wanted to drink, RedBull.

As soon as I gave him the RedBull and turned the TV on, the phone rang. The damn house phone.

"You have a collect call from 'your baby'."

I couldn't even get a hello in there before Jay started going slam the fuck off. The volume on the phone was up high, and I knew Ced could hear him. But to be honest, right then, I didn't even care.

"Where the fuck you been, yo?"

"Well, damn, hello to you too."

"Mane, answer the fuckin' question, yo. I ain't even playin'."

"I never said you was playin', but you gonna calm down before you hear the dial tone."

I had to leave Ced, so I went to my room to get my clothes together so I could hit the shower and get fresh. I had to get Jay off the phone before a shower could take place though. Fuck it, I could get my clothes together while we talked.

"Look, I ain't tryin' to fight with you, baby. I just been stressed and ready to come home to you. Shit is just crazy."

"And, Jay?"

"I'm sorry for goin' off on you. I don't want to lose you, Sweets."

"I hear you."

"What you doin'?"

"Gettin' ready to take a shower and go see Beauty. Her daddy's keepin' her for the week."

"What you got planned?"

"Shit, nothin'. Work."

Hell naw, I wasn't telling him I was off work.

"I spoke to my ma today, and my baby-ma was over there."

"You claimin' that baby without a blood test, even when the little girl looks just like your friend, Lambo?"

"Until a blood test say she ain't mines, then I'll stop. But for now, she's mines."

"What the fuck ever. Do you. I don't care." I didn't feel guilty for spending time with Ced, or even having him in the next room while I talked to Jay, but I was fucking mad that I was giving money to his mother for a child that I didn't even know was his.

"I mean, damn, Sweets. I'm tellin' you, and you gettin' mad."

Now he's screaming? That's when he got the dial tone. I warned his ass, but he never listened. Some women mean what they say.

I left the phone in the bedroom while I hit the shower. I could hear the phone ringing again, but I paid it no mind. Shit, I was busy. I got dressed and went to let Ced know I was ready.

"Pack a bag 'cause I want you to spend the rest of the week with me."

That nigga needed to see a doctor. But shit, okay, maybe I did too. A few minutes later, I had a bag packed. I forwarded the house phone to my cell.

"You look amazin'," Ced told me.

"Thank you."

He took my bag to put it in the car. I checked my stash to make sure that shit was still the same. Then I armed the alarm system and locked the door. It was time to roll.

Jay just pushed me into Ced's arms, even though I was already there last night. I was tired of fighting about stupid things. If he couldn't respect me or give in about a blood test, then I was not gonna ride. Plus, his actions lately had me questioning his reasons for having me around while he was doing his time...

Jamaica

Chapter 20
This Is How I Do

Dressing was like a hobby. I took pride in it. I could dress any which way and still look sexy. No bitch could see me. A fresh perm had my hair looking just right. Polo all the way down, I was so official, I should have changed my name to horse. I was wearing an all-white short sleeved tee with a V-neck to show a little cleavage on top of a light blue skirt so short it showed a lot of thigh. With legs like mine, I didn't need heels. I was rocking some all-white flip-flops.

On my momma, on my hood, I looked fly. I looked good. Every *boss* nigga deserved a *boss* woman. Knowing that he wanted me around made me smile. When I got in the car, he bit his bottom lip as he looked me up and down.

"Damn."

"Well, thank you for the unspoken compliment."

"Since you can read my mind, you must already know that you're very welcome."

"All Polo just like you."

He gave me that million dollar smile again. How could a nigga so sexy and so well-mannered be single? It was a mind blowing thought. I just wouldn't have minded him blowing my body.

I texted Beauty's dad to let him know I was on my way and just to get the nasty thoughts out of my head.

Ced pulled into the storage facility, and I pulled my skirt down before I got out. But my ass pulled it back up again. I knew he was watching me as I climbed the stairs to get to the office, so I let it ride up. I liked the thought of giving him a little show.

"Hey, girl," A'Dasia greeted me as I walked in. No one was around. I handed her a stack.

"Good lookin' out with them numbers."

"Girl, you know we family. You ain't never gotta do that."

"Shit, I never know when I might need you again."

"A'ight, tell my cousin I love him."

"Sure will," and with that, I left.

Ced was on the phone when I got back in the car.

"Hell yeah. I'll be there in an hour, so make sure that shit correct. A'ight?"

He never stopped his conversations when I was around. It seemed that he trusted me.

"I gotta go to them apartments over there by Virginia Baptist Hospital," I said when he got off the phone.

"The ones in the bottom?"

"Yeah. Today is a beautiful day. The sun is shining, and everythin' feels right," I said as I looked out the window.

"Couldn't be better. I got the most beautiful woman in my car."

"Are you always this sweet?"

"Yeah, when it comes to you, but I do have an impure side."

"Hope I never see it."

He didn't respond to my last statement. Instead, he let Yo Gotti talk through the speakers.

I spotted Beauty, Traymon, and Regina at the playground as we pulled into the parking lot. Ced watched my face light up when I saw Beauty.

"She looks just like you. Gonna make a nigga real happy one day."

"One day." *And that nigga better treat her like a Queen and better,* I thought.

I couldn't wait to get out of the car and hug my princess. Damn, I'd missed her. As soon as she saw me, she ran in my direction.

"Mommy. Mommy," she screamed at the top of her lungs as she grabbed my leg.

"Hey, baby. I miss you."

"Mommy, I miss you more. Guess what?"

Beauty always told me everything she knew or heard. I loved our relationship. Why didn't I have this with my mother? Why didn't she love me enough to take me with her? You would have thought that carrying me for nine months was special, but I could see it wasn't. If she was around I probably wouldn't have suffered from Damien's hands. I wouldn't have seen my father's habits come alive in front of me. I wouldn't have had to ask a friend to tell me about sex, relationships, or anything else. My mother's rejection hurt the worst. But just like the rest, she too would pay in due time. I'd make sure of it.

Beauty would never have to worry about rejection, pain or anything harmful because I was going to be there to protect her.

"Daddy got me ice cream and some new games."

Traymon and Regina were a few feet away. Ced stayed in the car. You couldn't see inside because the windows were jet black. I wanted Traymon to see him *so* bad because he'd never seen me with any nigga, but he knew I'd been holding Jay down.

"He did? Do you like them?"

"Ma, I love them."

It made me feel good to know that Traymon had stepped his game up with being a father.

"Dag, you riding clean," Traymon was paying attention to that white on white. I couldn't blame him.

"Hell yeah. Hey, girl," I said to Regina after I answered him.

"Hey, you look good," she said, knowing she was fake as fuck.

That bitch recognized I was still the shit. She wasn't ugly, but she wasn't all that either, and she damn sure wasn't me. We were about the same height, but my skin was a little darker than hers, and my body left her wishing for a miracle.

"760, all white everythin', damn," Traymon sounded jealous.

I turned around to look at Ced's 760. Yeah it was beautiful inside and out. So was its owner, I wanted to say it but didn't.

"Beauty, your daddy's crazy."

"Ma, you crazy, too."

We all laughed. Nobody could help that little smart mouth of hers.

"Give me some sugar." I wrapped my arms around her and kissed her all over her face until she squirmed and begged me to stop.

"Ma, can I stay with daddy?"

"Yeah, you can, but you better be good."

"A'ight, ma, I will. I love you, but I'm going back to play."

And then she was off, with Regina right behind her. As soon as she was out of ear's reach, Traymon turned to me. "You look good. You eatin' good?"

"Always. With or without a nigga, I am always gonna look good."

He shook his head at my comment. He knew it was the truth.

"Who you with?"

"A friend."

"Oh, yea? I told you a long time ago to let me hit that, but naw…" He let his words trail off.

"Get the hell away from me. You the one with the wife from Mars, and Traymon, real talk, we been over a long time ago." *Why do I always have to tell him this? Is it ever gonna sink in?* "Call me if you need anythin' for Beauty."

"Corona, before you go, let me tell you somethin' funny."

I saw something move from the corner of my eye. Ced had cracked his window. I could actually see the top of his fitted hat. Traymon hadn't noticed, or he wouldn't have kept talking.

"Beauty's teacher said some little girl pushed Beauty, so Beauty two pieced the little girl in the mouth and nose. I told Beauty to tell the little girl sorry, but she, said, 'Naw, daddy.' So I asked her why not. She said, 'She snitched on me, so naw, I ain't tellin' her sorry.'"

"That's our child. She got that temper from you, damn sure not from me," I reminded him.

"Hell yeah. She looks like you, but acts just like me."

I shook my head and started walking back to the car. I knew Traymon was watching, so I did my stunt walk. As I opened the car door, Ced spoke.

"Can you drive me?"

"Now?"

"Yeah. Right now."

This nigga wants my baby daddy to see him. "Okay."

Ced got out of the car and walked around the front of it. I saw how he kept his head facing Traymon, and I smiled at him.

If looks could kill, I swear I would have been a dead bitch right then.

I adjusted my seat and put my seat belt on. When Ced got in on the passenger side he pushed his seat all the way back and propped his right foot up on the dashboard. As I pulled out, I let the window down to speak to Traymon one more time.

"Call me later, before Beauty goes to sleep."

He was silent. He just threw a peace sign my way. I blew the horn at Beauty and Regina, and they both waved at me. Ced broke the silence first.

"You know them apartments on Wards Road?" he asked.

"No."

"Drive to Target, and I'll show you how to get where we goin'."

I knew what apartments he was talking about, but I played dumb. You just gotta play the game right. You never know when the card up your sleeve can turn into an ace in the hole.

"He still wants you," he said next.

"What?"

"You can tell by the way he looks at you."

My eyes were on the road, but I heard him loud and clear. "Why you say that?" I was curious to know what he saw.

"He'd be a fool if he didn't want you back."

"Not interested."

"I had to let him know that you are in good hands. I'll protect you with my life."

"So that's why you wanted me to drive? So he could see you?"

"You think you know me, don't you?"

"I'm tryin' to know you, Ced, every part of you." I took my eyes off the road for a moment to meet his eyes and let him know that I was serious, dead ass serious.

"Don't worry, you will. You just make sure you're ready."

He didn't give me a chance to reply that time. He just turned the music up. We listened to rap all the way to Wards Road. I sang along while he bounced his head. If he only knew I was 'bout that life. I had an idea what he was about but I wanted to know every detail.

We got to Wards Road in no time. He directed me to the apartments by moving his hands, gesturing left or right.

Chapter 21
He Da Boss

"Yo, I'm outside." Ced was on his cell.

"I know damn well you ain't gonna leave me out here by myself?" I had to ask him.

"I told you once, but I see I gotta tell you again, I want you in my sight forever."

"A'ight, I'm just sayin'..."

He cut me off with a kiss. "Let's go. I have business to handle."

The door was already open. He stepped in first, and I closed the door behind us. Damn! Niggas were every fucking where, like fifteen of them. Ced leaned close and whispered in my ear, "Stay here."

"Okay."

I stayed standing at the door. Weed smoke filled the air, and I could smell alcohol, too. I mean, that shit right there was crazy.

Ced walked in front of the TV, and I heard him tell two niggas to pause the game. They were playing. As I watched Ced, I had to say that his demeanor was priceless. That right there was a boss nigga.

Young Jeezy was blazing through the system.

Mel man you my heart I swear to god (swear to god)

Knew you was real man, I saw it from the start (from the start)

Even when I was wrong my nigga had my back (yeah)

We used to laugh, wasn't shit funny (flaw)

Late night at my grandma house countin' money...

Someone turned the music off, and everyone got quiet. I swear, I could damn near hear hearts beating. Then Ced spoke up.

"Yo Butter, you got the paperwork ready?"

The nigga who was leaning on the counter was the shade of butter for real, so it didn't surprise me when he was the one who answered. "Yeah. I gave that shit to Slim last night."

"Oh, a'ight. So what the fuck's goin' on with Clap now?"

"That nigga holdin' on, but he got four holes in him. His shawty down there with him as we speak." It was the nigga by the radio who relayed that message. I counted the niggas while they talked. There were twelve, not fifteen. I didn't count Ced.

When Ced spoke, the room went dead silent again.

"I want y'all to lay low for the rest of the week. Today's Wednesday, I want shit back to normal by Monday."

A'ight's, okay's, and yup's erupted throughout the room.

"So what we gonna do about the situation with Clap?" the nigga by the window asked.

"You know who's responsible for that fuckery?" Ced asked, sounding mad as hell.

"Word on the street, they say some nigga name BU did that shit," Butter said.

"Make sure for a fact before you handle that shit, Trigger," Ced told this one skinny ass nigga.

"You already know, my nigga," Trigger responded.

"Y'all stay out the way, lay low, relax, and chill. Don't get caught slippin'. Be here Monday at 10am."

"Who that?" the only white boy in the room asked, referring to me.

Everyone turned around to look at me, but I kept my eyes focused on Ced and waited to see what he said. He motioned with his head for me to come over. *Damn. I got this short ass skirt on, and all eyes on me.*

I heard someone say, "Hel-lo," and laughter exploded. When I got to where Ced stood, he put his arms around my waist.

"She off limits, way off limits."

He flicked a military salute at the men, and they returned it.

I kept my arm looped through his, and we exited the way that we'd come.

"I'll drive, boo." He opened the passenger door for me, and I adjusted my seat back to its original position when I got in.

"Girl, you look so good, I could tear you to pieces right here right now."

"Believe me, the feelin' is mutual." I couldn't even lie.

"You think you ready?"

"I was born ready, and I stay ready."

"I'll see if you ready in due time."

I changed the subject fast, before it got any hotter in that 760.

"Where we goin' now?"

"Don't worry, Sweets. I won't hurt you."

Hearing his words smoothed over my secret pain. I had a gut feeling he was telling me the truth, and I wondered if he could sense that I'd been through hell and back. Did my eyes give him a story that my soul wanted to tell? I needed to hear those words from him. He said his word was all he had and I prayed he let his actions prove those words.

Deep down inside of me. I was glowing. How did he always know when to say all the right things?

"I'll take you at your word, just let me think on it. You know I got that nigga, and I've always kept it real with myself, so give me time."

"Have as much time as you need, boo. I ain't goin' nowhere, and you ain't goin' nowhere either. So think, and plan it all out for our future."

Damn! How can this nigga possibly say all of this to me?

"Oh, don't worry, Ged. I got us. As you say, as long as we keep it real with each other, then we good, right?"

He just smiled that perfect smile at me and turned the music up.

That was his way of letting me know that he agreed. *Damn. So do I want to do this nigga in, or cherish him to the fullest? Fuck. I'm stuck.*

I closed my eyes, picturing us together, and the shit was so good that I dozed the fuck off. After a while, I woke up because my phone kept vibrating. Six missed calls. *What the fuck? Where the fuck am I at?*

"You know you look so beautiful when you're asleep, and even more beautifuller when you're awake."

"Thank you, but is beautifuller even a word?"

"In my book to describe you, it sure is." The nigga had the sexiest sweet talk ever.

"I know you thinkin' I'm crazy. Strength, stability, power, loyalty, trust, and respect are all hard to find, but I have all of those in me."

I didn't even give him time to say anything else.

"Let me tell you somethin', Mr. Williams. I've got all those things and more, you just haven't seen them yourself yet. So don't ever put me on the back burner because I go just as hard as a real nigga. And if you ask me, I go harder than any nigga."

He smiled. "I can dig that all the way, boo. The chemistry we have is off the meter. It feels like I can show and tell you anythin'. I've never felt this way. Ever since I laid my eyes on you, I knew we were meant to be."

This nigga's getting deep. "We gonna give time some time, and see what happens. Even if it's us against da world, then I'm down. Right after I close up this other problem I got goin' on."

He nodded his head up and down.

We finally reached where the hell we were headed. We pulled up a long straight driveway to a two story brick house that was really too big to be called a house to begin with. *This is MTV Cribs worthy, for real. This nigga's got a mansion.*

"Damn," I said. "Who lives all the way out here?" I didn't mean to sound so excited, but damn.

"This my other spot. Besides my kids, no one else knows it exists but you."

This nigga's taste equals money. He opened up the door and my eyes 'bout jumped the fuck out of my head. *This shit is laid.*

Green and white were the main colors of the décor. The shit was beautiful, better yet, enchanting. He told me that the house had seven bedrooms, seven bathrooms, two kitchens, and two game rooms, one for children, one for adults. There was one dining room, and a living room that could each fit one hundred people easily, a gym in the basement, a recording studio, and a backyard the size of a football field, let's not forget to mention the four car garage. Me and that nigga equaled *greatness*, or me by myself equaled *one lucky bitch.* I was in such deep thought that I didn't even hear him ask me if I wanted something to drink the first time.

"Girl, I've asked you twice already if you want somethin' to drink."

"Yes. Yes, please." *Get it together,* I told myself.

Damn. There goes my phone. That fucking thing would not stop ringing for shit. It was my sperm donor. The nigga was trying to be funny, so I answered.

155

"Yo."

"Damn, yo, I called you three times," he sounded mad.

"Beauty okay?" I asked him, knowing damn well she was good.

"Yeah, she good. So you fuckin' with that nigga now?"

"Damn, last time I checked, I'm a grown ass woman. I don't question you about how you live your life, do I?" *This nigga is losing his mind.*

"You can give that nigga Jay a chance, and now this other nigga, but you refuse to give me a chance again so we can raise our daughter and be a family."

I know he ain't copping a plea, for real now. "Look, T, I don't know how many times I'm gonna have to tell you this, but please, let this time stick in your head. What we had is dead. The only blessin' that came out of it was Beauty. I can't go back, and I will *not* go back." With that being said, I ended the call.

I knew that Ced had heard the entire conversation, and to be honest, I didn't give a fuck.

He handed me my drink. "I got you some fruit punch, didn't know if you wanted a real drink so early in the day."

"Thanks. This is just fine. I love your house, and I admire your style. You have a lot of skills. Did you come up with all this on your own?"

"You might think I'm lyin' but yeah, I did. Green was my mother's favorite color, and since she's no longer around, I thought I'd hold her extra close to me by puttin' green all around me."

Awww, he loves his mother.

"I also love white, as you can tell."

"Well, you did a wonderful job. And yeah, I figure white was your favorite color."

The question wouldn't leave my head, why was this nigga single? What the fuck was wrong with him? I wished I could have read his effects. Damn. The nigga had me speechless.

"I wanna know this though, why did you pick me, out of all the other women, to share this moment with?"

"As I said before, there's somethin' about you that pulls me to you. I've never felt this before in my life. Ever."

My mind wasn't working any more. My pussy wanted to do the thinking so I let it take the lead. It had been a minute since I'd felt anything sexual towards anyone besides Jay. I pushed my lips against his and then whispered, "I think I might be ready."

"Naw, you gotta be fully ready. I mean all the way ready, Sweets."

"Well, I am."

To show him I was ready, I pushed my tongue into his mouth as I brought my body closer to his. I could feel his dick getting hard. I took his hat off, and then I let my hands roam through his dreads. My lips never left his. But after I took my hands from his head, I used them to unbuckle his pants. I wanted to see what he was working with. That nigga was not 99.9, but 100 percent *all* wood. It felt like he had a .45 and a 9mm down there, so I took my lips off his face to make sure I was not tripping out.

"God blessed me, baby."

I dropped to my knees and glanced up at him. I looked at it, and then I smelled it. Dimples taught me that. She said, "Bitch if it looks funny, that's okay. But if it *smells* bad, hit the door."

I grabbed half of it because, truth be told, how the fuck was I gonna put ten and a half inches all the way in my mouth at one time? Fuck it. I was willing to try.

I sucked the head real slow, as I used my right hand to beat the rest of it and my left hand to massage his balls. Call me a masseuse if you want to, I was about to show that nigga I was ready. I heard a moan escape from his mouth. I licked his dick carefully, and then I sucked it like I had nothing but gums, section by section until he put his hands at the base of my neck, guiding me up and down. I felt like I was almost swallowing the whole damn thing. I gagged, but I kept going. He was already taking his shirt off when he lifted my head up and I release the wood from my mouth. I kissed him from his dick all the way up his body until I was face to face with him again.

"You got some freak inside of you," he said with a smile, and I smiled back.

He carried me up the stairs and into one of the bedrooms, where he lay me on the bed and undressed me until I was butter ball naked. "Sweets, you better than a full course meal."

"Oh yeah?"

"Hell yeah."

"Once you eat some of this you gonna be straight." I didn't know how he turned on the music because he didn't leave me, but Usher's *Trading Places* came on loud and clear.

I'd never had my toes sucked before, and I didn't expect it to make me cum, but it did. When he finished with my toes, he made his way up my legs and thighs where he stopped. I was trying to get my breathing together. I heard him say, 'beautiful,' and I knew he was talking about my pussy because I thought it was beautiful, too.

He dug his whole face between my legs. He licked me wet, and practically licked me dry, but when he turned me over and told me to put my ass in the air, I swear I went to heaven. My pussy ached to be fucked so bad I wanted to cry, but he continued to punish me with his tongue.

"Please. Please, just fuck me," I begged him. But he was not listening to a word I said. He licked my pussy, then my ass, and then my pussy. I swear his tongue was better than a wash cloth. I came twice without him even using his fingers. His face did all the work. Finally, he kissed my pussy like he kissed my lips, and then he licked my navel. He pulled each of my nipples into his mouth, like a baby sucking milk. I could feel his dick on my pussy and I needed it inside of me so bad.

"Don't move," he commanded me. I was so weak already, damn.

I lay still and watched him. Well, I watched the dick between his thighs as he walked to what seemed to be a closet. He returned with a condom in his hand. He ripped it open and put it on without ever taking his eyes off mine. He eased his body on top of mine as we kept our eyes locked on one another. His eyes held a story that I wanted to know more about.

He gently pushed my legs apart, and then he slid his dick into me. It was a tight fit, and it hurt enough that I bit my lip and tried to move away, but he didn't let me. He took his time, nice and slow, and it started to feel so good. I hoped he never stopped.

Once he was in, the rest was history. I was seeing stars, two moons, the sun, and some more shit, all put together.

He knocked my walls like he was laying bricks. Stroke for stroke he gave it to me, and I matched his rhythm. I took it like a champ, closed my eyes, dug my nails into his back, thanked God, and even hollered Amen.

"I don't think you ready?" he asked.

"My turn," I told him. He'd already had the first two quarters. "Let me finish the game," I said in my bedroom voice.

"Do you," he responded.

"Lay on your back. Grab a pillow while you're at it, and put it behind your head. Like Wacka Flocka said, *no hands*, so you can't touch me in any way."

A smile came across his face. Damn, that nigga was sexy.

I got on top of him, but from the back, with my ass facing him.

I rode him like I was driving a five speed. He tries to hold on to me, but I turned my upper body to stare at him, and then I shook my head no. I grabbed his ankles, arched my back, and rode my dick. Yeah, I said it, *my dick*.

"Damn, yo. What the fuck?" I heard him say just as I was about to cum.

I did a one hundred eighty degree turn on that dick so I could face him.

"Can I please touch you?"

"No."

I bounced up and down, and rocked side to side, until I felt his legs shaking. I watched him close his eyes, and I knew he was near climaxing. So I leaned down, kissed his lips, and whispered, "Let me see you cum all up in this pussy." My words pushed him over the edge.

He grabbed my ass, dug real deep in my guts, and stared into my eyes. I couldn't take it anymore, and neither could he. We had orgasms together to the sound of Rick Ross and Nicki Minaj singing, "You the boss."

We laid together, chests heaving, and tried to catch our breath.

"Damn, you can cook, you can do hair, you can dance, you can dress, and you can fuck. Damn, boo. Where you been at all my life?"

"You got jokes, as always, but I've just been waitin' on you to find me."

"Really?"

"Hell yeah."

We lay in bed, just listening to music and holding each other.

"I'm hungry, and I'm pretty sure I just heard your stomach talkin' to your back," I said after I heard his belly growl.

"Let's take a shower, and you make us some dinner. Then we'll watch a movie and catch up with each other," he said in a bossy way.

"Okay."

He got dressed and left the room. I got up and looked around in the closet, naked. I had to make sure he wasn't trying to be someone else in their shit. The closet was big as hell, and his clothes and shoes were all in order. Damn, that nigga was the nigga for real.

I carried my ass to the bathroom, where I noticed, just as I had in his apartment, that there were no lady items anywhere. *Damn, I wonder how much he paid for this house.* I stepped into the shower, pressed the hot water button, and let it relax me. I closed my eyes to enjoyed the heat of the water on my body.

When I opened my eyes, Ced was standing there watching me. "Join me," I offered, and he did. He washed me from head to toe, ass crack and all. I couldn't help but wonder again, why was this nigga single? He was perfect in every way. *I guess I am just one luck bitch.*

I washed him from head to toe also, but I left his ass alone because I damn sure wasn't trying to make him uncomfortable or disrespect him in any way.

"I'm diggin' everythin' about you, Sweets. I want you in my life forever," he confessed.

The dick was splendid. He was sexy, perfect in every way. Plus, he was paid. The two of us together might equal *greatness* for real.

"God knows I am feelin' you too, Ced. I don't know what it is but I'm ready and willin' to give it a try, but…"

"There goes that word that I hate."

"You know I gotta end this other thing I got goin' on, anyway."

"I know you do, and I'm waitin' on you, real talk."

We got out of the shower. He wrapped me up in a towel and sent me to get dressed. He had left my bag on the bed when he brought it in. but instead of putting my clothes on, I slid into his closet and grabbed me a t-shirt and a pair of boxers. No need for a bra and panties. I pulled my hair into a neat ponytail and headed to search.

The house was so damn big, the shit was crazy. I almost got lost but I eventually found my phone exactly where I left it with my glass of fruit punch.

Thirteen missed calls. Dimples and Black had each called once, but the rest were from Jay. I made my way into the kitchen as I called Dimples back.

"Damn, bitch. Where you at?" she asked me as soon as she answered.

"I'm with Ced."

Dimples wasted no time telling me how she thought I was creeping. I didn't even pay her statement any attention. She claimed Black had some jobs lined up, so we called her on three-way as I made my way around the kitchen. I was so amazed at the house, and the man who owned it had gotten me thinking. I was lost in a world by myself with Ced, and it had me speechless for real.

As Black answered, she questioned Dimples about my whereabouts without even saying hello. I got straight to the point.

"Anyway, what's up with these jobs you got lined up?" I asked.

"Yo, girl, this shit is super sweet. This nigga who goes by Swoll, he's got one eye, so that's a plus, 'cause he'll never see us comin'. I heard he's got stupid cheddar, no kids, main bitch stay out of town, but the best part is that he only lives blocks from Dimples' parents."

After she gave me the run down on Swoll, I almost dropped the damn phone. That was my sperm donor's cousin. *What a small fucking world, full of nothing but money to be gained.*

Black dropped all Swoll's info on us like she'd been fucking him herself. I wanted to make sure her info was correct, but she dropped the bomb on us that she'd been getting all the info directly from his right hand man.

Dimples questioned her about trusting the nigga and she reminded us that she had never led us wrong. I really couldn't talk how I wanted to because I didn't know what Ced may have planted in his house. I just listened as she ran it down, and it made sense. So as far as I was concerned, it was a go. With nothing else to discuss, we ended the call.

Damn, this refrigerator is stacked. And since the kitchen is my favorite place to be, I'm 'bout to put on in here. Oh yeah, I thought. Thyme seared steak with sautéed onions, green peppers, and mushrooms, paired with mashed potatoes and some string beans sounded great. You know what they say, "The way to a man's heart is through his stomach." That man was about to love me, for real. I went to work.

I texted T's phone, telling him to tell my princess goodnight for me. As soon as the text went through, my phone rang.

"Hello?"

"You have a collect call from 'your baby'."

What a night it was shaping up to be.

I pressed zero.

"Damn, yo. 'Bout fuckin' time you answer my phone calls."

That nigga had been showing his ass off lately, like I was the one behind bars.

"Let me know when you're gonna stop cussin' at me, 'cause I am not in the mood for this shit today."

"And, bitch, you think I'm in the mood?"

"Call me another bitch, and I swear on your momma, I'm gonna show you a bitch for real. You done lost your mind talkin' to me like that!"

"Sweets, you actin' like I don't even matter to you any fuckin' more."

"Every time you call, you stay goin' off. You act like you the only one doing time. Nigga, I been doin' this time with you. When you call, I fuckin' answer. Visit comes, guess what? I'm fuckin' there. The money you get, I send it. The mail you get, I fuckin' write it. Tell me, when was the last time you actually wrote me a letter tellin' me thank you? How the fuck you think I feel, Jay? Nigga I try my best to make your time go by easy, and look how you treat me. Come the fuck on now, yo. I got feelings too, and I don't think you give a fuck about how I feel, or how I'm doin'. But you know what? I'm good, *always* good, remember that, 'cause a bitch like me is meant to last forever."

He was silent, not even an *I'm sorry* or anything.

"You ain't gotta come see me this weekend. My mother and them comin', so come next week or whenever," he said instead.

Yeah, I was born at night but not last night. Even though he'd been out of touch with her, all of a sudden he had a number for his mother. When he called her, his baby-ma was over there, so I was pretty sure he talked to the bitch too. Now his mom was going to visit him and I was not supposed to show up that weekend. Nigga thought he had me fooled.

"Cool, I can do that." I pressed the *end* button, and stopped wasting my time. My life was a book, and the pages wouldn't stop turning.

I was still at the stove when Ced came up and grabbed me from behind.

"Damn, you got this joint smellin' good, like you," he said.

"I know you hungry, so you better leave me alone before I don't finish, and we start somethin' else," I told him as I arched my back and pushed my ass up on his dick.

"Yeah right, I'm hungry, but I wouldn't mind gettin' some more of this," he said, reaching around   and   grabbing   my pussy.

"No panties?" he asked me.

I smiled, ignoring his question.

"Don't worry, you will, as soon as I finish feedin' you some food."

"I'm gonna be crazy over you fa' real."

And once again, I smiled.

Dinner was off the chain. He cleaned his plate and helped clean mine too. We cleaned the kitchen up together, with not a word being said between the two of us. But the chemistry was like electricity.

Eventually, he asked, "*Shottas* or *Boyz N Da Hood*?"

"Oh, since I'm the guest here, you want me to pick?"

"Please."

"Shottas." Shottas was the shit, no matter how many times I saw it. Mad Max was amazing and crazy beyond explaining. That nigga didn't take shit from anyone.

After a while, he pulled out a bottle of Patron, and we drank it straight, shot after shot. I squeezed my little body under his on the sofa and let the liquor work its magic. My body was aching for his touch, and as soon as his hand touched my pussy, I rocked my hips forward to let him know that I was ready for round two. It was going down, and I mean all the way down. It was ridiculous. He was a beast in bed, had me screaming Jesus and Amen like I thought it was a revival.

Chapter 22
Back to Grinding

It was the light through the blinds that woke me up. It was 7:30 in the morning and Ced wasn't in the bed with me. My head was bouncing and my body definitely felt the workout from last night. *Damn, I'm sore.* I found his shirt, pulled it over my head, and ran to the bathroom to release the pressure from my bladder. As I washed and dried my hands, I heard Ced's voice.

"'Bout time you wake up, Sleeping Beauty."

"Why?"

"I made you breakfast. I can't cook like you, but I tried my best."

I had to smile.

"You are an amazing man."

"Naw, you are amazingly better."

"You and your words. Let me guess, that's in your dictionary, too?"

"You know it," he laughed.

Breakfast was pretty good. He made some pancakes with scrambled eggs and grits. I asked myself for the millionth time, *why is this man single?*

It didn't matter that he was single, or why, because he was not going to be for long. I could handle that.

"Look, Ced, on Saturday I gotta go see this nigga, 'cause I gotta set things straight. I am gonna tell him that I'm seein' someone else."

Ced nodded his head, but he didn't say anything.

"I'm not gonna say who you are, 'cause that's none of his business, and I don't want no drama comin' to you."

"I respect your gangsta all the way, but I don't give a fuck if you tell him who I am 'cause at the end of the day, no nigga puts fear in my heart. I only fear God."

"I understand, and I hear you loud and clear. I also told Dimples that I'd help her pack, 'cause she's goin' out of town with her parents. I'm drivin' her to the airport on Friday."

That was a straight up lie, but what I was I supposed to do? Tell him I had to go hit a lick? It wasn't time for all that. I continued what I was saying. "So, I got Dimples Friday, that nigga on Saturday, so I won't be back until that evenin'."

"That's cool. I'll grab my kids and take them out somewhere. What time I gotta take you back home?"

"Later. Are you mad?"

"Naw, never. When you give me a reason to be mad at you, then I will be, but for now, I'm good."

"Will you always agree to everythin' I say?"

"Only if it helps the both of us, then it's whatever you want and like, baby."

Our day was beautiful. I re-twisted his dreads and braided them back. We played a few games, cleaned the house, talked, and just enjoyed each other's company in general. Leaving him for two days was gonna be hard, super hard.

When we pulled up in front of his apartment to get my car, we kissed like the end of the world was on its way. When I finally pulled away from him, he looked into my eyes and said, "I'm gonna check up on you, but if you ever need me for anythin', I'm just a button away. Call me."

As soon as I got home, I texted his phone. "Crossin' paths with you has been a blessin'. You have everythin' that I want in a man, there is no word to describe you, but you are perfect for me in every way. I had so much fun with you, and I can't wait to get back to you :)"

I forward the calls back to my house phone and texted my bitches to let them know that I was back at the house. Then I called Beauty to see how she was doing.

She practically shouted into my ear, telling me how many toys her daddy had bought her and how he was taking her shopping. She was having fun and I loved that her father was showing and giving her his love and attention.

I could see her being daddy's little girl, and she needed that. It was something I couldn't give her, especially since I didn't even get it from my father. If I was a daddy's girl, my life would have been different. He would have protected me and made sure I was taken care of, if he was a good father.

Beauty ended our conversation with an *I love you* before she passed the phone back to Traymon. I was not in the mood to talk to him, so I ended the call in his ear.

As I ended the call, Ced texted me back. "I am gonna make you carry my last name as soon as you give me the green light. Can't wait to have you back in my presence."

He had got to have a Webster's response book memorized because he had all the right answers.

I checked my stash. I couldn't complain at all. Shit was looking sugary. Free money always needed an owner, and I was happy that owner was me. I'd forgotten about giving T that work that I'd gotten from the last lick. Even though I was not hungry, I knew that T may as well be starving because he was trying to be a boss, and at the end of the day, he was still just my sperm donor.

I texted him to see if he could handle the work. "Yo, what you doin', nigga?"

"Shit. 'Bout to make a run real quick."

Oh so he'll be out. Great, I thought to myself.

"Meet me on Memorial Ave in ten minutes, and you better riot bring our child or that bitch."

"A'ight."

I pulled the work from my stash and drove to Memorial. I parked in the Family Dollar parking lot and texted him again, so he know where I was. Thirty seconds later, his car pulled up with Joey driving. He was one of our friends, a cool ass white boy who went super hard when he was high. He loved smoking crack, so we called him The Tester. Even though that nigga weighed a good four hundred pounds, he stayed fly, and all that crack didn't take any of his weight off. He thought he was the next Eminem. And I can't lie, the white boy had skills with the beat. As soon as I saw him, I ask him how his wife was doing. He said she was good. I passed the work to T and drove off. Two minutes later, my phone was ringing off the hook.

"Yo."

"Damn, nigga, the snow that heavy?"

"Maybe today. You ain't gotta pay to get that shit shoveled either, just enjoy the weather," I said.

"Nice lookin' out, yo."

Sometimes I thought I missed him. That nigga showed me everything about the street life, and for that I respected him to the fullest. But he wasn't for me. He and Regina deserved each other. Two pieces of shit equaled one pile.

I got back home just in time because Black and Dimples pulled up right behind me.

"So tonight's the night, huh?" I asked Black.

"Hell yeah. Me and Swoll's right hand man, Cuzzo, been kickin' it hard. Cuzzo say that Swoll ain't breakin' bread like he supposed to, and he treats his workers like they ain't shit."

Damn, right hand man wasn't shit either, nigga hating, and it wasn't cool. The closest were the ones that got you first. It was a fucked up world, I kept telling myself.

"Cuzzo's baby-ma's brother got on Swoll's team. Long story short, the little nigga got picked up and Swoll turned his back on him. The little nigga so loyal that he didn't even tell."

"Damn, now that's fucked up, yo. The game changes every minute," Dimples said with dismay.

"Anyway, what else is new?" I wanted to know.

"Look, I know this shit might sound crazy, but I got a job lined up for us."

Me and Black just looked at each other. Dimples lined something up.

"So what's up, Dimples?" Black asked.

"I met this bitch named D'Wonda at the strip club the other night. We talked the whole night about me joining, but she said that I didn't look like the stripper type. I should be the one collecting all the money, she said. Let's just say the bitch got extra mustard. She's pushing weight for somebody, 'cause the whole club was rollin' like a motherfucker thanks to her."

"Well," I was getting real impatient with the story already.

"She invited me back to her crib, and we were chillin'. Shawty kept talkin' like a parrot, tellin' me how many pills she's pushin' a week."

"How many?" Black was getting real impatient too.

"Five thousand pills a week, hittin' the streets at twenty dollars a pop, so if you do the math, that bitch makin' forty stacks a month, easy, and let's not forget she bad on the pole, too. So you know she's paid the fuck up."

That shit was crazy. I was thinking so hard, I could actually hear my mind talking to me. But the look on Black's face showed jealousy.

She stared at Dimples like she was disgusting, and shook her head.

Something was up. I knew it because I saw it on Black's face.

"What you think, Black?" I asked her, trying to get up inside her head.

"That bitch is a target, and I'm ready to hit her."

"So, tonight we hit Swoll, and then tomorrow we smack D'Wonda," I told them. It sounded good, but was it really? Seeing how Black was looking at Dimples had me questioning how close they really were to each other. Black's attitude with Dimples jumped out the box as soon as Dimples said she met D'Wonda at the strip club. She couldn't have been there because she would've known.

I got my shit together, and we left the crib to go to Dimples parents' spot. Something was up. If it wasn't clear before, it was clear now.

The ride was so quiet that it kinda scared me. What was going on with my bitches? No one sang along to Young Jeezy's *Focus*. Could they just be nervous?

When we got to Dimples' parents' house, we got dressed and waited. It was 12:30 in the morning when Black finally got the text from Cuzzo.

We walked through the bushes and other people's backyards all the way to the nigga's house. A light was on in the bathroom.

"They all in the basement and the door's open," Black told us.

I pulled my mask over my face, adjusted my mouthpiece, and made it my business to have one in the head of my P89. If I had to empty that bitch, then I would.

I turn the knob, and it turned. Those niggas couldn't even hear us because they were too busy watching Kevin Durant dunk on James.

"Lay the fuck down, bitch." I yelled at the nigga closest to me.

Dimples and Black laid the other two niggas down.

172

"I ain't gonna say this shit too many times 'cause I hate sounding like a scratched up CD, so where the fuck the money at?" My words were met with silence. No one said shit, so I went into action like a Tasmanian Devil. I shot the nigga to my left in the leg. The P89 barked like a pit bull on steroids. The nigga started to holler like a bitch.

"Shut the fuck up. If you don't, I'm gonna shoot the other leg, and make my way up."

"Swoll, just give them the money, yo," I heard the nigga beside Swoll say.

"I agree," Black said, putting her two cents in.

The nigga Swoll really had one eye. I wondered how he lost it. Since the nigga wasn't talking or giving shit up, I felt like he needed a little incentive. I shot the nigga in his other leg, and then I shot him in his right hand. That nigga was gonna have some trouble wiping his ass for a little while, because I was gonna get that other hand of his if he wasn't careful. No money, more blood to let loose. Dimples and Black kept looking at me like I was crazy.

Maybe I was. Maybe I was losing my fucking mind all the way.

"A'ight, a'ight, yo. It's in the sofa, in the middle seat. There's a button on the right arm rest. The middle seat will lift up."

Dimples followed Swoll's directions, and *bam* there it was, free money. I pulled the three trash bags that I'd brought along out of my pocket.

"Cuff then up, my nigga," I told Black. I kept my P89 on those niggas. Dimples loaded up the trash bags, and we left the same way. We went in. I was so glad when we saw Dimples' house light come into view because the damn trash bag had some weight to it.

Once we got inside the house, the questions came at me direct. "Damn, what the fuck was that all about, Sweets?" Black asked.

"What the fuck you talkin' 'bout?"

"You hit that nigga up three times. For what?"

I didn't know what my friend was thinking, but I had to let her ass know.

"Them nigga's wasn't movin' until that P89 got to talkin'. I had to show them that we meant business and not games. We didn't go over there for a slumber party."

To my surprise, Dimples didn't say a word, like she wasn't even there.

"Damn, Dimples. Do you have somethin' to say?" I asked her, surprised by her silence.

"Yeah, we safe, but y'all goin' at each other's throats like sharks."

"Fuck that. Let's count this bitch up and split it, then I am out," I told them.

We could hear sirens flying up the street. That nigga Swoll had almost got his homeboy bodied.

"Pussy ass nigga, I should've shot his ass in the other eye," I exclaimed.

Dimples took a long deep breath like she couldn't breathe. Black just rolled her eyes at me. Something was up with those bitches, I swear.

It was six in the morning, and we were still counting money. I felt like Jeezy for real. I should have changed my name to Lil Miss Jeezy.

One hundred eighty thousand dollars, damn, that shit was magical. I felt like I deserved more because I sure did put in work, but fuck it, I wasn't tripping. We split the shit three ways, sixty thousand dollars each. I gave Black ten thousand dollars to give to Cuzzo for looking out.

I called a cab, and left. As soon as I got to the house, I texted Ced as I walked through the front door, letting him know that I was thinking about him. *Tomorrow that bitch D'Wonda is gonna get smoked if she didn't give it up, I swear on everything I love.*

Since Black had been acting funny ever since Dimples brought that stripper bitch up as a victim, I texted Dimples to let her know I made it home. As I was counting my money, the more I thought about it, I realized both of them bitches were acting strange. Dimples looked like she wished she'd never brought the stripper into the situation.

I fell asleep counting my stash and woke up looking for my phone. It was under the money. I could hear it ringing. It was my fucking sperm donor.

I listened to him pour his heart out about Swoll getting robbed and E getting hit up last night. I just sat and listened because there was no need to comment, and I wasn't trying to hear the shit for real.

It was crazy how shit hit close to home, and niggas got all soft and shit. T sounded like he wanted to break down. Bitch ass nigga. Now you tell me, what the fuck could I do with him after he made my heart cold? *Nigga's nowadays ain't built to last. They forget that Eve made Adam eat the fruit. This is a woman's world,* I thought.

I got me a new stash spot for all the money I had now. I wanted to change the lock on my room, but I was not going to because that would let them know that I was aware of their antics. I was one step ahead of them bitches, and I wanted to keep it that way, especially since I thought Black didn't want me to be a part of that mission with the stripper bitch. My mind was running wild.

Better safe than sorry.

Jamaica

Chapter 23
Can't Be

That bitch D'Wonda gave the shit up easy. Caught her coming home late and she took me in. Now that was how business was supposed to operate. Ten thousand pills, and fifty thousand in cash. Yea, for a single black woman, that bitch was living large, waiting on someone like me to come take it, and that was exactly what I did.

"Just give me fifteen thousand dollars and two thousand pills, Dimples." Shit, it was free, plus it was Dimples' lick.

"Sweets, you sure that's all you want?"

"Yea, I'm good with that."

Once I got my share, I dipped away from them.

I gave the pills to T.

"Christmas in summer, yo?"

"Get your bank roll up, playa, and don't let that bitch know shit."

"You a real ass bitch, Sweets. No disrespect, but I swear the nigga that gets you is gonna be a lucky ass nigga."

It was Saturday morning, and I had things to do. I got dressed, and I knew from head to toe I was the shit. The skin tight True Religion jeans showed my ass perfectly. When I wore them with my white fitted T that said "You can't touch this" across the chest, it made my waist look crazy small. They say dope man's are for trappers, but shit I was a motherfucking killer in the all-white Air Force Ones. When I left the crib, I went to Payday to send a Money Gram to Jay for two thousand dollars. Crazy right?

I jammed all the way to Dillwyn, listening to Jeezy and Lil Bossie *Better Believe It* and some other songs of theirs. When I finally arrived, I saw his mother's car in the parking lot, but I didn't see anyone, which meant they were already inside.

When I got inside, I still didn't see them. They were in the back with Jay already. The officer processed and searched me. Then someone came to escort me to the visiting room.

When Jay saw me, he looked like he'd seen a ghost. His mouth dropped open, but what I saw had my hands sweating. His mother was holding his so-called little girl. Damn.

"Hello everyone," I said.

"How you doin'?" his mother asked me.

"Great, and you?"

She didn't get the chance to respond because Jay jumped in.

"Yo, I know I told you not to come this weekend."

I knew that bitch ass nigga didn't have the nerve to say that. My feelings were hurt because I didn't want to leave him alone doing his bid. Plus, I loved him, I really did. But lately my actions had shown me maybe I was wrong. I fucked Ced. So instead of crying because Jay had hurt my feelings, I was gonna laugh this off, since I had one over him anyway.

"Yea, you did tell me not to come. But for real, I've been comin' up here for two years, and this is what you say to me?"

My brother always told me to use logic over emotions. Damn, I missed King. But when the little girl's mother came out of the restroom, I knew what time it was.

Now all eyes were on us.

"Nigga, you done fucked the church's money all the way up. How could you actually play me like a lotto? How could you take my mind and fuck it crazy? I motivated you, I dedicated my time, fuck that, my life to you, and this is what you give me?"

Now the bitch was sitting down and I was in his face.

"Nigga, you so funny, Kevin Hart ain't have shit on you at all."

With that being said, I walked off to take a picture.

"Yo Slim, how you doin'?"

"Good."

Slim was the picture dude, old but sexy. He'd been down for like sixteen years, had four left. He didn't have no family. I'd been knowing him since Jay got moved there.

"That's what's up. Do me a favor, 'cause I know Jay got picture tickets."

"What's up?"

"Can you take a picture of me?"

"Yea."

I mean, everyone was looking at me, but I didn't give a fuck. They were lucky I didn't turn the fuck up. I flashed my middle finger in the picture. That was something he'd never get because no inappropriate pictures were allowed. Only thing he'd be getting was a letter from the staff.

"Thanks Slim. Keep that head held high."

"You too, shawty."

I walked my fine ass back over to Jay's table to say something but headed to the exit instead. His nasty ass so-called baby-ma felt like she had to speak up.

"Thanks for all the hard earned money."

I stopped dead in my tracks and looked back to smile. I swear all thirty-two of my pearly whites were showing. By the time I got to my car, tears were flooding my shirt. Why did that even bother me? I was gonna break it off anyway. Damn, he'd been giving that bitch my money. Damn, another nigga had just made my heart even colder. I wanted to flatten every fucking tire on his mother's car, but prisons had cameras every damn where.

I got in my car to drive but my nerves had me paralyzed. So I called Ced.

"Hello."

"Can you please come get me?"

"Where are you? What's wrong?"

"Dillwyn."

"Don't move."

I heard him telling someone they had to drive him because he had to drive another car back. I hung the phone up and held my head down while I cried my heart out. Once again, I was hurt by a man.

I turned the music on and listened to Lil Boosie's *Betrayed* because that was exactly how I felt, but the conclusion that I had come up with had me smiling like nothing had even happened.

When a bitch is real, is nothing anyone can do about it. You can either be down with her, hate on her, or you can sit back and give that bitch the utmost respect. Some niggas and bitches are haters, while others would do anything to have a real ass bitch on their team. Real ass people salute realness, but some snakes claim they real till they show their heads. I am a real ass bitch with what's getting to be a cold ass heart, I thought as I sat in my car, waiting.

Ced finally showed up with that white boy. He got in my car and his people drove off.

"Damn, you got here quick," I told him.

"If I could've flown, I would've been here faster. Now tell me what's wrong."

I gave him the story, start to finish.

"Sweets, I apologize for dude but I'm glad that's over with 'cause you mine now."

"Really?"

"Really. And I don't want you doin' nothing. Just take care of your daughter, yourself, and me, with my help!"

"Thanks, but no thanks. To be honest, I was taught to depend on no one, especially not a man."

"You just got caught up with the wrong niggas."

"Let me think about it."

"Cool. Let me drive 'cause you ain't stable."

"Funny. Since I'm not stable, can you make me stable?"

He grabbed my face in both hands and we let our mouths dance. My pussy was already wet just from looking at him, so I told him between kisses, "We can do it now, right here in the prison parking lot and go to jail for havin' sex in public, or we can do it when we touch the front door."

"Jail will keep us apart, and that I don't want, so I'd rather wait."

The ride back home seemed long. My body was there, but my mind was far away.

"You know, I just sent that nigga two stacks before I got there, and for that dusty bird brain bitch to tell me *thank you* means he's sending my money home to her."

"Well, not anymore. Everythin' he got in his account you can get back."

"How can I do that?" Now my mind was coming back. Money was involved.

"My people's girlfriend, Lex, works up there as an accountant. I can get her to wipe his account clean. She can send you the check and make the purpose of it a gift."

"Could you please?"

"Hell yea. No problem, you know that any nigga in his right mind should be savin' if he got a rider dropping bread like that in his account."

Nowadays it was not what you knew, it was who you knew. Ced got on his phone and handled that for me.

"Lex, said first thing Monday morning it will be on her to do list."

That nigga Jay had just gone from stunting to being dead ass broke and didn't even know it yet. I hoped he had that bitch saving some, but knowing that bitch, she probably spent it. At the end of the day, I was still good. But having Ced, I was gravy.

If I wanted to become a warrior, I had to maintain a peaceful mind, use intelligence over emotions, and stay strong, or the world was gonna eat me alive.

We didn't go back to the mansion, we went to his other spot. As the door opened, we attacked each other like vampires. From the living room to the kitchen, I grabbed some ice from the freezer and hit my knees to suck his dick like a mad woman. I rubbed ice on his balls as I attempt to drain him of everything he had inside of his body.

"Baby, I'm 'bout to bust."

I didn't say anything. I just let my mouth do the talking. I pulled his dick into my mouth with my lips and locked my tongue around it.

When he released inside my mouth. I thought for a second that I was drinking RedBull. I licked up every drop. What was the point in wasting good juices? I tried to find the words to say, but all I came up with was, "You have the potential to hold a huge piece of my heart forever."

Shit. What was I doing? I asked myself. He smiled at me as he lifted me up, and put me on the counter. He reached inside the freezer and grabbed a jolly rancher popsicle. He pulled the stick out and inserted the whole popsicle into my pussy.

"Oh my," I gasped.

He put his face between my legs and sucked the whole thing out before pushing it in again and repeating the process until it was all gone. When he finished, he carried me to the shower, where he straight fucked my brains out. I bent over, holding on to the toilet as I let him man handle me. But I started throwing that shit back at him like a pitcher out for revenge. We made it to the shower where he let the wall hold me while he fucked me some more. I didn't want to stop. I hit the shower button and, as the water hit our bodies, he slid his dick out of me to use his face to suck my pussy some more.

"I can't take..." I came so hard I slid straight down the wall, my knees buckling under my weight.

"My turn," I told him. I pushed him against the wall and I sucked the whole ten and a half. I grabbed his hand and put it behind my head.

I let him fuck my mouth like an open pussy, and I didn't even gag. I felt his legs shaking like he was warming up for a track meet, and I knew I had more RedBull coming. He let loose in my mouth and all I could think was *RedBull; it gives you wings.*

"Damn," he panted.

We washed each other from head to toe. I could have fallen in love with his dick, him, or maybe both. We laid up all weekend. Pillow talk was a motherfucker.

Jamaica

Chapter 24
Come Clean

"You may or may not know what I do for a livin', but I am a hustler. More like a money maker," he said.

I gave him a look like, *keep talking.*

"I push almost everythin', but my choice is cocaine and crack." They forget to say that pussy would make a man confess. It was true. It was happening right then.

"I get it right off the boat myself, because I got a Mexican plug that loves me like family. My father turned me on to them. Since my dad was so loyal to them, they cherish me and treat me like their own. I push everythin' in this city; and in two others, also. Nothin' little, all major. In a week, I average almost a million, so do the math."

Damn. That nigga could write a book about money if he wanted to.

"I treat my crew like I would want to be treated. When somethin' happens to them, it happens to me also. But at the same time, I don't sleep on none of them 'cause this is a crazy world. Everyone wants to be a boss. I respect them, I treat them well, and I pray that they never try to cross me in any way, 'cause if I live to see the next day, they will not be so lucky, and I make that clear as day to them."

Sometimes silence is the best. Why interrupt him? He was on a roll.

"Yeah, I have competition everywhere, 'cause everyone needs to eat, but I keep the peace," he said.

What could I actually say to him that he hadn't heard before? I questioned myself. But before I even finished that thought, the words flew out of my mouth on their own.

"We could be a hell of a team, together." I watched his face, but he was playing poker. His reply said he was interested anyway.

"How?"

"Since you came clean with me, I'm gonna come clean with you. The only people who know the truth are my girls. I'm a stick up bitch."

This nigga was still wearing that poker face, so I couldn't read him.

"Yeah, I work at the salon, but that's to throw everyone off. I go out and see who's doin' what, my bitches get in good with the victim, and then we go from there. Does that mean that I am watchin' you? No. At first, I didn't know we was gonna be close, but as I said, my *girls* get in good with the niggas, and then we go from there. You're not a target. You've never been a target."

"So how can we be a great team?"

"You show me your competitors, and I take them out."

"And?"

"And I'll split everythin' with you straight down the middle."

His poker face was on. "Sweets, I am astounded. I never would've thought you had that in you. In the bed, you a beast, so I can only imagine you with a strap in your hand."

"Don't worry, you'll see for yourself if we become a team. As you say, don't no nigga put fear in your heart. Well, not one person puts fear in me, and I mean no nigga or bitch at all. If we become a team, I will have the final say so on how the missions should be completed."

"And why is that?" he asked.

I hated it when a motherfucker questioned my gangsta. "Because this is my hustle. This is what I do. I truly enjoy this.

It's somethin' I'm blessed to know, and I know you understand so I don't have to explain myself."

"I respect that. The less I know the, better it is, so let me give you the rundown," he said.

"I'm all ears."

"Corona, don't get it fucked up though. I got your back 103%, and that will never change unless you cross me in any way. Then I gotta handle my end to the fullest, 'cause you damn sure ain't no average woman to be played with."

That nigga was not gonna be sleeping on me, and for some reason, that turned me on even more. "We both on a different level, but at the end of the day, we want the same thing from each other."

"And what would that be, Miss Lady?"

I finally told him what I knew he wanted to hear.

"Each other. We want each other forever."

As soon as I let those words leave my mouth, I realized that I meant it. I know that we were perfect for one another.

Me + Him = Greatness, I pictured the equation in my mind.

"I can dig that. So here's what you need to know. I got six niggas in my way. I don't care how you handle your business, as long as you come back to me in one piece, 'cause then life will still be worth livin'."

"Don't worry. I'm gonna be good 'cause I got a little girl to live for. Now that I have you, I'm comin' back home to you untouched. And if I don't, you better clean the entire city until you're satisfied."

"On my mother's grave, I can promise you that."

We sealed our conversation with a kiss, and then I encouraged him to get my pussy wet by telling me about this money we were gonna share together.

"Ain't no words to describe you girl, I swear."

"Anythin' is good, but Bad Bitch says it best."

Chapter 25
Count Down

"The first nigga go by Milk. He's pushin' heavy weight. We ain't beefin' or nothing, but he dropped his prices, so he's got way more people than me. He tried stuntin' on me one night, hard. Had too many witnesses, so I couldn't really do anything but walk away. My nigga Trappa's girlfriend, Lex, got a baby by him. He don't even claim her kid, don't do shit for lil man. My nigga Trappa raisin' his kid."

I saw the hurt in his eyes for that lil boy.

"I'm gonna make you proud, so don't worry, baby."

He gave me the rundown on where Milk lived and everything he thought that I needed to know. I was born ready and real, so yeah, I put my bitches on the lick with me. Ced was cool with that.

Milk was a straight up bitch ass nigga. I had caught that nigga slipping super hard. He was living large, I mean dumb large. The shit had me zoned the fuck out. I kept thinking that nigga was Tony Montana, but Tony could get his ass touched if he was around too. I got in his crib through the back door by kicking the motherfucker off the hinges. Then I posted up in the nigga's tub, waiting on him to come home from the bar. As soon as he came in the house, the first thing he did was head to the bathroom to release that liquor.

When I heard his piss hitting the water, I popped up like a jack in the box and put the burner on his ass. His piss dried up quick. "You know you should always check your home when you get in, no matter what," I told his dumb ass.

"If it's money you want, you can get it. You can get the work, too."

I laughed at him.

"Let me tell you off the top, my people's already searched the house. They found the drugs, but no money. So yeah, I want it all, baby!"

Dimples' and Black's masks were down, but mine was not. I wondered why they were being sloppy, but guess it didn't matter. I'd already got the feeling that nigga wouldn't be telling any stories anytime soon.

I escorted him to the kitchen. Dimples and Black were talking like nothing was going on.

I barked my orders. "Somebody give this nigga a chair and cuff his feet. Cuff his hands behind his back too."

As they complied, I went to the sink. I wet the sponge so it was soft and stuffed it in his mouth. Then I told him exactly what I expected to happen.

"When I ask you a question, I'll take it out of your mouth. Tell the truth and don't lie about anythin'. Agree?"

He nodded his head *yes* like he thought he had a choice. He didn't.

"First question. Where's the money at?" I removed the sponge.

"Bitch, fuck you."

Oh hell no. It was not a good time for him to get balls. "What did you say? Let me ask you that again. Where is the money?" I just knew that nigga didn't say what I thought he said.

"I said, bitch, fuck you."

I stuffed the sponge back in his mouth.

"Yo, one of y'all bring me a knife."

Dimples put a knife in my hand. I cut that nigga's pants straight the fuck off of him. He was wearing some Bugs Bunny boxers. I pulled his dick out, spit on my leather glove, and beat it to get it hard. Once it firmed up, I sliced the very tip off. Oh man, that nigga was screaming like he was giving birth. Blood spurted, but it was not as bad as I thought it would be. I took the sponge out of his mouth so I could get an answer. I put it on top of his dick so it could soak up some of the blood.

"It's a 32-inch old school TV in the closet of my bedroom. The money's in there."

"Go get that," I told my bitches as I stuffed his mouth back up with the bloody sponge. Yep, I was cold.

When they left, I got to talking to him again.

"How old is your son?"

"I don't have a son."

He was in pain, but he better not had start screaming.

"Yes, you do, Milk. He's seven years old, you don't do shit for him or his mom, another nigga's playin' daddy to your seed and you have the nerve to say that you don't have a son? Nigga, you don't deserve to have a dick."

I solved that problem by taking it off for him. He was screaming and fighting, but the cuffs wouldn't give.

When Dimples and Black came back, they were in shock to see his dick lying on the floor beside him.

"Bitch, you done lost your mind," Black yelled.

Why was that bitch always questioning my gangsta? "Yeah, I done lost it. Take that shit apart, and see if the money is in there.

They busted it open and there wasn't one wire in that thing. With all that money, who needed wires?

"Put that shit up, grab the drugs, and load the car up. I'll be out in a few." Milk was losing so much blood that he kept fading in and out. I was glad that he wasn't screaming anymore. That was getting on my nerves. I leaned in real close to ask him my next question.

"Do you know Ced?" He heard me. His eyes flew open and he nodded his head *yes*.

"Well, this nigga's raisin' the son you have with Lex, takin' real good care of him too. You tried to stunt on Ced one night. Then you dropped your prices so low that it started fuckin' up his bread. I don't give a fuck 'bout none of that, though. What I *do* care about is that you lied to me about your only seed, so you shall not live." I pulled the sponge out of his mouth so that I could hear his plea.

"I gave you everythin' that you asked for."

That nigga couldn't even say that he had a son that he needed to live for.

"Do me a favor. When you get to hell, tell all the other fake ass niggas I'm sorry I didn't get to meet them."

I let my P89 speak exactly how I felt. Brains splattered, and blood ran. I even shot his dick once, just for good measure.

Dimples and Black were waiting in the car when I came out of the house. Black drove, and no one said a word until we were about five minutes from our place.

"You killed him, didn't you?" Black asked.

I gave her a look like, *bitch don't ask me no questions.* I could say that Milk had it going on. Twenty-five thousand two hundred grams. That's twenty-five bricks flat, plus eighty thousand dollars.

Damn.

"I'm keepin' all the work, and the money's gotta be split four ways." I waited for someone to say something, but no one spoke up. They got their bread and dipped. I called Ced as soon as they were gone, He lets me know he would be here soon. We kept it short and sweet.

It wasn't long before he pulled up outside.

"There was twenty-five bricks, plus twenty thousand dollars for you. I sliced the bread four ways. I didn't touch the work, 'cause that's not me."

"Yo, I swear you somethin' else," he told me with a smile. "Don't judge me, just get this shit out of my house."

His homeboy had driven him, so Ced spoke to dude in the living room, and dude loaded up the bricks and left.

"Let's go, I'm gonna stay at your house with you, cause I don't want to go to sleep here."

With Black questioning me about killing Milk, I had a hard time trusting her.

"Cool."

We got in my car and left. No words had to be spoken.

***

When we got to his mansion, he turned my face towards his and finally told me the truth.

"I've been worried sick about you."

"I told you not to be 'cause I would return in one piece, right?"

"Right. You did that, Miss Lady."

"Can we take a shower and make love until morning?" I asked.

When two people understood each other, words were extra. We made love until just before dawn, when my body gave out and gave up. I finally slept the sleep of a working woman.

I woke up to the sound of a newscaster. Ced was watching the flatscreen.

"This is Helen Short reporting to you live from Forest Road. Around 6:30 this morning Devone Shaw was found dead by his brother, Marcus Shaw. Reporting officers say that Devone suffered a cruel and painful death. The deceased's genitals were not only removed from his body, but also suffered a gunshot wound. As you can see, family and friends are arriving here now at the scene. At noon, there will be more details. As of now, there are no suspects in this horrifying tragedy. Back to you Oswald."

"I couldn't let him live 'cause for one, he lied, for two, he disrespected you, for three, most of all, he didn't deserve to live 'cause he wasn't doin' nothing for his son."

The words tumbled out of my mouth faster than I would've thought possible.

"Baby, you ain't ever gotta explain yourself to me. You got this under control."

I felt sorry for the lil' boy. I didn't have any parents around to make me feel protected, so I could relate to him. Hearing Milk deny him made me angry.

"You kept your word with me about the money I sent Jay, and your people put herself in danger to send me that check. All I can do is help her live in peace now."

Jay had had almost ten stacks on his books. When Ced had that money returned to me, I'd given every dime of it to Lex. "That's my thank you gift," I told her.

It had been weeks since I'd heard from Jay. He had tried calling me at first, but I hadn't answered. I'd also told Traymon that he had to keep Beauty for the next two months. He was cool with that because I kept blessing the nigga. It was sad I had to pay his ass to keep his child, but fuck it.

Chapter 26
Number 5

"The next nigga comes from New York, so you know he's about that Big Apple money. This nigga Sham stays strapped even when he's fuckin'. It's hard to catch him slippin', and he's trigger happy."

"There's always a way to get a nigga with money," I said.

Ced's face was unreadable, so I continued, "Nigga's with mad money always think they can't be touched, but they fail to realize that's just a sayin' and not a fact. Pussy is a powerful thing. They say this is a man's world, but pussy runs this shit. If they only knew, and if you don't believe me, let me show you."

Two bad bitches at the same time was something that no sane nigga would pass up. I watched the nigga Sham for a week nonstop. Every bar he went to, Dimples and Black were there. Every sale he made, I saw it. Every bitch he fucked, I saw them. I was his GPS.

I could have been the alphabet boys. He wouldn't even have had a clue. But soon, and very soon, I was gonna be his worst nightmare.

On Saturday nights, Big Licks stays packed 'cause drinks are super cheap. Bitches outnumbered the niggas four to one, so you already know shit was going smooth as ever.

I watched as Dimples and Black work on Sham. They were acting gay, like they were a couple. Only thing missing was that solid dick of Sham's. If I didn't know them bitches, I would've thought that they were gay for real. They could have gotten a Grammy for the best acting ever because them bitches were definitely putting on for the team. Pussy was a powerful thing. If pussy told the hard dick it needed to be touched, that hard dick was gonna try to be superman. Two pussies at one time was heaven sent, that was what that nigga was thinking.

I watched them getting into his car. They all piled into the backseat. As I wondered who the fuck was driving I saw big ass Trill come out of Big Licks. Damn, he was hit too. My question was why the fuck were they together? The nigga Big Trill got into the driver's seat of Sham's car. Mane, what the fuck was going on?

The car started and then pulled out of the parking lot. I followed them for a few minutes, and they pulled into the first hotel they saw, The Lodge. It was an okay joint. Niggas and bitches went there to get their freak on because they could pay by the hour. Trill got out and went to the hotel's office. Sham's charger was moving like they were already fucking. Trill got back in the car, and drove around to park in front of room 123. The back door opened and Dimples came out first, then Sham and Black followed. Together they headed to room 123, but Trill stayed in the car.

Tell me this nigga's leaving, I think to myself.

Yup. When 123's door closed behind Sham, Trill drove away. I watched and waited just to see if the nigga was coming back. Twenty minutes later, still a no show.

Krystal, this girl from around the way, was working in the office. When I went in, she didn't recognize me because I had six braids in my head, covered by a fitted hat, with my breasts taped down. And I was wearing some black Dickie's with black Timberlands. I was looking like a pretty ass nigga.

I put some bass in my voice and said, "Yo, shawty, I just lost the key to my room."

She was all into her phone.

"What room is that?"

"123."

She lifted her head up. "I just gave Mr. Flex a key to that room about thirty minutes ago."

"Well, I left to go to the store while my nigga took a shower. I ain't on no homo shit," I answered as she laughed.

"Ok, that will be five dollars for an extra card."

I handed her a twenty, told her to keep the change, and she gave me a new card. I walked away and just as I was about to step outside the door, Krystal hollered, "Have a good night," after me.

I didn't turn around, but I did toss a "You too shawty" over my shoulder. I pulled the fitted hat down over my eyes a little more. I was ready to get this shit cracking.

I slid the card into the slot slowly, trying not to be heard. The lights were off, but the TV was up loud. I couldn't hear shit except Dimples hollering like a motherfucker, at least I thought it was her.

When I flipped the light switch on, I almost ran the fuck back through the door. Sham was getting his dick sucked by Dimples, and Black was eating Dimples' pussy from the back.

What the fuck? So who the fuck was hollering? Was it that bitch ass nigga?

"Nigga, if you as much as blink, I swear tomorrow you'll be the guest of honor at your own wake."

His dick went soft immediately.

"Cuff that nigga to the bed and put some fuckin' clothes on, 'cause y'all bitches on another cloud."

Black laughed, and Dimples cracked a smile. I had to give it to them though, they had it going on. Even had my pussy itching for a minute and missing Ced's touch for real.

"What's good, nigga?" I asked Sham.

"This gotta be a fuckin' freak show! Ya'll bitches done lost ya minds, got me cuffed to this damn bed. Y'all got me fucked up.

I couldn't help but smile, hadn't enough pussy got him in trouble?

"And how is that, sir?" I asked him because I really wanted to hear what the fuck he had to say.

"Do you know who the fuck I am?" he screamed.

He was just another nigga that bleeds.

"Y'all take the sheets off the bed, tie one around each ankle, and pull his legs apart."

That nigga had way too much mouth and I was about to shut him up. I got his pants off the chair and search his pockets, a wad of dead Presidents, a cell phone, a bag of X pills, and a 9mm.

So that was what was going on.

"Text Trill and let that nigga know you gonna take a cab home."

His eyes searched me, wondering how I knew Big Trill. He better not ask me either.

"How the fuck am I goin' to do that if I'm cuffed up like this, bitch?"

"The next time you call me a bitch, make sure you say Miss Bitch, you bitch ass nigga."

He still had heart.

"Pull his legs apart some more," I told Dimples and Black. He was hollering like a bitch now for real.

"Nigga, I told you to shut the fuck up." I put the head of my P89 at his ass and told him, "You scream again, and I swear this baby goin' inside your ass nigga."

I saw tears in that nigga's eyes and he shut the fuck up too.

"A hard dick can always get you in trouble, and that's for real. You got greedy tryin' to have two instead of one, but in the end, look at who got their legs apart, your bitch ass."

Niggas like that made me sick.

"She gonna uncuff one hand so you can text Trill. If you try anything funny, you can do me a favor and tell Milk when you get to hell that as long as I'm alive, his son gonna be good without his bitch ass."

Black uncuffed his hand so he could text Trill.

Trill texted back, "Ok."

He had to be the biggest bitch ass nigga ever because as soon as I asked him a question, he would answer. I had to do this nigga in because no nigga or bitch in their right mind would not be out to get revenge. I had the keys to his stash spot. He told me where the money, X pills, and guns were. I knew the nigga wasn't lying because I'd been watching him like a hawk.

"I've got two 9mm in the car. If anyone gets in y'all's way, don't wait, smoke their ass," I told them.

"You already know we comin' back in one piece to get you," Black said.

"That means a lot to me."

They left and I re-tied the sheets, one to the vent, and the other to the bathroom door. I knew the nigga wanted to scream, and I was surprised that he didn't. He must have remembered what I told him about putting my baby in his ass, and I meant all the way up in that shit.

I took a seat on top of the dresser and just looked at him. "How do you know Trill?" I asked him.

"We have the same baby mother."

"Damn, she's one lucky bitch. She's got the best of the same world with the both of y'all."

"Instead of us beefin', I thought we could be parents and partners."

Damn. Thank God this nigga hasn't gotten picked up by the feds because God only knows his ass would be singing

Amazing Grace like no tomorrow. Ugh! He made me sick just looking at him.

"How much bread you sittin' on?"

"Five hundred thousand." His voice cracked as he said that.

"How many pills?"

"Probably two hundred fifty thousand."

"How many guns?"

"Thirty."

"Damn, you a one stop shop."

"Why you askin' me all these questions, since you gonna have it all?"

"You want me to keep it a stack with you, Sham?"

"Yea."

"For one, I dont' trust my bitches like I used to. They acting too funny. Second, I wanna see for myself how loyal they are, not only to themselves, but to me. Loyalty is a must in my life."

He nodded his head, agreeing to what I was saying.

"If a nigga or a bitch did this to me and let me live, I know in my heart I would kill everyone close to them until I get them. So, truth be told, I can't let you live." I watched the nigga swallow the lump in his throat. Damn. Knowing that he was about to die was mind fucking blowing.

"Ma, on some real gangsta shit, I respect you 'cause you a gangsta motherfucker. You real, brave as hell, and sexy as ever."

Men and their sweet talk, sad it won't work with me. "Well, thank you, but I've been told all that before. The only way I'll let you live is if you let me fuck you in the ass with my P89."

"And you'll let me live?" That nigga didn't waste any time thinking about it.

"Yea."

"Well, come on then."

He was a bitch in sheep's clothing, fa real.

My phone rang. It was Black saying shit was straight. So I told her to meet me at our place in an hour. I hung up the phone and returned my attention to Sham.

I rammed my gun straight up in his ass and that nigga didn't flinch, move, or scream. It was like he was enjoying it, and I knew for a fact that I had to smoke his ass.

"You know, I wish you had told me to fuck myself, then I could've respected your gangsta. But instead, you told me to fuck you with a damn gun, a P89 at that. How can I let you live after I done took your pride like that?"

Before he could even answer, I rammed my gun harder up in his ass again. As he started screaming, I put two bullets in him and they ripped his belly open. I could smell his shit and see pieces of his intestines on the blood soaked sheets. I put two more in his head, just for GP.

I got to the house, cleaned up, took a shower, and waited for my bitches. As usual, I texted Ced to let him know I was safe and at home. Dimples and Black pulled up just as Ced's text came through, letting me know he was on his way. They carried everything into the house.

"That's all that was there?" I asked.

Black answered, "Yea."

Four hundred thousand dollars, one hundred fifty thousand pills, and thirty guns. The numbers didn't match, so I asked them again.

"Was that everythin' in the house?" These treacherous as bitches.

"I told you, yea. You keep askin' the same question, like we lyin'."

My head dropped. *Why lie to me*, I wanted to ask them, but I didn't.

"We gonna split the money four ways, pills and guns goin' to the person."

Once again, Black spoke up, "Cool, we can live with that."

We? Who the fuck was we? And why the fuck did she say it like that? Mane, them bitches must have been fucking each other. The bitch said, "We can live with that." I had no choice but to look at it that way.

Dimples hadn't said shit. What the fuck was going on? They left when they got their cut. What was there for me to do but shake my damn head because the president of America couldn't pay me enough to believe that they were actually stealing and betraying me like I was nobody? It was taking everything in me not to smoke both their asses.

Finally, Ced showed up in his car with Snow driving. I watched Snow park the car in the driveway through my kitchen window. I wondered how he ended up with the name Snow because nothing on him was white, not even his teeth. Snow stayed in the car when Ced came in the house. I explained everything to him, except for how I killed Sham.

"Damn, your home girls are dangerous."

"Them bitches don't scare me. I help them bitches eat. I put them on. When did money and drugs become such a big problem between us? I always had their backs, no matter what."

Tears were in my eyes, but I swear to God I refused to let that shit drop, fuck that.

"It's all good, though. I'm gonna use them to get the rest of these niggas, then I got a surprise for them both."

"The ball in your court, play with it baby, but always remember I got your back, Sweets. You ain't never alone."

'Tomorrow's Sunday. How about we get your kids and I get Beauty, and we go out and have some fun?" I asked him.

"Yeah, we can do that. Grab some of your shit, 'cause you damn sure ain't gonna sleep here no more."

I gave him his share.

"Let me put Snow up on what's goin' on," Ced told me.

As I was getting my things together, Snow was loading Ced's share of the profit into the car.

"Snow's gonna take my car, so we're takin' yours to the mansion because he's gotta take the shit back to the trap."

"Ok," I said as I nodded at him.

I texted T as soon as we got there, letting him know I was coming to get Beauty in the morning so have her ready at eight.

All I wanted to do was go to sleep, but Ced had something planned for me. He ran my bath water, placed candles all around the tub, and told me to relax, before leaving me alone in the bathroom.

My mind was working overtime. Dimples and Black were fucking around, had to be, but I just didn't understand why they lied to me about the money and the pills, but not the guns. That shit didn't make any sense at all to me. No matter how hard I tried to figure the shit out, it still wasn't coming to me. All that thinking had me so tired. I could feel myself drifting off to sleep in the heat.

Ced returned. "Damn, you wanna drown yourself, baby?"

"Naw, just tired."

He washed me and dried my body before carrying me to the bed. Once we were there, he put lotion on me. Then he grabbed one of his t-shirts and put it on me. Then he carried me downstairs. He had candles on the table, plus roses, and dinner. Well, not dinner, but a snack, chicken fingers with fries.

"You have such a soft side to you, and I love everythin' about this. Thank you for takin' care of me. I love it, Ced. You're the best, baby. Everyday just brings me closer and closer to you." The light in his eyes made me smile. He was happy that I was happy.

"The night just started."

We ate and discussed how tomorrow was gonna go down. Then he carried me back up the stairs.

No panties, no bra, or nothing, so I knew it was going down for real. He lay me on the bed and walked away. What was he doing? I was confused. He walked back over to me and handed me a small gift box. I opened it and gasped.

"Four and a half karat green diamond stud earrings," he told me as my mouth hung open.

"They're beautiful. I love them, and thank you so very much." I put them on and looked at myself in the mirror above my head.

"Even sexier. Come let Daddy put you to sleep now."

I hit the stereo remote and waited until I heard Ace Hood's *Body to Body* playing. *Tonight I am going every angle in bed, but first, I want to tease him.*

I danced a little.

"Damn, pop that ass on this dick like that."

"Don't worry, I plan on doin' that, too."

The sex was off the chain, no condoms, just body to body. I came three times, and he came once.

Just as I began to doze off, I heard him say, "I love you. You're the best thing that's ever happened to me beside my kids."

What the fuck did he want me to say?

We woke to the sound of my phone ringing. I mean, the shit wouldn't stop ringing. I looked at the alarm clock and it said 6-:45am. I answered my phone, not even looking to see who was calling.

"Damn, you had to kill the nigga like that? What the fuck is wrong with you, Sweets?"

I didn't say shit. I just hang up on Black's crazy ass. That bitch would not hear me say I did anything. I didn't do shit. That was my story and I was fucking sticking to it.

Breaking News

"Early this morning, police were called to The Lodge Hotel on Main Street. Dispatch received the call around 5:00am saying a dead body was discovered in one of the rooms. No names have been released as yet to the public. Coverage and updates will continue throughout the day..."

The damn TV stayed on.

"You plan on takin' them all out, don't you?" he asked me.

"Stay tuned, and don't turn the channel."

I'd be stupid if I let these motherfuckers live. Damn right every one of them that I touched was gonna pay for trying to stop or slow down my man's money. I took this seriously because Ced showed me nothing but love, and I had wanted to be loved since I was little.

"We have kids we gotta get today."

"Get ready then, soon to be Mrs. Williams."

I stopped dead in my tracks and looked at him.

"Did I say somethin' wrong, Sweets?"

"Naw, but we got a long day ahead though."

***

Beauty was dressed and ready to go. We pulled up in the all-white Expedition and all T could do was shake his head. I got out of the truck to talk to him for a minute.

"I'm bringing her back later 'cause I still got shit to do."

"Cool."

"And make sure you stay sucka duckin', nigga," I told him once I closed Beauty's door.

He didn't respond, so I climbed into the truck.

"Ma, who with you?" Her little smart ass mouth had to say.

"My friend, Cedrick. Say hello."

"Hey pretty girl, you gonna play with my girls?" he asked her.

"You have kids too?"

All I could do was smile.

"Yea, I do. Two girls and one boy."

"Ma, you gonna give me a brother?"

"You want a brother?"

"Yea, ma."

"Ok, let mommie think about it and I'll let you know, ok?"

"Ok."

I could hear the excitement in her voice. Her ass was too damn smart for me. Ced couldn't stop smiling. He looked at me and winked.

We pulled in front of a green house on Taylor Street, 2736 to be exact. He called to say he was outside. The front door flew open, and the kids came running out with a woman behind them. She was pretty, with a lot of ass. I could see it from the front. I tried not to stare but it was hard. Ced was already out of the truck talking to her.

"You act like every time I come 'round here I gotta give you money. I just gave you eight stacks last week."

"You did, but damn. You act like you ain't got three kids with me. You have kids somewhere else?"

"Look, Tarsha, I ain't goin' there with you. Y'all get in the truck."

"And whatever bitch you have ain't got shit on me."

He left her standing there and got in the truck. The passenger side of the truck was facing her. He rolled the window down because they were black as tar and you couldn't see through them at all. When she saw my face, all she could do was look and shut up.

"A'ight, Tarsha, I'll bring them back later."

She turned around and walked away. She was mad and I mean heated. Soon after we pulled off, his phone started ringing. He didn't answer. Must have been her. Christina, Cobra, and Ced Jr. were all three spitting images of their father. Cobra and Beauty stuck to each other like glue, already like old best friends.

***

The whole time we were at the fair. I kept catching Ced smiling as I played with the kids. When he told me how great I was with them, my heart fluttered with joy. Kids should always feel loved.

Spending time with Ced and the kids made me happy and that was what I wanted Beauty to have, a real, loving family.

We dropped Beauty off first. It was around 11pm when we got her back to T's place. He didn't say shit to me out the way, but said, "Be careful, yo. Niggas droppin' like flies out there."

"You should already know me," I answered on the way out.

Cobra got up as soon as we got in front of her house.

"When can Beauty come see me again?" she asked.

"Whenever you want to see her, you tell your daddy, and he'll let me know. Ok, darling?"

"Ok."

Tarsha opened up the door and Ced carried them inside one by one. Christina and Ced Jr. were both fast asleep. I got the bags out of the truck, and waited for him. Now this bitch Tarsha had the nerve to start talking shit.

"Nigga, I know you ain't bringing this bitch back here?"

She was acting like she knew me, but I was glad she remembered my face.

"I don't say shit with you having fifty different niggas around my kids, do I?"

I'd already had enough of that big ass bitch. "You know what?"

"What?"

If you weren't his baby-ma I'd drag your ass from here to Africa and back. You better recognize real when you see real. We can get along, or we can get this shit crackin' right now, so you let me know."

Ced looked at her and laughed. "Come on, Sweets. She ain't worth it."

The bitch ain't say shit. She walked her fat ass back in the house and we got back in the truck and drove off.

"You know something funny? Her ass didn't know what to say or do. She thinks she's crazy, but you brainsick, got her beat ten times over."

"Well, Ced, you crazy twenty times over for fucking with me to begin with."

He turned the music up and winked at me.

Young Jeezy's *Everything* blasted.

I coun't help but to think about Dimples and Black, so I decided to text them.

"The store still open up tomorrow? We gotta go shopping."

Black texted back, saying, "Yea, meet you at the laundry mat on Campbell Avenue at 6pm."

Dimples texted back, "Okay."

I let her know where to meet and what time. Me and Ced chilled for the rest of the night. We talked and fucked, fucked and talked.

Jamaica

Chapter 27
Number 4

I met up with Dimples and Black and gave them the run down about our next mission. Truth be told, I wanted to do the shit by my damn self, but fuck it, they were in it and I coulf use the hands.

Jimmy was our next target, a Haitian nigga who lived in Atlanta but pushed his weight in Virginia. He was a real black ass nigga, too. He looked like a jet black statue, but money made him look like a sexy chocolate bar. That was the power of paper.

At first I was kinda scared to do this one because them Haitians were some crazy ass fucks, and they were on that voodoo shit. Plus, I didn't really know for a fact if my bitches had my back or what. I was ready for anything.

The nigga lived on a dead end street called Federal, the last house on the left. Why was a big time drug dealer living on a street called Federal? There were no alphabet boys here, though. It was just me and my bitches.

The front door was wide fucking open, and the only thing in our way was a mesh screen door. I lifted my right leg and kicked the motherfucker open.

Cheap ass lock.

The sound brought a bitch down the stairs. When she saw our masks, she screamed and tried to run back up the stairs. But I was too fast for her. I took the stairs two at a time.

"Scream again and you won't even remember it, I promise," I told her.

"Please don't hurt me," she whimpered.

We were masked the fuck up like the DEA. Them Haitians could put a root on you from the grave, from what I heard, so I wasn't letting anyone see my face.

"Please, please, just don't hurt me."

"Bitch, I heard you the first time," I said.

"Where's the money?" Dimples asked her.

Black was tearing shit up already.

"I don't know where anything at."

I kind of believed her, but you couldn't put shit past a bitch.

"Where's that nigga at?"

"He went to make a run, should be back any minute now."

I heard a car door slam.

"That's him outside," the bitch said.

"Take the bitch in the closet, B, and if she screams, tell her goodnight."

Black did as she was told. I was halfway surprised she didn't question my gangsta.

"D, get in the bed, cover your head, and lay there. I'm gonna be behind the door," I whispered.

"Baby. Baby, I'm back," Jimmy yelled as he came into the house.

"Tammy, wake the fuck up. What happen to the screen door?"

As soon as he came through the bedroom door, I put my glock to his head.

"Bring that bitch out," I yelled,

The closet door opened and Black had the bitch in hand. She has her nine shoved into Tammy's mouth.

Dimples came out from under the covers.

"I know what you're thinkin', but please don't try it 'cause you will not make it. Jimmy, all I want is the money and drugs, and you can live with your Tammy forever in peace. Just give me what I ask for."

"I don't have shit here."

"Lie to me again and I'll show you that I mean business, nigga."

"How the fuck you gonna tell me I'm lyin'?"

"Cause your bitch told me already, so I'm gonna ask one mere time, where's the money and drugs at?"

He looked at Tammy and shook his head. She hadn't told me shit.

"It's not here."

"Oh, really? Since you wanna play games, let me show you that I am not in the mood for games."

Black's gun was pointed at him now. I walked over to where Black was holding Tammy and shot that bitch in the head twice. She fell from Black's hands like hot fries.

Brains, blood, and pieces of her skull flew every fucking where. Dimples had her hands over her mouth, Black was stuck, and Jimmy was on his knees, begging Tammy not to leave him. But she was already gone. It was too late for all that.

"If you would've listened to me, she would still be here. Now that you know that I ain't playin', tell me where the money and drugs are at? Or you gonna meet her on the other side."

He let go of her body.

"Under my dog house outside."

"What the fuck we waitin' for then? Let's go."

Thank God the nigga had a fence around his house. Black and Dimples better be inside searching that motherfucker down. "Rocky. Rocky," he called his dog.

That big motherfucking dog didn't even bark, he just wagged his tail. I knew one thing about dogs, they didn't like anyone but their owner.

Rocky was a big ass red and black pit bull, chained to a snub into the ground. What the fuck was he feeding that dog?

"Get that shit 'cause I don't have all day, nigga."

This nigga better not try to run and jump this fence 'cause these bullets gonna catch him and his dog both, I thought.

He moved the dog house to the left, and pulled up two big ass suitcases from under that shit.

"There you go," he said.

"Nigga, if you don't carry that shit in the house, you and Rocky both gonna see Tammy."

He grabbed the suitcases and carried them into the den as I followed.

"Open the motherfucker. You act like my life in danger and not yours, nigga."

When he opened them both up, all I could do was plan my dream for tomorrow. I didn't know how long it took him to make all that, but I knew it wasn't gonna take me long to claim it.

Six seconds, that was how long.

I shot his ass six times, closed both of the suitcases, and left him where he lay. Black saw me smoke him so I knew Dimples was only two seconds off her ass.

"Y'all ready?" I asked them as they looked at the dead body.

Neither one of them spoke.

"Y'all follow me. It's time to go."

I can't be nothing other than what I am, I am one cold hearted bitch on a mission.

Back at the spot, I opened up the suitcases and smiled. Thank God I had invested in a money counting machine because I don't know how long it would've taken me to count a million dollars.

I split the shit into four shares.

"Keep ya'll phones on. The next job ain't far," I told them.

Our relationship sure had changed, just wasn't the same. I could feel it in the air when we were together. They must have sensed that I was feeling a bad vibe because Black called the cab service, and five minutes later, they were gone.

As always, I called Ced. "Dinner's ready, baby."

"A'ight, boo. I'll be home in a minute."

A minute is sixty seconds, and sixty seconds later, he was standing in front of me.

"Damn, yo. Nigga's really eating in this small ass town," he said with surprise in his voice.

"I'm glad they eating 'cause that means we're eating too."

I gave him his share and told him, "I need some work, it doesn't matter how much. That nigga Jimmy had had fifty bricks, so give me twenty- five."

"That's all you want?" he asked.

"Yeah, 'cause that's all that nigga T getting."

"Yo, you are a real ass bitch. Don't ever forget that."

"Don't worry, I won't."

I texted T and told him to meet me at the Family Dollar in twenty minutes. Ced's worker, Snow, got the money and work and left right before we did. Ced drove, and on the way we saw like twenty police cars flying towards downtown. I told T to drive   Park Lane Street instead.

His car pulled up, and I saw that Joey was driving. That meant Beauty was with shawty. I could dig that. T got out and came to the passenger side of my Impala, thinking that I was alone. I let the window down and gave him the bag.

"Call me, nigga," I said to him as he was looking at Ced. Mane, that look he was giving Ced, I knew right then that I had to check that nigga myself or there were gonna be problems.

T called me in less than thirty minutes, just as we walked through the door of Ced's little apartment.

"Damn, you must still love me?"

"Naw, nigga. Don't get it fucked up, I eat, you eat, so get that shit straight. I don't disrespect ol' girl, so don't cross that line on my end."

"I'm listening, Sweets."

"Traymon, you can listen, but I want you to understand me. I am not playing."

"I understand." He sounded mad, but I was glad he checked his temper, because sperm donor or not, he could get it too.

"Good. Enjoy ya gift, kiss my princess for me when you touch the door, and be careful, nigga."

"I got you, baby-ma and nice look."

Ced didn't waste any time. He undressed me right then and there in the living room. We fucked like friends, no feelings at all. Ain't nothing better than some good hard core fucking.

***

Lynchburg was on lockdown and people were scared to even open the door to get the mail. The city was on fire and probably hotter than hell. Satan didn't have shit on me. I was stunting on that nigga, and only God could intervene. But there was a developing situation. Niggas had made my heart cold, but my bitches were making it colder. So on the next mission, I decided to leave them out of it. I had to do it by myself. Ced was worried, and he wanted to come with me, but I couldn't let him do that.

Chapter 28
Number 3

Big Trill wasn't an average size nigga. They called him big for a reason. At 5'9" and three hundred pounds, no one could call that nigga little. I knew I had to catch him nigga slipping, and eventually, I did. I caught him coming back from his baby's mother's house, but not that same bitch that he and Sham both had a kid by. This was a different female. That dirty dick motherfucker.

The piece of shit had left the doors of his truck unlocked. That was good. Sometimes other people's stupidity came in handy.

I opened the back door, and climbed in. I searched the truck, looking for anything and everything that might interest me. But all I really found was a .38 under the driver's seat. Okay. I had that nigga. I kicked back in the back seat for around two hours, just waiting on him to come back. The element of surprise was priceless, especially when a dumb motherfucker thought he was safe.

When he finally got in the truck and started driving, I spoke up.

"You know, I can't stand a dirty dick nigga. I can't stand a nigga that lies and cheats. A nigga like that don't deserve to breathe," I said as I put my baby to his head.

He swerved the truck but managed to keep it under control.

"And how you figure that out?"

"Well, for one, you have a main bitch, but you choose to keep fuckin' each and every baby-ma of yours. Ain't you scared of gettin' an STD or AIDS?"

"Huh?"

"Nigga, I know you don't think that you the only nigga they fuckin'."

Silence. I could see the thought had never crossed his mind.

"Cat got your tongue?" I asked.

"What the fuck you want?"

"Talk to me without respect, and watch this mother-fuckin' .45 knock the waves out your fuckin' head."

"I got you."

He better believe me. "Good, now that we have that clear, let's handle business."

"What business is that?"

I hate it when people ain't on the same page as me. "Nigga, don't act slow, or try to lose your memory all of a sudden, 'cause that shit ain't gonna work with me. I hate repeatin' myself, so listen closely if you wanna live. Understand?"

No reaction. I took that to mean that he was listening. Not that he had a choice or anything.

"Where's the money at?" I asked.

"My nigga got killed the other day. He had everythin'."

"Nigga, if you think I'm gonna believe you, then you're stupid. You and I both know that you've got somethin' put up somewhere for a rainy day."

"I mean..."

I cut him off, fuck what he had to say. "You lie to me, and you'll see who else is in hell when you get there."

I was not a woman to be played with. Games were for kids. If I wanted to play a game, I knew Beauty would've been happy to play with me. But I was not with her. I was sitting there with ol' dirty dick. There were no games in me for that nigga.

He drove to Beford Avenue. I could smell fear coming off of him. He turned right onto Boston Avenue, where he parked on the left hand side in front of the very first house, 1927.

"Let me tell you somethin'. You listenin'?" I asked.

"Yea."

Nigga better be.

"Your baby-mas don't know, about this spot. I know this is where you keep everythin'. None of your niggas know about this place either, except Sham, and since he's gone, that leaves you and me. So let's handle business. This is how this is gonna work. I'm gonna climb over this seat, and when I get out, you're gonna climb over here and exit through this door. Act stupid or froggy, and I swear on Sham that you will be left right here."

That nigga must've been a bitch. He didn't try to attack me or nothing, but maybe he was just smart. He kept a little of his dignity by keeping his mouth shut, not that it mattered. If I wanted it I would've taken that too.

We entered his house together, like I was a wanted guest. When we got into the house, the first thing I noticed was that it was clean, like a bitch was living there.

"I don't have all night, so let's get going. Give me what I ask for, and I'll leave."

All of a sudden it seemed like this nigga had lost his mind because he started talking cash money shit.

"Bitch, I ain't giving you shit. Go fuck yourself."

"Oh, yeah? I like that."

He pulled the .38 from his pocket and pointed it at me. He must've grabbed it on his way out of the truck. I just kept my glock on his ass.

"Now you looking like a real bitch 'posed to look," he said with a dumb fucking smile on his face.

"Nigga, I'm looking like this 'cause you got caught slippin' hard."

He pulled the hammer, but a good weapon wasn't shit without ammo. When he realized it was empty, he rushed at me, and that is a big ass nigga, but he ain't big enough to run through these bullets. I lit his ass up like the Fourth of July.

I texted Ced and told him to be at the end of the block. He texted back one word, "Done."

I searched the whole crib, and find *nothing*. I was so mad. All this for nothing? I kicked this big dead motherfucker as hard as I could, expecting his ass to be like Jello, but it was not.

He felt firm against my foot, and it almost sounded like I was kicking a wall.

"What the fuck?" I said out loud. I kicked him again, knowing that this motherfucker didn't have muscle like that. I pulled his shirt up and saw stacks strapped to his belly. That nigga was wrapped up like a mummy and I couldn't stop laughing about it.

"Ced, you ain't gonna believe what I'm about to tell you, but it's the God's honest truth."

"Tell me."

"Trill had the money strapped to his big ass with plastic wrap all around his chest and waist. I couldn't believe the shit my damn self. I rolled his ass over and cut the plastic off."

Ced was laughing at me telling him the story.

"Funny, right?"

He nodded his head and continued to laugh.

We went to his apartment and counted the bread up. Some of the bills had holes in them, looking like New York pot holes. Altogether, the nigga had fifty stacks on him. We split that shit down the middle. He tried to push forty on me, but I told him no.

"Why don't we just put the whole fifty towards our future?" He suggested after I refused the extra money.

"Meanin' until death do us part?"

"Yeah. Actually, that sounds better than what I was gonna say."

"So what are you saying, Ced?"

"I want you to be my wife, Sweets. You're perfect for me. You make me happy. You go harder than any nigga I've ever known. My kids already dig you, and I can't live without you, my Black Diamond."

"Is that really how you feel, Mr. Williams?"

"Yes, Mrs. Williams, that is exactly how I feel. I'm in love with you. From the very first night, I knew I had to have you."

"I hear you loud and clear."

And just like that, a smile jumped on my face.

He fucked me doggy style on top of the money, which was something I'd never done before, and wouldn't soon forget. Then he made love to me from the front.

"You gonna be my wife?"

He was looking dead into my eyes. I could feel his love, and I'd heard those words before, but when I felt him enter me again, I knew my answer.

"Yes, I'll be your wife, Ced."

Tears dripped from his eyes and onto my face when I spoke my answer to him. His emotion moved me.

"Yes, I'll be your wife forever."

The first thing we did as a man and woman engaged was cum together.

Jamaica

Chapter 29
Number 2

Lip was sexy. He had to be one of the sexiest men alive, I swear. He looked like an angel from heaven, but that was too bad because that nigga was headed to hell, and I was the one sending him.

The nigga was a cornball, a straight up pussy, and sexy or not, his mama should've swallowed the batch that made him. Nigga was so terrified he couldn't stop shaking. Even his damn lips were shaking. No wonder they called him Lip. He was a yellow bone nigga with hazel eyes. He was about 5'7", 165 pounds. I mean a real pretty, sexy nigga. He had Ced beat. I hated to say it, but it was true.

I caught that pretty boy nigga sitting in the trap on 5th. He was waiting on the fiends to come through, but the only person who was coming through right then was me. I knocked on the door and waited. I knew where he was at because I'd been following him for the past five hours.

"Who dat?" he yelled when he came to the door.

"It's Cupcake. I need a twenty rock." I was hoping he just opened the door.

"Cupcake?"

"Yea, Cupcake. Lala sent me up here." Lala was the pipe head I'd met a few minutes before.

"Oh, okay."

I heard him throw the dead bolt back and I got ready to move. As he cracked the door, I rushed his ass. That nigga wasn't even strapped. He didn't even try to push back on the door.

"Rule #1, always stay strapped." My baby was all in his space.

"Who is you?" he asked me.

"Fuck questioning me, nigga. This is my house now. I ask all the questions, and you answer."

"A'ight, ma," he said, shaking like a leaf.

"Where the bread at?"

"Shawty, I don't have none."

"You don't have none? So how the fuck you hustling?"

"I'm just making a little something, nothing major."

He started running off at the mouth, just telling everything, his connect, and this, and that, blah, blah, blah. Niggas and bitches kill me. Just because they were getting a little money, they wanted to act and put on like they had it. Where they do that at? He was just a flunky trying to pretend that he was balling. Altogether, that nigga didn't have but five fucking thousand dollars to his damn name. After I collected the money, I gave him something in exchange for his cooperation. I gave him four shots to the head. I was giving head shots all day.

A nigga or a bitch who couldn't hold water in their mouth when they were under pressure didn't need to live. It was sad but true because they were the same ones screaming "Death Before Dishonor", or "Snitching Ain't In My Blood." That was why I said move your lips, get your soul transported.

Chapter 30
Number 1

This last lick had to be done proper because the shit that I heard was that this nigga played no games. Since I was going for him, I was going correct. I didn't start doing this shit yesterday, and I felt like I was born with this gift, so that meant that I was *ready*.

This nigga lived out in Boons Borough, I mean all the way out in the cut, on some hide and seek shit. How the fuck did Ced know where this nigga lived? When you in the game, you ain't never safe.

This money paid drug dealer niggas had it going on. His place looked like a single spot of civilization out in the middle of nowhere. There were two Suburban's, two old school Chevy's, an all-black 745, and an all-white Maybach. This nigga wasn't just balling. This nigga was the plug himself.

I parked about a mile away from his place. I had a surprise for the King of this castle, and I couldn't wait to show him either.

The only light in the house looked like it was coming from a TV somewhere upstairs. I walked around the whole house looking for an open window or a door, but my luck wasn't hitting on shit and everything was locked. Good thing I was always prepared. I pulled out my glass cutter and cut a whole fucking window out. I held my breath as I did so, knowing I couldn't afford any sound. I leaned the glass against the side of the house, and entered into what looked like a playroom. There was a pool table, a stripper pole, a dice area, I mean this nigga had every fucking thing.

I kept my P89 in front of me at all times. I searched the entire ground floor and found nothing. Next step, second floor. I made my way up the stairs, and halfway up, I saw a woman's shadow. The bitch looked like she had some curves. I backed up against the wall, and breathed through my mouth. Whoever she was, she was in the wrong place at the wrong time. But that was how life went. You won some and you lost some. But fuck that, I had a daughter I had to get back to, and a nigga who claimed to love me. A nigga I believed. I couldn't afford to lose.

I could hear three different voices, but the TV was on so loud that it was hard to tell. It could have been more. Fuck it.

"I was born for this," I told myself under my breath. The bedroom door was open, and I could hear more clearly as I crept closer.

"So you sayin' you never had a threesome before?" A woman asked.

"Naw, never. I swear," the nigga said, his voice deep. That had to be Rell, unless there was another nigga in there.

"You tellin' me that tonight was your first time ever?"

That was a different female's voice. So far the future body count's at three.

"Yeah, I ain't lyin' to y'all."

"How long you think we can last for?" the first female voice asked.

"Shit, if we keep rollin', we can last till next week," he answered with a laugh.

"I got us some water," the female said.

"I'm poppin' four this time." This nigga must really not be trying to last till next week.

"Well, we gonna take two a piece then," one of the females answered.

I peeked into the cracked door just in time to watch three silhouettes pop their pills. All three of them were in the bed together.

Damn.

They were slipping hard. This was why I was drug fucking free. I pulled my flashlight from my Dickies pants and exhaled slowly. It was time.

Ready. Set. Go.

I had my flashlight hand stacked on top of my P89. Niggas and bitches didn't know nothing about tactics these days. The first thing I did was shoot the light out of the TV. The bitches started screaming under the covers. Rell tried to make a run for it, but he didn't know who he was fucking with. Running from me was like trying to run from your mama when she was trying to whip your ass.

It was only gonna piss me off, and I was not using my hand, a shoe, or a switch.

Pow.

"And if you so much as breathe, your ass will not remember it. Y'all bitches shut the fuck up." I used my flashlight to find the light switch that was right by me, thank God. I turned it on. Rell was holding one leg, and blood was everywhere. I knew I'd hit a vessel for sure.

"Ya'll bitches come out from under the covers, 'cause only Jesus himself can save you now, and I ain't seen him lately."

My eyes had be playing tricks on me.

"What the fuck?" I shook my head, hoping my eyes were wrong. Dimples and Black. Let me handle the nigga first.

"Nigga, get your ass up and get between them bitches on the bed."

"Bitch, you got me fucked up."

He didn't know that I was Satan himself.

"She ain't playin', yo. Just come over here," Black told him.

It was nice to hear her doing something other than questioning my gangsta for a change.

"You better listen to her 'cause I know for a fact *you* got *me* fucked up, all the way up, nigga."

Them bitches wasn't even strapped. And how the fuck they know that nigga?

I watched him drag himself to the bed, and I follow him with my P89.

"Ya'll bitches better start thinkin' about the explanation y'all 'bout to give me, 'cause I want to know what's goin' on."

They were just looking at me.

"Where the money at, Rell? You know, money over everything is my motto."

Those bitches were in there naked. They had be fucking each other, for real. One of the Suburbans out front must have belonged to Dimples.

My mind was racing as I watched Black help Rell into the bed. I heard Dimples praying.

"You think I'm gonna hustle my ass off for you to come in here and demand my shit after I done survived the game this long?"

"You can't knock a bitch for trying, can you?"

"I mean, to each their own, but if you want it, you're damn sure gonna have to kill me before I give it up."

He wass brave.

"How sure are you about that?" I asked him.

"A hundred and fifty percent sure, shawty. You think 'cause you shot me already I should just get to talkin'?"

He didn't even seem to be in pain.

"I mean, you are a grown ass man. This is your shit, so do and say as you please, but remember I am the one in charge.

Dimples was crying, but Black was just holding her head. They already knew I was not the one to be played with. I was giving that nigga six seconds to tell me what I wanted to hear. I started counting him down.

"One. Two. Three. Fuck you, nigga. Six."

And just like that, I stopped his heart. What they say is true, real gangstas don't live to see thirty because they're either dead or doing life. Dimples was crying so hard she was shaking. It was starting to get on my nerves. Brain matter and blood was all over the place, even on Black.

"Why the fuck you had to kill him?" Black asked. She seemed calm, cool, and collected, but Dimples was crying even harder now.

"Why the fuck you had to steal from the team like that? Y'all took an extra cut of everything but the guns. Y'all think I'm stupid? And while we're on 'why the fucks,' why the fuck y'all on drugs? And when the hell y'all start fuckin'? Ya'll gay now?" I was yelling at them and I couldn't help it. Good thing we were out in the cut.

"Ever since you got with that nigga, Ced, you been brand new," Black said with disgust.

"How you figure?" I was lost now. I had been good to those bitches.

"You don't have time for us anymore."

"I have time for y'all. We getting money and living good. All them licks we did, Ced put me on. And guess what? I put y'all on. But look at y'all. I put y'all on everything. I taught y'all how to do this shit. All I ever showed y'all was love and loyalty, but look at what y'all showing me."

"Sweets, I hated you from the moment I opened my eyes. I wanted to kill you then, but Dimples talked me out of it."

"What?" I was shocked, hurt, and confused for a split second before the coldness began to sink back in to my heart where it seemed to belong.

"I knew about you before you even knew me. I knew your life from start till now. When you helped me in Hardee's that day, it was all planned out. Dimples been gay. This ain't nothin' new. She didn't know how to bring me around you, so we came up with a story and a plan."

She was still talking, but I was done listening.

Fuck what she was saying. One to the head would keep her speechless forever.

Pow.

The left side of her face opened up. Blood flew all over the place. Her eyes were still open. I wondered if she heard the bark of my P89 before her body hit the floor. I'd be sure to ask her when I saw her in hell, but that was gonna be a long time from now. I pulled my bottom lip between my teeth and shook my head at that disgusting ass bitch.

Dimples brought her knees up to her chest, as if to hold her heart in. Her eyes were big as golf balls, and her mouth was wide open. She must have been in shock because her whole body was shaking like a leaf.

"What did I do to you, Dimples?"

Silence.

"Bitch, you better say somethin'."

Silence.

I took a deep breath.

Silence.

Finger on the trigger.

"I know you hate me, and you have good reasons to, but please, know that I'm truly sorry."

I was so mad. I was ready to let my P89 speak again but I asked her again, "What did I do to you, Dimples?"

"Nothin'. It's what happened, to me."

"What happened?"

"I've been hurt by the ones who were supposed to love and protect me. My parents ain't even my parents, Sweets. I know you think that you know them, but you don't. Not really. I hate the ground they walk on. My so-called father, the pastor, he's…" her words trailed off for a second as a brief flash of pain crossed her face before she continued.

"They adopted me when I was six, and used me to get to where they're at now. Every deacon you see on the list at church has had their way with me, and not only them, but my fake ass parents too. They would offer me to people of high standing, people of influence, people with money and power who were willing to help them get the things that they wanted. Anytime somebody wanted me, they had me. I hate men, I hate them." She practically spit the words when she said them.

That was some heavy shit. What the fuck was going on here?

"They buy me everything to cover their dirt up, Sweets. They even wanted me and you to sleep together so they could watch, but I think they were really setting it up so they could ask to join."

"Naw, Dimples. You lying to me."

"I swear, I put it on Beauty's life."

Silence.

She was still shaking. She knew Beauty was my world, so she used that to let me know she was telling me the truth.

This shit was crazy.

"I met Black years ago. Her boyfriend tried to kill her when he found out that she was gay, but I helped her out. She was the only person that I was ever with who didn't use me or abuse me. Her love for me was real love, but she hated how close me and you got. She was so jealous of you that we came up with the Hardee's situation to have her closer to me, and it worked, but I never meant for things to happen this way."

A part of me felt sorry for Dimples. We'd been friends for years, and she was as close to a sister as I'd ever had. Cold hearted or not, I couldn't kill her. I decided not to pull the trigger. Instead, I left her in the bed until I found what I came for to begin with. The place was huge, and it took me almost an hour to find it. But when I did, I could hardly believe my eyes. Jackpot. I got on the phone immediately because I knew I was gonna need help. I told Ced to get up here. There was no way I'd be able to load up all that shit by myself. I headed back up the stairs to check on Dimples, but to my surprise, she was gone, and what was left of the woman formerly known as Black was gone, too.

Now she would only be known as that dead bitch I used to know.

I ran down the stairs two at a time, following the line of blood. I made it out the door just in time to see her struggling to get that dead bitch into the truck.

"Bitch, I tried to give you a break, but I see you don't want one." I was starting to think they made a pretty good couple, Dumb Bitch and Dead Bitch, but if she was gonna test me, Dumb Bitch would be Dead Bitch, too.

She dropped Black, and when she hit the ground, I noticed that she was still breathing. Dead Bitch wasn't dead after all. That was okay, I could fix that. I put two more in her. Nobody could live with that much lead in their head. Dimples covered her eyes but didn't scream. Good! I was sick of hearing that kind of shit.

Now I was thinking that, that bitch only told me her story so I wouldn't shoot her and maybe shoot Black again. She must have seen that Black was still breathing, so she used that sad ass story to distract me. It worked, but not for long.

I smacked her ass in the face with the gun, and blood poured from her nose. She grabbed her face, but no sounds escaped from her body. Nothing!

"Carry your ass on. You get in that truck, and carry yourself somewhere far from here, Dimples. Move away, and don't ever come back, 'cause the end results won't be pretty."

Tears flooded her face, but she heeded my words. She got in her truck and drove away. A few minutes later, Ced pulled up.

"Who the fuck is that?" he asked, tilting his head towards the body on the ground.

"A bitch that was in my way."

Something in my voice must have given me away because Ced pulled me to him.

"It's gonna be alright. Real gangsta bitches like yourself don't cry."

We got to work, loading everything up, and then we left.

I had left one of my best friends back there. Dimples was gone forever, and there wasn't any coming back. But that fake ass bitch deserved it. Fuck it. That was just one less fake bitch to worry about.

I couldn't drive, so Ced took the driver's seat and drove to Snow's house, where we counted the money and drugs. In the end, we'd gotten two million cash, a thousand pounds of hydro, and five hundred bricks of pure white cocaine, just like my name.

***

"I need to get out of these clothes," I told Ced. I was exhausted.

"A'ight, let's go to my crib. Snow, handle this shit and I'll holla at you later."

The ride to his place was silent, and I faced the window to hide my tears. I couldn't believe how the night had turned out. Both my bitches were gone. One was dead, and the other was gone with the wind.

I couldn't stop asking myself what the fuck was really wrong with me. I always lost everyone to *disloyalty*.

As soon as we got into Ced's crib, I headed to the bathroom, removing my clothes as I went. I got in the shower and scrubbed myself from head to toe. It didn't matter if my eyes were open or closed, all I could see was Dimples' face streaked with tears. I heard every word she said again and again, echoing in my head. But it seemed like I didn't hear the right words. How could this be real?

I knew Black was in hell already, probably waiting on me so we could go ham on each other. But for right now, I was holding the realest bitch down, *my damn self.*

All of a sudden, I felt Ced's hands on my hips. I knew he had to be thinking some crazy shit. I turned around so I could read his eyes, and when I looked into them, they just looked cold and calculating. "Do you regret anythin' you ever did?" He asked.

"No. I don't regret shit. Everythin' that happened was meant to happen so that life can go on," I answered.

"I have been through so much, I have seen a lot, and I've heard it all before, but I swear on my mother I ain't never met a woman like you before."

"And you wanna know why?"

He nodded his head *yes.*

"'Cause I am one of a fucking kind, baby. Not too many bitches can say they've done or seen the shit that I have done and seen. Don't get me wrong though, I know I can be touched. I'm not invincible. But for right now, I am just living and doing all the touching.''

"You are the realest bitch ever."

I was glad he knew that.

"Real recognize real, as always, 'cause I know you are the realest nigga ever."

Ced used his mouth to wash me all over again, and then he made me cum with that beautiful dick of his. But I was so tired, I didn't even let him get his in. He didn't trip either. Nigga better not. Shit. I needed that to the fullest.

Jamaica

Chapter 31
For Real

I heard the front door coming off the hinges. "FBI. Lynchburg Ploice Department. Don't move."

I tried to move anyway, but the police were already holding me down. They had Ced down on the floor.

"Ms. Corona Cocaine Cash aka Sweets, you are under arrest for seven murders," the man who was holding me down said to me.

"I ain't kill nobody, motherfucker."

"Not only did you kill them, but you took their drugs and money also."

"Fuck you, you dumb motherfucker."

Deny, deny, deny. That was the only way to deal with this, and I knew it. All of a sudden I realized that Ced was down there talking, and his words were making sense to me. He was telling them how I killed everyone.

"That motherfucker's lyin'."

I screamed as I struggled against the hands that held me down.

"You lyin' piece of shit!"

"Ms. Cash, don't plead your case to me, plead it to the judge."

"Suck my pussy when I'm red from the back, you cracker motherfucker."

***

"Baby. Baby, wake up. You havin' a bad dream."

Ced was shaking me awake.

"You're talkin' in your sleep and everythin'."

"That was a dream straight from the pits of hell."

I got up from the bed, grabbed his shirt, and pulled it over my head as I walked to the kitchen to get something to drink. I knew he was on my ass, I could feel his presence. That nigga told on me in my dream.

I took two shots of Ciroc back to back. Damn!

"I gotta make sure my daughter's okay."

"So call and find out."

My cell phone was plugged into a charger on the kitchen counter. I picked it up and pressed two. Speed dial. Ced sure was sexy early in the morning. I licked my lips.

"Sweets, its five in the morning and you calling me?"

Traymon sounded sleepy and irritated. I had the phone on speaker, and I was looking Ced dead in his eyes.

"Yea, I know what time it is. Y'all good?"

"Yeah, we good. You callin' 'cause you want me to come put you to sleep?"

Ced's eyes got bloodshot red in an instant. I was tired of putting Traymon in his place. He just wouldn't give up. So I reminded his ass.

"I have a man to do that already, so stop disrespecting him."

T hung up on me.

Ced smiled, and then he picked me up. He carried me to the sofa in the living room, and sat himself without letting me go. I was comfortable in his lap, wrapped in his arms.

"Whenever you wanna talk, Sweets, I am all ears."

He could see it all over me. I was hurting from all the lack of trust from people. We sat in silence for a few minutes before I finally said something.

"I don't think I can ever love you like you say you love me."

"Why, be…"

I cut him off. "I've been hurt by so many, it's crazy. It's hard for me to trust anyone. When love comes to me, I try to push it away, or run away from it, 'cause it always ends up no good for me. You've seen my good side and my bad. You know my secrets. They say fear God, love no nigga, and trust no bitch. But for me, I fear God, I trust no bitch, but I love and trust you, and I put that on everything. You are the man of my dreams, and I'm sorry that it took me so long to find you."

His lips touched mine, and I closed my eyes.

We made love like tomorrow was never going to show up. We fucked each other from the living room to the bedroom. And when the sun came up, we still weren't finished.

Finally, we ended up falling asleep. When I woke up, it was 1:00pm. Ced was nowhere in sight, but there was a note on the dresser with some green and yellow flowers in a crystal vase.

I searched everywhere to find you, but I wasn't searching hard enough. Then, just like magic, you pop up, and look where you at now. I love you, Sweets.

Ced

My baby daddy used to cheat, beat on me, and dog me out back then, but now look at me. I had a real, live, trill ass nigga who was down for me no matter what. How could I go wrong?

The phone interrupted my thoughts. It was Jay. Shit.

I pressed 0.

"Hello?"

"You got some nerve to say hello, bitch, when you left me high and dry," he screamed.

"Naw, nigga, you mean low and dry. You played me like a sucka, a real sucka. I feel like you gave me a stupid ass pill, and I took it."

"It wasn't even like that." His voice was low now, so I let him continue to beg. "You came up here and started thinkin' crazy. You ain't even let me explain it to you."

Begging season was over, and what the fuck was there to explain? "Jay, do us both a favor and delete this number. I am no longer yours. Change the address on your release papers, 'cause you will not be there. Don't waste your stamps, pen ink, pencil lead, paper, or envelopes on me, 'cause it will be returned to you, and when you get home, please don't start no shit, 'cause I will not even spare your momma."

"Bitch, fuck you."

"You better be careful, 'cause I might get you fucked for real."

I hung the phone up on that note. That dumb ass nigga tried calling back to back, but I ignored his ass.

Fuck that nigga.

***

When Ced got back, he asked me to move into his house with him.

"Is that what you really want?"

"Sweets, I know what I am askin' you. Just give me an answer."

"Yes."

"Well, we got a lot to do then, so let's get goin'." That man was a blessing and amazing.

***

We rented a U-Haul truck, and packed up my house. When it was time to go, I headed to the back yard to dig up my flower garden.

"Baby, what are you doin'?" Ced asked, coming up behind me while my hands were still in the dirt.

"Pay attention," I said without stopping.

I dug all the flowers up, and a few inches beneath them until I saw a wooden box. It was heavy, so he helped me lift it out of the ground and take it to the truck. He never asked what was in it, and we never said a word to each other about it. I looked back at my house as we drove away, and a tear fell from my right eye, but a smile came across my face. One chapter ended as another began. I turned the music up just in time to hear Jeezy's new hit, *I Do's*. Ced and I smiled at each other as we listened to the words.

Remember the night we first met,
I caught a contact, now she my ride or die.
It's us against the world,
You know we both hustlin', so hustlin' is our word...

When we finally arrived at my new home, we unloaded the truck, and unpacked everything in Ced's mansion. I even put Beauty's room together, and I knew that she was gonna love it. After we finished, Ced pulled me into his arms.

"Let's relax and take the truck back tomorrow," he said.

I nodded my head okay.

"Do you really think you can let me live with you after everythin' you've seen?"

I searched his eyes with mines. Nothing!

"Yes. If you seen half the shit that I've done, you might not want to be here either. What can I say? We both have the same hustle, just on different levels, and we not here to judge each other. We're here to love each other through the good and the bad, right?"

"You right, Ced."

I smiled because his words came from the heart. I could see and feel it, and it gave me goose bumps. Why was this man single? I pulled myself away from him.

"Ced, let me show you somethin'."

I opened the wooden box and smiled up at him. Ced's eyes didn't budge from the box when he spoke to me.

"How long you been doing this?"

He was shocked. I could tell. His words were low but powerful. I smiled before I answered because I knew he'd never had a female like me before.

"For a hot minute. I only spend what I have to 'cause when I leave this life, I want my daughter to be stable more that anythin' in the world. She's the only reason why I do this shit like this. I kill because I don't want to have to watch my back everywhere I go. If they're dead, they can only haunt me in my dreams."

He was just looking at me. I had a wooden box worth five million. Three from all the random jobs I'd pulled over time, and the two we got from Rell. Shit was looking damn good. I changed the subject. "I'm ready for a vacation."

He looked at me and showed me that fucking smile I have come to love so much.

"How 'bout we and the crew take a trip?" he suggested.

"Yeah? To where?"

"New York City."

Just what I was thinking. "Cool. I was thinkin' the same thing 'cause I have some unfinished business to handle."

He pulled me into his arms and shook his head, knowing I didn't ever give up.

"On a vacation you're supposed to be relaxin', not workin', Sweets. That's why it's called a vacation, you're supposed to rest and have fun."

"I will, as soon as I finish what they started wit me."

"Huh?"

I knew he is lost. In due time, he would find out. "I'll relax, baby."

"You better, 'cause this is our world, baby girl."

I knew it was. "So when we leaving?" I asked him.

"How 'bout tomorrow?"

"What? Ced, you had this planned already?"

I was shocked by his response.

"Naw, I just got it like that, and money talks, so everyone except you gotta move when I speak. Boss niggas do *boss* things, so enjoy life, baby. I'm gonna show you nothing but the best."

"You are something else, boy, I swear."

"Trappa, Snow, and Clap coming with us. They'll probably have their ladies."

"So?"

"I'm just letting you know. I don't leave town without them."

As long as they weren't in my way, I was good. I had a lot on my agenda, even if no one knew it yet.

"Where am I gonna put this money at?" I asked him, changing the subject again and leaving his embrace.

"You have a whole house and ten acres of land at your disposal. Pick a spot and do you."

"Where's your safe at?"

"Sweets, is that a safe question to answer?"

A question with a question. "Well, you have a choice. You can tell me, or I can find it myself. Pick one."

He shook his head. I was one of a kind for real.

"Since you have such a smart mouth, I'll just show you."

He better had.

"Come on, Sweets."

I followed him to his secret stash spot while taking his body view in. Damn he was fucking sexy! My pussy was wet just thinking dirty. Let's just say little box didn't have shit on his money. His money could count itself. I was dead ass serious. This nigga was *paid.*

"I'm not gonna ask how much is there."

"Good. When you become Mrs. Corona Williams, it's all yours. Until then, no more questions."

That was all I needed to do? "I'm gonna put mines in there with yours."

He didn't even hesitate. "Fine with me," he said.

'Cause when I come to take it, I am taking all of it. This devil on my shoulder is a greedy little motherfucker, I thought to myself.

"How did you come up with an idea like this to hide your money?"

"No questions."

He walked away and left me standing there, still looking at all that money. There had to be at least twenty million in there.

Damn. My pussy was soaking wet.

***

I called Traymon and told him he had to keep Beauty for a minute because I was stepping out of town. He didn't trip. He handled the situation better than I expected he would, and I was impressed. Wow. Maybe the nigga was really working on changing. For real though, I didn't give a fuck. He didn't change for me, and I wasn't gonna hold it over his head because Karma was gonna catch up to him in due time.

Until then, the life that I was living would only get better than his to me.

Chapter 32
New York

Instead of driving, we flew. There were eight of us since everybody brought their women. Trappa brought his girl, Lex. Snow brought his wife, Jade. Clap brought his down ass bitch, Jasmine. The plane was okay, not as bad as I thought it would be. And since it was my first time flying, Ced held me the entire ride. He was perfect. When we arrived in New York, a limo was waiting on us.

"Where are we stayin'?" I asked Ced.

"Bronx, baby."

''Bronx?" My voice lifted up.

"You seem worried, are you okay with that?"

I knew I sounded worried but I was *not*. I was actually happy because Brooklyn was not far from there.

"I'm fine with that."

"My peoples have a four bedroom house in the Bronx, on Eastchester Road. It has enough space for all of us. The shit is mad big."

"How much space we talkin' 'bout, baby?"

"Four bedrooms, four bathrooms, a big ass kitchen that can hold at least twelve people comfortably at one time. It's carpet all the way from the living room to the front of the house, then the porch is hard wood, you'll see. It's real open. Nothin' like the mansion we got though."

"Okay, sounds good."

Everyone was just enjoying the view and the city lights. New York City is beautiful to me, but I hated that state. I knew that I would come to love it again before I left.

***

Ced's Uncle Shevan was so glad to see him.

"Boy, luk pon yuh," (Boy, look at you) his uncle said with a heavy Jamaican accent, as a wide smile covered his face. Shevan looked just like a real damn Jamaican. He had dreads down past his ass, with a Jamaican flag printed wrap used to tie his hair back out of his face. He had a goatee that covered his chin, but no mustache to go with it. I knew they said that Jamaicans were black, but that motherfucker was so black he looked purple.

It was amazing. But I swear, when Ced started speaking, I came in my panties.

"Yuh know seh mi can't stay little fi eva." (You know I can't stay little forever.)

Next time we fuck he's gonna talk to me like that! Hell yeah! Damn it, that's sexy, I thought to myself while he talked to his uncle.

It seemed like a family reunion. I meet so many people that I couldn't even remember their names. We did a little running around and shopping. We were just enjoying New York in general. Each couple split up to do their own thing for a while. Jasmine tried to get friendly with me, but I let her know that I was not in need of any friends. She said she understood and gave me my space. Fuck letting another bitch into my life. All I needed was my child and my man.

"Ced, I need to take a trip into Brooklyn," I told him over dinner at a restaurant in the city.

"By yourself?"

"Yes, by myself."

"Do you need anythin'?"

"Yeah, a .45 and a silencer."

"Sweets, can you promise me that you'll come back?"

"I promise you I am coming back."

"Can I come with you?"

"No. I have to clean this up by myself, but don't worry. You are always with me 'cause I am carryin' you in my heart." He showed me that beautiful smile. "I'll take your word." "You better 'cause my word is my life."

It was 6am. I was dressed all in black, so you already know what kind of mission I was on. I'd done a little research on the man who had turned my life upside down before we left for New York. God bless the Internet.

That fool hadn't changed for nothing, except to get even uglier. I followed him from his job all the way to his house.

He lived in the back of an apartment complex on President Street.

It had taken me a long time to get around to this, but I'd always known the day was coming. When he parked, I pulled up right beside him and got out of my rental car to face the man who raped me when I was a little girl. I didn't even give him time to get out of his car, much less turn the engine off.

In my head, all I could see was me in my room that night when that ugly motherfucker took my pride. Now I felt no pain. Matter of fact, I was not even thinking. What was there to think about? The motherfucker didn't think about me back then, but I was glad to show him that he should have. He may not have changed, but I had. I was no longer defenseless. There were no words, just the sound of me emptying the .45 on his ass. I got back in the rental and drove away. I had one more stop to make.

It was 7:30 in the morning, and I was on a mission. My father, Richie, lived by himself. I guess he ran out of women to fuck. His address was 1038 Nostrand Avenue, which was an apartment on top of an old printing shop that appeared to be out of business. I needed a key to get in, but I was lucky because the side door was unlocked. I climbed the stairs as quietly as possible. But for real, I didn't give a fuck if he heard me or not, because he was about to meet his maker.

I rang the bell, and put my back to the door so that I faced the stairs.

"Who is it?" I heard his voice muffled by the door that separated us.

"Sir," I said loudly in response.

As he opened the door, I rushed my way in with my .45 aimed at his head.

"Corona," he exclaimed like he was surprised to see me.

Yeah, me too. "Oh what a surprise. You know my fuckin' name?"

"You are my child. Why wouldn't I know your name?"

"Shit, you tell me."

This was the same man who didn't do nothing for me when his bitch's son raped me.

"You have grown."

"Spare me the bullshit, Richie. You ain't my father. What the fuck did you do for me as a child besides providin' a roof over my head? The government could've done that."

I couldn't keep the tears from falling, and that pissed me off. My soul had a hole in it from the hurt, all the hate and pain that I suffered as a child.

"I hate you," I shouted at him.

"Everythin' about you makes me sick. I am so sick I can't even stand myself. But you know what? I have a child to live for, or else I would've killed myself thanks to you. My grand-mother should've pushed you out in the toilet."

"Corona, I know I was the worst father ever, but I've changed. I'm sorry for all the pain that you went through, but your mother should have aborted you."

My heart stopped in my chest for a second. *I know this motherfucker didn't just say that.*

"Fuck you," I screamed at him, unable to control myself. Those were the last words that he heard from my lips, or from anyone else's for that matter. Father or no father, I had shown that nigga that I was one bitch who deserved to live. Too bad he didn't.

Now when I visit New York, I'll love it to the fullest.

***

A whole week had flown by, just like that. I missed Beauty so much it hurt. I had to get back home to my princess.

Ced was holding a family meeting on our last night in New York. "I'm glad to have all of y'all here today. We started at the bottom, but now we stand at the top. We have one hell of a team. Untouchable," Ced announced.

Clap had finally gotten out of the hospital just in time for this vacation. He had a sideways stance, and you could tell that something bad had happened to him. He was one of Ced's best and most trusted workers, had been on the team since day one. He got shot four times, but he'd made it through. Now that he was standing, I wondered what he had to say.

"This year so far has been crazy, but I'm blessed to have my freedom, blessed to be alive, and I'm blessed to have a family like y'all who care, who would lay down their life for me. I don't know where we would be if it wasn't for the love that we have for each other."

Mane, this was some real deep shit. Ced kept his eyes on him, and so did everyone else. We could tell that he wasn't finished.

"Jasmine, I love you. Don't ever think different. You are the bullets to my glock, and for that I am very thankful."

Jasmine was crying.

"Ced, my nigga, even through the rain, we still standin'. I love you, no homo, same to the rest of y'all niggas."

At those last words, everyone burst into laughter. When the happy sounds died down, he finished what he had to say.

"Blood doesn't make us related, but *loyalty* makes us family."

Everyone cheered for the sentiment that he'd shared.

Their team was loving and trustful, but most of all loyal. Damn, I actually missed my bitches. Ced must be a mind reader because he leaned over and said, "We gonna have us some fun, so cheer up." He hit the music as he led the way, and we started dancing to some old school jams in the living room. Just like that, everyone else followed.

"You are the most beautiful woman ever, and I am super blessed to have such a diamond in my life. I really do love you."

"I love you too, Ced."

"Yo, Snow, hit the button to the system for a minute. I have somethin' else to say," Ced told Snow and walked away from me towards Clap.

"I hope everyone is enjoyin' themselves. I love and cherish each and every one of y'all, so I didn't want y'all to hear this from someone else. I'd rather y'all witness it for yourselves.

"Corona."

I was holding my breath. Was he really?

"You are the most beautiful woman I have ever seen. You are the definition of real. You go just as hard as a real nigga, and even harder. I don't ever have to worry about my back, 'cause I know you got me all the way. I never thought I would find someone like you, but God proved me wrong, since you're here now. I'd like to keep you in my life forever. So with that said, will you be my wife?"

He was standing right in front of me now, all the ladies were crying. I could hardly breathe, and I felt like I had to keep one hand over my heart to make sure that it didn't jump out of my chest.

"Yes, I would love to be your wife, Ced."

He got down on one knee and pulled a black box from his pocket.

"They say diamonds are a girl's best friend, right?"

After he slipped it on my finger, everyone went wild with applause, and I had a feeling it was as much because of how big my ring was as how happy they were for us.

"That's a seven carat marquis cut diamond set in white gold, baby."

Ced told me as I looked at it. My left ring finger had to cost at least two hundred stacks because it was sure shining. That was a night I'd never forget. We get twisted and head to the bedroom to tear it up.

Ced pushed me gently to the bed and slowly removed my clothing piece by piece. He kissed me from my mouth to my breasts, and trailed down my stomach, between my legs, and down to my toes.

My pussy was so wet and ready for him. I wanted him to touch me, at least breathe on it, shit, but he didn't. He just covered me with kisses, every part of me, back to front.

"Please, Ced, stop teasin' me."

"Yuh sure, yuh whan did?" (You sure you want this?)

Oh, hell yeah. That Jamaican talk.

"Whatever you say, I say yes. Please, Ced!"

"How it feels?" he asked me.

"Good, baby, but can you make it great?"

It felt as if he put his whole tongue inside my pussy. It felt so good. I couldn't take it. I tried to back up, but Ced wouldn't let me. He hooked his arms around my upper thighs and pulled me closer so he could eat my pussy and ass at the same time until I begged him to fuck me.

"Please. Baby, just fuck me."

"In every hole, Mrs. Williams?"

"I ain't never been fucked back there, but since I am about to be Mrs. Williams, Mr. Williams, do as you please."

He fucked my pussy so good from the back that it made me cry. He got me over the side of the bed, and hammered away. He nut right on my asshole. It was warm and it felt so good. Damn! I couldn't wait for him to fuck me in my ass now. His dick was hard and ready to go again in like a minute. He was a beast.

"Just relax and breathe. It's gonna hurt at first, but once it's in, it's gonna be great."

He ain't never lied. That shit hurt like a motherfucker. My ass expanded so far his whole dick fit inside of me. My pussy got so wet that it felt like I pissed myself. As he was fucking me in my ass, I was playing with my pussy. He grabbed my hair, and I threw my ass back. He fucked me so damn good I got to shaking.

"A fi mi, pum pum, des?" (Is this my pussy?)

"Yes, daddy."

"Yuh whan mi feh buss in deh?" (Do you want me to buss in it?)

"Yes."

When I heard his breathing speeding up, I knew he wasn't far behind. He fucked me harder. The strokes got longer, and we came together. I came so good I cried like a baby wanting a bottle.

On the way to the airport, Ced stopped at the store to get a bottle of water, but he came back with a newspaper, also. He read part of it before he passed it to me. I read where it was opened to.

32 year old, Damien Fuller was found in his car by a member of the community. He was killed by multiple gunshot wounds.

Richie Cash was found in his apartment by a friend. He was killed by a gunshot wound.

I loved the way things turned out. I knew Ced wass looking at me, so I looked back at him and winked.

"New York will be better next time, boo," I whispered in his ear. A smile was spread all over my face.

That little vacation had been amazing. I had gotten engaged and cleaned up my dirty laundry.

Jamaica

Chapter 33
Back N Da Burg

Life was hell in Lynchburg, Virginia. So much had been discovered while we were gone. Traymon filled me in immediately. He told me about how the police were looking for me. Black's body had been found, but Dimples was missing. In an effort remove myself from the light, the first people I called were Dimples' parents.

"Hello?"

"Can I speak with Mrs. Marshall, please?"

"Who is calling?" she asked.

I held my breath for about five seconds. "This is Sweets."

"I am not going to ask you how you are doing, 'cause you didn't even have the nerve to come and say goodbye to your so called sister."

Mane, that bitch was crazy, all the shit that she'd done to Dimples.

"I didn't even know anythin' until I came back last night. That's when I heard the news."

"Oh yeah?" she said, sounding like she had an attitude. That bitch really had some nerve.

"I am sorry that I didn't make it to the funeral, but I am much more worried about findin' Dimples."

"Funny how Black is dead, Dimples can't be found, and you just getting back in town."

"What you want me to say, Mrs. Marshall?"

She got quiet, I mean dead silent on the other end of the line.

"Mrs. Marshall, I apologize. Black can't come back, but I'll try my best to find out where Dimples is at."

"If you need to make a call, please hang up and try again. If you need help press zero," the operator told me.

I know that Chester the Molester ass bitch didn't hang up on me.

Pastor or no Pastor, that bitch wasn't invincible. I ran the whole thing down to Ced.

"Just relax, baby," he said in a soothing tone.

"Oh, I am relaxed. Don't question that."

"Call the police station and see if they have a warrant for your arrest. If they do, go down there and hear what they have to say. If they don't have anythin' for you, then good. Fuck the world."

I knew that nigga was going crazy.

"Go down there? Them motherfuckers gotta come get me they damn self."

"Look, baby, if you go to them, then they'll know you're innocent and have nothing to hide, but if you run from them, they'll hold you as suspect. You gotta think and act smart. Whatever you do, I got your back all the way."

"So I may as well call and see if they want me, right?"

Ced was right, why run.

"Yeah, and don't worry, you'll have the best lawyer ever."

"What the fuck you mean the best lawyer ever, Ced? You know somethin' I don't know?"

"Naw, but just in case."

"Just in case my ass. Listen to how that shit sounds. You want me to go to jail, Ced?" I screamed.

"Calm the fuck down, baby."

I was in his arms. I felt safe.

"You makin' yourself scared. You're gonna be alright, yo. And no, I don't want you to go to jail, Mrs. Williams."

I felt so sick to my stomach. I had to run to the bathroom to throw up. I felt so weak, so tired. Thank God Ced was with me because he helped me clean up, and then put me to bed. My nerves were all in pieces.

"First thing in the morning I'm gonna call those people and see what they want," I said to him as he pulled the blankets up over me.

"Okay."

I knew I'd covered all my tracks, so why was I worried? I call T and put him onto game.

"Damn, babyma, I got your back. Me and shawty gonna keep Beauty till this shit is clear, so you don't have to worry about her."

A whole flashback came over me. I thought about all those times my father left me and King to be watched by Carlenee and how she treated us. Wait until I find that bitch.

"Yeah, do that, and make sure shawty don't do shit to my daughter, cause on everything I love she will not be able to fix it."

"Come the fuck on, yo. Don't carry me, Beauty's mines too."

"A'ight then."

I ended the call. I would smoke that bitch's ass in a heartbeat, and not even think about it.

***

I called the police station. They told me to hold on, and just when I was ready to hang up the phone, the lady picked up and said, "Yes, Mrs. Cash, Detective Harris would like to speak with you in person."

"Is today a good day?"

"Hold on a second, let me check the calendar."

Sweets, what the fuck are you doing?

"Yes, you can come down here to the West building at 2:00 this afternoon."

Damn. It was already noon.

"Okay, I'll be there at two."

"I'll let him know that you are coming."

"Thank you."

***

Ced wanted to drive me, but I'd rather drive myself. I had to get my thoughts together, and I didn't want us to be seen together by those motherfucking devils. Police stations made me sick. Why the hell did they make places like that?

When I arrived, I text Ced to let him know I'd made it safely. Mr. Harris, or must I say, Detective Harris, was already waiting for me.

"You must be Ms. Cash?"

Motherfucker knew good and damn well he already looked me up, so he knew exactly who I was. I can play games too.

"Yes, and who are you?"

"I am Detective Harris."

"Well, nice to meet you."

"Likewise."

'I could tell that he was blown away by my looks because he just couldn't stop staring. Aside from a desk, two chairs, and a map of Lynchburg on the wall, the room was empty. I took a seat and waited. After about five minutes, he returned.

"Sorry about that. I had to get myself a cup of coffee. I didn't know if you would want any, so just to be on the safe side I brought a cup for you also."

"Thank you, but I don't drink coffee."

"Would, you like me to get you something else?"

"No, thank you. I'm not trying to be rude, but my daughter gets out of school at three and I have to pick her up."

"I understand. Well, your name has come up in an investigation, and I would like to ask you a few questions. I know you, Black, and Dimples go way back."

258

I didn't know why these motherfuckers always wanted to seem like they were down with us and they knew damn well we and them wasn't cool. My thoughts were killing me. *Play the game, Sweets. Play the game.*

"Yes, we're friends, more like sisters."

I wasn't giving any more information than I had to. He was gonna have to work for it.

"So I know this has to be hard for you and their families?"

"Yes, it sure is."

"Where were you on the night of Black's death?"

"I don't even know what night she was killed." I guess he thought I was stuck on stupid.

"Well, the autopsy says between Sunday night and Tuesday morning, so I need to know where you were on those days."

Easy, I think to myself.

"Sunday night I was at Buffalo Wild Wings on Ward's Road. Monday I was packing for my trip, to New York, and Tuesday I was in New York."

The detective looked like some shit out of the movies, and they all say the exact same thing. This dumbfounded, retarded motherfucker thought I was gonna tell on myself. He had me fucked up, I mean all the way up, and he needed to hurry the fuck up. "And do you have proof for those nights, Sweets?"

"Yes, I do and that's Ms. Cash to you." *Motherfucker, me and you ain't friends,* I thought. Just because I didn't say it didn't mean that I wasn't thinking it. I could tell he knew it.

"You can get the video from BBW, and check with the airline that I flew on. Don't mean to be rude, but you already know I have to get my daughter from school."

"Yes, I know you do, but I have one more question for you."

I wanted to just smoke his ass, right there, right then. Fuck all the questions.

"Why did you move, and where are you living at now?"

Motherfucker, that's two questions. "I moved because I wanted to, and I am living where I want to. You can take my phone number. Call me anytime and I'll show up. But aside from that, if I'm not under arrest for anything, my life is my own, and I'm allowed privacy. Is that correct?" *Don't get it fucked up. I know my rights.* I really wished I could say everything I was thinking.

"Yes, Ms. Cash, you are correct."

"Here is my number. Feel free to contact me if you need me."

"Thank you, Ms. Cash, but I must warn you the next time we meet probably won't be this lovely," he told me as he showed me the door. I wanted to smile, because I knew that I'd won that round, but I kept it to myself. As soon as I got to the car, I let out a sigh of relief. I refused to let them see me sweat. Something was up. I just had to put my finger on it, and once I did that, I knew I'd be able to fix it. This shit was getting out of hand, fast.

I texted Ced to let him know I'd be home soon. He texted back saying he was in a meeting. Next, I called Traymon.

"I'm gonna pick Beauty up from school," I said as soon as he answered his phone.

I missed my daughter. I wanted and needed her with me. She was my only peace of mind. She kept me sane and on track. I didn't know where I would be if it wasn't for her. I wanted her to know just how much I loved her, to show her just how much she meant to me.

At the end of the day, she was the only person that I had to be loyal to. I pulled up at her school and waited for her to come out.

Chapter 34
Family

She looked just like me, my image for sure.

"Beauty," I exclaimed as I squatted down so she could jump into my arms.

"Ma, you come to get me?"

"Yes, baby."

I wanted to break down and cry just holding my daughter and thinking about why I didn't have a mom. Fuck it. My heart was soft only for Beauty.

"We gonna go chill and have some fun, just you and me, ok?"

"Ok, ma, I'm ready."

We went to Chucky Cheese and the mall, where we got our nails and toes done before we did some shopping. Just me and my lil nigga having fun while blowing some money. On the way home she said, "Ma, put that Lil Boosie song on."

"Which one, Beauty?"

I was a Jeezy fan and she was a Boosie fan. Mane!

"Wipe me down."

I had to laugh because she had to brush her chest off while telling me that. I put it on for her, and she went ham singing Lil' Boosie's verse...

"B-O-O-S-I-E-B-A-D-A-Z-Z, that's me," she said, pointing to herself. When I said she was a little monster in the making, I ain't never lied. By the time we get home, her ass was out like light. Ced carried her into the house and took her into her room, where he put her to bed.

"Hey, baby," I greeted him when he came back downstairs.

"I miss you girl. How did things go today?"

"Just as planned, did you tell your peoples to handle that?"

"Yea, they changed the date and time on the video. You should already know   I'm on top of that. I ain't no slouch ass nigga. I'm a warrior, boo," he said as he pulled me into his arms for a kiss.

"I got you a gift, Mr. Warrior."

He smiled. "Oh yea? Let me find out you had a nigga on your mind."

Nigga, you know about my life, damn right I have you on my mind all the time, was what I thought to myself but, "Oh, believe me, you stay on it," was what I actually said out loud.

I had gotten got him a bracelet for his arm. Yea, he had a watch, but you could tell how jealous his right hand was, so I had to balance it out for him. That shit costed me twenty stacks. I wasn't balling for nothing.

"Baby, it goes perfect. Thank you."

"No problem at all. Every Boss deserves to shine, and as long as we together, I'm gonna make sure you glow all the time."

"Already."

He knew I meant every word I said.

"Tomorrow's Friday. How about you get your kids after school and bring them back here so we can enjoy the weekend together?" I asked.

"Yea, I can do that, Mrs. Williams."

***

I kept Beauty home from school the next day and let her roam the whole house. She loved her room so much she didn't want to leave it.

"Cobra comin' over later," I told her.

"For real, ma?"

"Yes, baby."

Beauty was so excited about seeing Cobra later, so we cooked dinner and waited for them-to come running through the door.

Can you say one happy family? We played every game you could think of. By 12:30 they all were fast asleep, Ced included, so I decided it was my time to go. Just as I was closing the door behind me, I heard Ced's voice.

"Make sure you come back.to me in one piece, Sweets."

I was dressed in all-black, so he knew the devil in me was ready to come out.

"Don't worry. I will."

Jamaica

Chapter 35
I'm Judging You

As I traveled up Timberlake Road, I realized I knew what had to be done. There was just no way around it.

Once I got to where I wanted to be, I noticed all the lights in the house were off. I didn't know why rich people who lived around other rich people hated locking their doors, but they did. I guess they figured no one needed to steal or kill because they had it all among themselves.

They never locked their door. It was always open. I turned the knob, and the lock was unlocked just like I figured it would be. The house was quiet. I knew my way around the house like I knew the back of my hand. This was not my first visit, but it would be my last.

As I climbed the stairs, I could hear someone snoring. They were sleeping. Either way, they were gonna stay asleep so it didn't matter. They were just gonna have a little red sauce to go with it.

I'd gotten my silencer on, and one was already in the head. My finger was just itching to pull the trigger. I could tell who was who by the way that they lay together. She had her head tucked under his chin. I figured I'd do him first. My itchy finger pulled the trigger twice. She must have felt the blood as it began to drip down the side of his head because she opened her eyes. She didn't scream or anything, but her eyes told it all. She was scared, and maybe she even knew why I was there. I told her anyway. I'd hate for her to die confused.

"I'm here to judge y'all. She was only a child. She did what she was told, and that killed her. She just ain't laying down."

I didn't give her a chance to say a word. Instead, I put her back to sleep and let myself out of the house.

On my drive back home, I felt better knowing those motherfuckers weren't breathing any more. I had to kill Dimples' so-called parents based on principle alone. They had cost Dimples so much. I knew I did her a favor, but now I needed her to resurface so I could finish what I'd started.

***

Ced was asleep on the sofa when I got back to the house. I went upstairs to check on the kids, and then I hit the shower. By the time I got out of the bathroom, Ced was in the bed.

"I hope I didn't take too long to get back to you."

"Naw, never. I'm glad you're back in one piece, because if one piece of this family is missing, then we ain't complete at all."

I loved that man. "Well, let me show you that I ain't goin' nowhere, baby."

We made love, sweet, sexy, juicy love, all the way into the early morning. By the time we got up, Christina had the other three kids at the table eating cereal. As the oldest child, she was definitely the most responsible. She was a good big sister, and they loved her.

After breakfast, Ced cut the grass, while the kids spent the day riding their bikes and playing outside. We fired the grill up for dinner, and after the kids ate and got their baths, I did everybody's hair, Ced included. Afterwards, we ate popcorn while we watched 'Fast and the Furious'. Around 11:30, I tucked them all into bed. Christina and Lil Ced had their own rooms, but Beauty and Cobra slept together. Those two were attached at the hip.

I went back downstairs to clean up. Ced was on his phone, doing what he did best, *handling business*. I cleaned the kitchen while he handled his business and played the Xbox 360.

"You know I ain't tryin' to leave, but I have somethin' that I really need to handle," I finally told him.

"Do you ever get tired?"

"No. Not when it come to my freedom. I'll never get tired."

"I understand, don't explain yourself, just…"

I cut him off because I knew what he was going to say.

"Make sure I come back in one piece."

"Yeah, you got it," he said as a smile broke across his face.

Jamaica

Chapter 36
Wrong Choice

I needed to pay a visit to Park Avenue. I had to see a nigga named Alphonso. He was Black's side meat, and since I now knew that Black and Dimples were sleeping together, I figured he may have been hitting them both off at the same time. Nasty bitches.

This nigga was on some late night shit, too. He didn't wanna go to sleep, because he was always thinking about the boys in blue. But he should have been thinking about the stickup boys. The police he couldn't beat, but he'd try his luck with those ski masked niggas.

I must've been my lucky day because that nigga was sleeping on the sofa with a blunt hanging out of his mouth. That was the reason I didn't do drugs. That shit just wasn't for me. I had to stay on point at all times, so drugs were out of the question for me.

He must have been cooking up because the kitchen window was wide open. Thank goodness he lived in the cut, too. That was even better. I climbed through the window while I kept my .45 on his ass. If he moved, I was touching him.

Yup, I was right. He'd just finished cooking up. Paper towels with crack were lined up all around the table. I walked over to the sofa, and just looked at him. He had to be 5'7" and around three hundred pounds solid. He had waves in his hair, and he was sharp from head to toe. He was so black he was purple like Barney. How could weed make a nigga not hear shit? I knew he was gonna feel that steel on his head.

"Sleep is for the weak, nigga," I yelled at him, expecting him to jump. But he didn't even open up his eyes, he just spoke.

"You better kill me, 'cause I ain't givin' up shit."

Another wanna be brave nigga. "How you figure?"

He opened his eyes to see my face. "Damn, Sweets. That's how we playin' now?"

I'd run into him on the streets before, spoke, and kept it moving. "You my lotto ticket and I'm gonna cash you in for a little change," I told him.

"This is a cold world, but I do wanna know why?"

"'Cause loyalty is a must. If I let you live, I know for a fact that you'll never let me live, nigga."

He tried to reach for the gun, but I rocked his ass to sleep. I searched his crib for almost a damn hour before I found the money in the fucking trash can under the trash.

He was a smart dead motherfucker.

I could feel sweat running down the crack of my ass, but once I glanced over at his leaking body, I felt at peace. Since I'd killed Black, I was assuming that Dimples had reached out to him and dropped a dime on me. I'd rather be good than dead. Damn sure wasn't trying to give a nigga a chance to come after me if I could hit him first.

I dumped the trash and used the bag to bag the money up. Then I threw some of the cooked crack all over the house so it would look like a drug deal gone wrong. I shot his ass one more time just because he didn't want me to go back to my daughter.

It is crazy how you know people, and just 'casue you know them, you have to suffer like them for their fucked up actions, I thought. Thanks to Black and Dimples, Alphonso was resting real good. It was a crazy fucking world.

Chapter 37
Questions

Sixty-four thousand dollars and five bricks. Shit, a nice little change. I gave the money to Ced, and the dope to Traymon. T was so happy he didn't even question me, but Ced did.

"What did I do to deserve this?"

"It's your world, baby," I said, using the same line on him that he used on me. My body count was getting off the chain because I was dropping them like flies. My heart was growing colder by the second, thanks to all the shit I'd gone through. My pockets, oh mane, they were looking beautiful, especially when I was pocketing everybody's money.

Lynchburg was off the fucking map right now. Bodies were coming up like flies from a pile of fresh shit. The city counselor Dick Duff had the nerve to get on TV with his cock sucking coworker, John Woody, and say, "We need to come together and find out who is responsible for all this blood. I promise you, when they are caught, they will never see the light of day again."

They were the original dick licking cocksuckers.

Aww, mane, I was so fucking scared. Ha, ha, that cracker truly thought his ass was the boss, huh? Imagine me being scared. As long as the sky was blue, my pockets were right, and my child was living, fuck the rest. At the end of the day, I was Sweets.

they say, "Hell hath no fury as a woman scorned." My heart had been scorned, so anyone who had anything to do with it had to pay, and I mean anyone. I'd rather die by the streets than live in a six by nine.

Months went by and not one case was solved. That just goes to show how much this world cared about them. *When you're dead and gone, that's it. Motherfuckers .move on with their lives, and the dead gotta fight their own case on judge-ment day,* I reasoned.

Chapter 38
Normal

I went back to being a full time mom again, not to one, but to four. Shit was crazy, but but I enjoyed those kids like they were actually mine. I would want Regina to treat Beauty like her own. My relationship with Ced was perfect. We didn't fight, and we didn't argue. We just kept it trill with one another to the fullest. When he went out to chill with his boys, I was cool with it because I trusted him. Like tonight, I waited up for him until 4am, but then I dozed the fuck off.

Eight in the morning and Ced was still a no show. Eight forty five, and he was pulling up in the driveway. The kids were upstairs playing and I was cleaning the kitchen when he walked through the door.

"Good mornin', beautiful."

"Good mornin', Ced. How was your night?"

He'd gone out with Clap to handle business. "Great, but I have to run somethin' by you."

I stopped doing what I was doing. "Go ahead, I'm all ears."

"So I'm at the bar with Clap, me and him just choppin' shit up when I see Regina and her friend. We pay them no mind, but next thing we know, they're walkin' in our direction. I keep talkin' to Clap. Regina and her friend come over to where we're at."

"And?" I was mad already.

"Baby, hold on. I'm gonna tell you the rest, just relax."

"Oh, I am relaxed," I said. *But I'm also super pissed,* I thought.

"She's like, 'how y'all doin'?' I ain't answer, so Clap speaks, sayin' we good and y'all? She says she's good but Ced, I'm talkin' to you. I look at the bitch, then I turn my head back to the bar, ignorin' her ass. Then she says, you need a real hood bitch in your life."

I was so hot steam was coming off of my feet because I was about to stomp that bitch wet.

"I wanted to smack the bitch, but I knew I wouldn't have made it home to you, so I got up and walked away. This joint has the nerve to grab me by my pants and say I can be your side bitch."

"Yeah." I was mad to the tenth power with a degree of 360.

"I told her, bitch, you got me fucked up. I wouldn't fuck you with someone else's dick. I have a real ass bitch, and don't ever touch me again, and then I walked off."

Before Ced could finish talking, I was on my way out the door. He didn't try to stop me. He knew better and I was glad he did.

Thank God, I didn't get pulled over because I know for a fact I was doing at least one hundred miles per hour in some places. I called T.

"Yo, I'm on my way."

"Okay:"

Six minutes later, I walked straight past Traymon at the door, no hello, no nothing. That bitch was in the kitchen. T was on my neck.

When she saw my face, she already knew what time it was. *Bop. Bop. Bop.*

I rocked that bitch with a fresh three-piece, and when she fell, I started kicking her ass.

"Bitch, you got me fucked up. You took my baby daddy, but I refuse to let you take this one. I will smoke your ass."

Traymon was in the middle of us at that point.

"What the fuck is goin' on, yo?" T asked as he faced me.

"That bitch right there ain't shit, and she better be thankful that it's your dick that's slidin' in her, 'cause you already know how I get down."

I walked out as I heard Traymon asking what the fuck that was all about.

Let her explain that shit to him, 'cause I didn't have the time, or the patience, but I knew that bitch had me fucked all the way up.

Ced didn't say shit when I walked through the door, but he made the mistake of laughing.

"You think this is a joke, Ced?"

"Naw, it ain't no joke, but who do you fear, Corona?"

"I fear God, but no humans, 'cause they bleed just like me. I promise you that bitch will never look at you again, much less speak, and if she decides to be superwoman 'cause she thinks she's brave enough, her ass won't live to tell about it."

"Thank you."

"Ced, ain't no need to thank me. That's my place and my job. A bitch or a nigga gets out of line, you should always run it by me, 'cause at the end of the day, it will be handled."

Jamaica

Chapter 39
Watch. Ride. Show.

Ced asked me to be his partner in business. At first, I felt a little hesitant. Me being the only female there was gonna be crazy. Some niggas didn't like to take orders from bitches at all, and I didn't want to be the one to break his shit up because I had my own shit going on. But he wanted me at his side so bad that I told him that I'd be happy to be his backbone.

He tried to school me on a few things, but I was already schooled. He put an ounce of cocaine in front of me and told me to cook it up. I did, and I got three extra grams back.

"Make that into fifty two grams," he told me.

I did that like it was nothing. Then he was amazed.

"Bring the thirty one grams back."

I did that, too.

"Where you learn to do that?"

"Ask no questions, Ced, 'cause I will tell you nothin' but the truth. Traymon. I used to watch him, and then I did it myself. If you want some fire ass crack, some shit that will have your phone jumpin' off the hook, I can do it. Say you know a nigga that you don't fuck with, but he needs some work like ASAP, I can bake his ass up too, in two different ways."

We both laughed.

"Damn, girl. What the fuck can you not do?"

"It's nothin' that I've tried that I can't do." I smile at him. Then it was my turn to school his ass for a minute. "First of all, there is always a snitch in a crew. You'll never know until shit hits the fan, then the shit gets to stinkin', so be on the lookout. I know you know your niggas, but pay close attention to them, they'll rotate."

His ears were taking in everything that I was saying, and he hadn't even blinked. I had his full attention.

"Then there's always one nigga who wants to take your place. Loyalty don't last forever unless they were born with it. That one hater can put a bug on you to the others. Next thing you know, it's them against you. I am here with you and for you. Four eyes are always better than two. Your crew probably thinks I don't know shit, so we gonna keep it like that."

"Damn," he said. He was blown away.

I'd gotten him stuck, but I needed him alert.

"Ced, always expect the unexpected 'cause no one is to be slept on"

He said his team was in check, but I wanted to make sure my damn self, so I took it upon myself to do a little private investigating, since my freedom was at risk. I was unwilling to leave my daughter. Hell naw. My instinct told me to search, and I was ready because it had never told me wrong. Ced had to understand that what I was doing was for us and our children.

I had a bad vibe about a nigga on the team named Worm, so I followed him around for a while. On the third day, the nigga got pull over by the boys in blue on Polk Street. I parked in the church parking lot nearby so I could watch what happened.

They had police dogs all around his car barking their asses off. They cuffed Worm and put him in the back of one of the police cars. Then they ripped Worm's car completely up until they found what they were looking for. Whatever they found, they put it in a brown bag. They drove away with Worm in their car. One of the police officers drove Worm's car away like nothing even happened.

Explaining the situation to Ced was hard.

"That nigga ain't gonna crumble." He sounded so certain.

"Shit, we'll find out, but I have a bad vibe about this nigga."

Ced was listening to me, but I knew he was thinking, too. "I hope he ain't tellin', but if he is, I'm gonna mute him."

The very next day, Ced called an emergency meeting to see how everyone was doing and everyone was there except for Christopher Lee Woodson, aka Worm.

"Loyalty is a code that should never be broken, no matter what situation you are in. When you die, your reputation lives on."

Out of the blue, Worm walked through the door. Ced continued his speech. If I was drowning, I would never pull any of y'all under, *never*. I hope the feelin' is mutual."

Worm took a seat by the door. I'd gathered basic info on him already. He was 5'7", 260 pounds, but for a big nigga, he had a nice little swag. He had a honey brown complexion, short curly hair, gray eyes, and a nice smile. He had two baby ma's and four kids, two boys and two girls. He seemed like an overall okay type of nigga. Clap interrupted Ced to ask Worm a question.

"Damn, nigga. Where you been at? I tried callin' you last night, but you never answered. I left you the code lettin' you know that we had a meetin' today."

Ced had already put the team on to Worm. Little did he know that I had seen the entire show.

"I know, yo. Me and shawty got into it real bad and shit, so I just cut my phone off and chilled," Worm answered.

"That's all that happened yesterday, Worm?" Ced questioned him.

"Yeah."

It was crazy to me how the nigga was gonna sit right there and lie like nothing happened. I knew for a fact that he was working after that.

Ced ended the meeting by telling his crew to chill out. Then he walked over to Worm and whispered something in his ear. Ced nodded his head at me.

"Drive up to Liberty Mountain," Ced told Worm once we were all seated in Worm's car.

I hoped he wasn't thinking to do nothing crazy. He'd better relax and do as he was told, or I'd send his thoughts back.

Dumb as dirt, nigga.

I was in the backseat and Ced was riding shotgun.

Silence.

I'd been ready to smoke that nigga since he walked through the door in the meeting, but naw, Ced seemed like he wanted to let him tell his side. When we got to the top of the mountain, Ced told him to turn on Rucker Fin Road and park under the tree. As soon as we were parked, Ced started talking.

"You know loyalty is all I live by in this game. Trust is somethin' that I give so that I can receive it, 'cause betrayal is nowhere in my lifetime."

Ced was talking way too much.

"Fuck that," I said. I shot that nigga in the back of the head, throwing his brains and head juices everywhere as he slumped over the steering wheel.

"Damn, Sweets. I wasn't even done talkin'."

"Baby, don't worry. He got the picture."

We drug his ass out of the car, and put him in the ground. The hole was dug last night. Too bad Worm didn't know it was for him. After we covered it back up, I emptied the .45 into the ground.

"I hate a fuckin' snitch!"

Ced just looked at me with one eyebrow cocked up a little, so spoke my mind.

"I mean, he wanted us to drown."

We cleaned the car up. Mr. Clean himself had nothing on us. Once that was handled, we drove the car to Clap's crib to get his truck so we could go trash Worm's car.

I drove Clap's truck, following Ced in Worm's ride. All the way to the chop shop, all I could think about was how I came to be caught up in this lifestyle. I hustled hard to get out of this game alive and still have my freedom, but I wondered if I'd be able to do that successfully. Yes, I was glad that I had Ced, but I was not a woman who was in need of a man, and I never had been. I was a woman that a man was in need of, but the two of us together were unbreakable, and unbelievable, because we knew way too much about each other. Physically and emotionally I was stable, but mentally, I was all fucked up, and I knew it. Too much time on my hands had gotten me thinking all kinds of shit, real crazy shit.

I watched Ced talk to dude about the car, and then he paid him to burn and crush it. It had been a productive day. We'd found and killed the snake before he even had a chance to attack. I couldn't get any better than that.

Jamaica

Chapter 40
Real Recognize Real

Business was good, great if you asked me. Everyone was playing their part. All the work in the city was coming from *our teams*. We were getting nothing but love and respect. Motherfuckers knew if they tried to disrespect us in anyway, they'd be handled, so they stayed in their own lane.

Traymon had finally gotten his money up, but he was still fucking with that bitch Regina. I guess she was his main joint because I'd seen him with a super high yellow skinny bone bitch named Shaquana.

I'd heard through the grapevine that old girl was a ho. every nigga and their daddy had hit that shit. She had hood pussy, no walls in that shit at all. What the fuck was he doing with a bitch like that? She must've been licking his ass for real. I had to give it to him though, his little side of town was on point. He was the man around the Bridge. But if the nigga wasn't my sperm donor, I would've touched his ass my damn self.

"Damn, nigga. You eating heavy around here, huh?" I asked him.

"Naw, I'm just trying to get to where you at."

"Shit, I'm broke, struggling to see tomorrow, and just tryin' to survive. You know the world we livin' in, so I'm just livin' it one day at a time."

"You really gonna start a family with that nigga, Sweets?"

That question came out of nowhere. Now I was just looking him up and down. Damn, we would have been one hell of a couple, but he hadn't wanted that. He gave me a baby, and then ran off to that other bitch.

"Let me worry about that. My life ain't your business."

"You right. I have enough problems in my life now. Regina hollerin' how she thinks she pregnant, and even that is too much for me to handle right now."

Pregnant? Mane, he had just crushed my feelings to the dirt, but refused to let him see it. That was supposed to be our city together, and I secretly wished it was just for Beauty's sake. Having us under the same roof would make her real fucking happy. The reality was that I'd never be able to forget his actions, even though I'd forgiven him on the strength of Beauty.

"Damn. You that lucky nigga then."

He wanted a reaction, and I knew it. Instead, I gave him a compliment, "You know that nigga Jay comes home in less than a year?" I changed the subject.

"Yeah, I heard. The question is, how you gonna handle that?"

"For me to know and for you to find out, nigga."

I brought him what he wanted, four bricks. I handed it over, got in my car, and drove away. I couldn't help but think about how things were gonna turn out because, truth be told, I knew Jay wasn't to be played with, but shit, there was no need to stop living my life either. Who the fuck was Jay?

"Nobody," I told myself out loud.

He was just another nigga who could be touched.

Chapter 41
Put On

I put Ced on just to keep him updated because I didn't want him in the dark. He was always gonna know first, no matter if it hurt or not.

"Baby, I'm glad you tellin' me this, but to be honest, I am not scared of that nigga."

I know he meant what he said. Our words were all we had, so if we said something, then we had to carry it out.

"By the way," he said, "My father comes home tomorrow."

I was glad he never got the chance to meet my father in person. Fuck that dead piece of shit.

"Hell yeah, I'm so happy for you. I'm excited 'cause I finally get the chance to meet him."

"I got him an apartment over there on Old Forest Road. Plus I have somebody doin' some shoppin' for him. I'm givin' him some bread, so he can be straight for a minute."

"That's what's up. At least you have him back in your life now." *Damn. What the fuck? I have no mother, no father; my only brother that loved me is gone. Beauty is all I have of my blood, I sadly recalled.*

"Yeah, I'm glad he's finally comin' home."

"Do you think he'll wanna take the business back over?"

His body was relaxed and he continued to rub my feet, not missing a spot.

"I don't know, but if he wants it back, he can have it. I ended up with what I wanted."

"And what is that Mr. Williams?" *Being a fucking multimillionaire,* I was thinking.

He smiled and my heart jumped.

"You. I got the best gift ever in this game."

And my heart beat overtime from joy.

That night, the sex was amazing. I knew life couldn't get any better than that.

Chapter 42
Home with Drama

Ced's father was a clown, just funny as hell, and they looked nothing alike. I could tell that time had turned him into an old man fast. But gray hair aside, he was a handsome man.

"Damn, boy. I left you with no kids. Come home and you got three and a model on your arm. I raised you right, I see," he said, smiling at his son.

"Glad you'll be able to enjoy your grandkids and your freedom. I want you to be a part of my wedding also," Ced told him.

"Congrats to you, my son's sweet lady."

"Thank you, Mr. Williams."

"No need for mister, you call me Steven. We're family now."

"Thank you for your blessin', it means a lot to us," I told him.

Ced wasted no time jumping back in.

"Yeah, dad, thanks. I wish mom was here to see it for herself, but I know she's lookin' down on me smilin'." The pain in Ced's voice said it all. He missed his mom.

I knew my father was looking up because he was damn sure in hell, but I didn't miss that motherfucker. I knew Ced was missing his mom though.

She was his best friend, and he was her only child.

"Look, Cedrick, I have somethin' very important to talk to you about. I can't keep it a secret any longer, 'cause it's goin' to eat me alive," Steven said.

What the fuck? Now he wanted his business back?

"So, Sweets, could you please excuse us?" Steven asked me.

I was ready to walk away, but Ced spoke up.

"Whatever you have to say, you can say it in front of her. We don't hold nothin' from each other."

He wrapped his arm around my lower back.

I looked at him and smiled. I was falling in love with him more and more. For him to stand up to his father like that for me, even on something little like that, showed me everything. Thank God he made me stay because I wanted to know. It sounded serious.

"Cedrick, I have another son."

My mouth dropped open. What the fuck? I looked at Ced and he had his poker face on, but he was tapping his right foot hard against the carpet.

Silence.

I breathed in and out slowly just to make sure I didn't pass out from shock.

More silence.

Mane, did I hear what I think he said?

"What?" Ced said, backing up a little from me. His eyes were blood shot red. Was I gonna see his fucked up side right there, right then? "Show me. Show me," I wanted to scream out, but Steven spoke up.

"Just listen, son, let me explain. Your mom wanted me to tell you a long time ago, but I couldn't. I ran into him in prison, and I knew I had to come clean with you."

That man had some fucking nerve. All I could do was be quiet, but was prepared to fire off if Ced wanted me to.

"You want me to stand here and listen to how you disrespected my mother? You had another child and say she is the only woman to possess your heart. But let me guess, not your dick? Listen to how that shit sounds. I know she begged you to tell me, but you didn't."

Ced was fuming. This was some real Jerry Springer mixed with Maury Povich shit, for real.

"Smoke his ass, Sweets, and don't let him cause Ced any-more hurt." That fucking red devil on my shoulder wouldn't stop screaming in my ear.

"I did your mother wrong, but she forgave me and stayed with me. She loved me, and I loved her back, 'cause she was a real woman, the realest woman God ever created. It kills me every day to know that because of my ways, she died."

Ced stepped toward his father and I prepared myself for the unexpected.

Silence.

"You damn fuckin' right. You killed my mother before her time. The love from her heart ate away at her soul, and because of that she ain't here."

I walked over to Ced to try to calm him down. "Baby, let's go," I told him.

"Shoot his ass Sweets," that fucking devil said again.

"Naw, fuck that. He's gonna hear what I have to say. You ain't even my father no more. You Steven to me. If you want the game back, you better get to lookin' for a team, and a new contact somewhere else. You are not gettin' that shit that I've lifted up. And you better move to a different state, 'cause Virginia is mines." He gave his father the business alright.

I smiled as I touched my strap behind my back.

"Boy, you don't scare me. I brought you into this world, and I'll take you out if I want to."

Not on my watch, I was sure of it.

Now Ced was face to face, nose to nose, with the man he called Steven.

Steven didn't even move. He seemed ready for whatever.

"Ma gave birth to me. She raised me. You just the water that helped her egg to hatch. You put no fear in my heart. And if I die today, I'll die a real nigga, somethin' you can never be.

and when I go, you better believe you goin' too. Sweets, let's go."

And I refused to let Ced die on my watch. Damn, how could everything turn upside down just like that?

"And the money that's in the room, just look at it as a gift from my mother, 'cause if it wasn't for her, your ass wouldn't get shit," he said to his father, and we walked through the door.

"Sweets, turn around and smoke that nigga," that fucking red devil urged.

Damn. That was all I could say. Damn.

"Sweets, you remind me so much of my mom. You're as strong as she used to be and you go just as hard as she did. She killed every nigga who told on my dad herself. I know for a fact that she is happy that you're in my life."

I smiled, even though I was lost in my thoughts. It was crazy. I felt closer to him now than ever.

"We would have been a hell of a team if she was alive." Mane, nobody would have been able to stop us.

"You damn right," he said, smiling broadly.

"Well, you and your brother will probably get along. See how shit works out and try to forgive your father. You have to remember we're humans, and we're far from perfect. Everyone makes mistakes. We just have to make sure they don't become our habits."

There I was speaking like I had forgiven those who hurt me. Oh well, at least I was telling him.

"You right, Corona,"

"Whatever you decide to do, Ced, I'm down to ride," I told him and he knew I meant it. I was riding till the wheels fell off and even when they were off, I was still riding.

"Oh, I already know. You stay ready, and I love that about you. I could never go worng with you by my side."

"Never." I couldn't hurt that nigga. Cross over on him? *Never.* And I damn sure wasn't gonna let anyone else hurt him. So, that shit his father had to say, I took it personal because I'd ride on his bitch ass.

When we got into the car, he broke down and cried. He needed me more than anything, and I wanted to let him know I was truly there for him. Right then, blood couldn't have made us any closer.

"Baby, if you want me to handle him, just say the word."

"Corona, I love you girl. You are one of the realest."

"Remember, real live trill ass niggas don't cry."

He smiled through his tears.

"Cryin' is good for the soul, and I miss my mom to the fullest. My dad couldn't do any wrong in my mom's eyes. Even when he used to beat her, she stayed with him. When he cheated, she stayed right there with him, playin' the scene like a real woman. When he got on drugs real bad, she took up the slack and took control. She found my dad a connect. She got him clean, and put him on top. But look how he repaid her."

"Damn. That is some cold ass shit for real."

This was proof that men needed women. This was supposed to be a woman's world.

"How about a small vacation, just us and the kids?" I suggested.

"Where ever you wanna go, let's go."

I chose Atlanta.

***

Atlanta was beautiful. Between there and New York, I didn't know which city was better. We stayed in Atlanta for an entire week, and the kids were so spoiled it was a shame. Between me and Ced, they got whatever they wanted.

Growing up, I didn't have shit. It hurt me to my heart to know that I had parents who just didn't give a fuck. Whenever I did run across my mother, boy oh boy, did I have a surprise for her. My past alone ate me alive daily, that was why my daughter would always have everything she needed.

Cedrick spoiled me, treated me like I was a queen, so I spoiled him back, and treated him like the king that he was.

On the way back to Virginia, Beauty told me, "Ma, when I get older, I wanna be just like you."

I wanted to tell her no, but how could I tell my child not to be like me? So I just told her, "I'll teach you whatever you need to know, baby."

Yea, and that meant pulling the trigger.

Chapter 43
No Visitors Allowed

Ced had put Clap, his right hand man, in charge while we were out of town.

"Mane, business is slow. Word around is that four Philly niggas visitin'," Clap told us over dinner to catch us up on everything.

"What's the word?" I asked.

"They don't have what we have. They got something better."

"Better?" Ced asked.

"Yea, they moving that PCP, also known as boat. Even the damn crack-heads smoking that shit, and let's not talk about the local small-time drug dealers."

"Word?" Ced asked.

"Word," Clap assured him.

"So what's the deal with them?" I asked.

"They getting mad money and they stuntin' in our city right in our face like this their shit. All up in Phase 2 every night like they ready to take over Lynchburg."

"No visitors allowed. No niggas disrespect our foundation. Ced was angry about the situation, but it was okay.

"I have a plan," I said.

***

Phase 2 on Wednesday night was wack. But with me in it, it was a different story. Dressed in some 8732 jeans and shirt with some J's, all I was doing was chilling. No need for attention, because I was just coming in and going out.

I saw my targets as soon as I walked through the front door. I could always tell out-of-town niggas because they tried to stunt on the niggas of that city.

Two with braids, one with shoulder-length dreads, and the other was rocking waves. I bet the main nigga of the crew was the one with the waves because all six eyes were eating up what he was saying. As I said, I'd just gone to see. Now that I had seen what I wanted, it was time for me to leave.

***

It was Friday night and Phase 2 was packed from front to back. Ced, Clap, and Trappa were already in.

As I walked through the door, all heads turned to look at me. I saw Ced and the crew. Hands down, I was the shit in an all-black mesh paneled knitted top by Alexander Wang with a black and gold Moschino patent leather belt that hugged my waist perfectly and a Marc Jacobs skirt, all-white denim mini, with black red bottoms on my feet. Bitches were hating, knowing I was walking around with all that money on my body, and niggas wanted a taste.

I knew Ced was watching all those other niggas watch me, and knowing that I belonged to him made him feel like a king.

As I got closer to the bar, I saw my visitors sitting in their favorite spot. I ordered a Jamaican Lizard and watched the bartender mix my drink.

"Excuse me, sexy, can I buy that for you?"

I didn't even turn around to answer whoever the hell it was. "No, thank you," I declined. But I could tell that the person was still standing there waiting for me to face them.

As I turned around with my drink in my hand, I could see Ced watching me. Just as I said, out of town niggas wanted everything in another town.

"Excuse me, please," I said to the man standing in front of me, blocking my path.

"A beautiful woman like you shouldn't be in a place like this."

This nigga's acting like he knows me. "Really? You shouldn't be in someone else's city tryin' to start a war."

"Excuse me?"

Now I had his full attention, so I was going in for the kill. "I am asking you nicely to take your crew back to Philly." My head tilted to the right as my fingers tapped the drink in my hand. My voice was level, but it expressed my attitude clearly.

"Do I know you?" he asked, cutting me off.

Silence.

I dropped my head and looked at his feet, and then worked my eyes back up to his. I straightened my head and stepped closer to him, leaning over to his left ear. I could see both the table with the Philly niggas and Ced with his crew from where I stood.

"No, you don't, but I know you very well. This is not your turf and you're fucking up my business. Once again, I am askin' you in a very nice manner to pack your things and leave." I stepped back so I could see his face.

He smiled. He had a missing front tooth.

"Orders comin' from a woman? I pay those no mind. You need to be at home watching TV with some kids."

Silence.

My fingers were twitching overtime. I smiled at him and shook my head.

"Well, this is my order for you. You have forty-eight hours to leave my city." My fingers were still tapping on my cup.

"If I don't?" His smile was gone.

That nigga really didn't know who he was fucking with. He should never judge a book by its cover.

"I'll show you that I am not a woman who needs to be in front of a TV with some kids. Now can you get out of my way?" My temper was up and all I wanted to do was smoke his ass right there, but I knew that was not the place.

He moved and I walked towards the dance floor with my drink in my hand, but my fingers continued to jump. Bitch ass nigga. I knew for a fact that he'd never had a woman talk to him like that before, because his eyes 'bout popped out their sockets.

No need for attention, the entire Philly table watched my every step, and Ced was watching them. I drank my Lizard and exited the building.

***

"Damn, T, what's wrong with you?"

I knew the nigga could hear me because he was looking dead at me. His body was as straight as an arrow.

"T,   what's wrong with you?" I asked him again as I waved my hand in front of his face.

Silence.

He and a couple of his boys were posted up on Holland Street. Those niggas were looking funny and even acting funny. One of the niggas was just staring at the sky.

"Why do you look like a zombie?"

I'd never seen no shit like this before, so I rubbed my eyes to make sure that I was looking at Traymon.

"Baby... ma... you... beautiful."

What the fuck was going on with him? His mouth dripped water as he spoke. He looked over at his boys in super slow motion, lifted his left hand, and waved for someone from across the street to come there.

A short, light skinned dude walked over.

"Baby... ma... this... my... nigga... BU..." he said after dude had been standing there for about thirty seconds.

BU, I'd heard that name before, but where?

BU extended his hand to shake mine. "Nice to meet you," I said.

That name, I knew that name.

"Likewise, heard nothing but good things about you. Sorry we have to link up like this, 'cause this nigga out here tripping," he said, pointing to Traymon.

Shit, the rest of those niggas were tripping too. The other nigga was taking off his clothes as slow as a snail. I was curious to know what he was talking about.

"What do you mean?" My eyes were still focusing on Traymon as his mouth continued leaking water. Soon there was gonna be a puddle.

"This nigga is wet."

I was brought back to BU by his words. "Wet?" I was lost as fuck.

"Yea, he smoking that boat."

Please tell me it's not true. My head dropped from shame.

"What the fuck?" I said out loud. BU jumped. "Nigga ain't living right."

"Same thing I said, too."

I knew what drugs could do. I'd seen it destroy my father's life. Damn, those Philly niggas had come down here, and now my baby daddy's a boat head? Oh hell no.

I looked T up and down, shook my fucking head, and walked off towards my car, feeling sick, sick because Beauty was gonna be upset. I had to tell her before someone else did. How could he choose a drug like that to do?

As I got in the car, I called Ced.

"Babe, you won't believe this shit."

"What?"

Silence.

I breathed in and out. "Traymon's fucking smoking boat."

I hoped Ced didn't hear the hurt in my voice, but that hurt was for Beauty.

"How you figure?" he asked with no emotion.

I shook my head as a tear rolled down my face. I was hurting because this was gonna hurt my daughter. "His home-boy, BU, told me."

"BU? Describe him to me, Sweets."

Was the volume up or was Ced's voice raised? "Light skin, short, has a scar on the left side of the bottom of his chin."

"Where you at?" he sighed heavily into the phone.

"I am on Holland Street. Why? What's goin' on, Ced?" Now I was trying to get to my best friend, aka my gun, that was in the glove box. Something was wrong. I could hear it in his voice.

"Get away. That's the same nigga that shot Clap up," he screamed into the phone. I knew I had heard that name before.

"Say no more," I told Ced and ended the call. I was not getting away before I got this nigga's info so I could holla at him in person.

I rolled my window down and called BU. As I watched him walk over to me, I could tell Clap was gonna love this.

"What's up, ma?"

"Wait until you see," I wanted to tell him.

"What's your number so we can vibe?"

"434-907-9807."

"Rite, I got you," I told him as I locked his number into my phone. *Don't worry, I got you alright. Real bitches do real things.*

Twenty-four hours left and those Philly niggas were still in the Burg. I knew exactly where they were laying their heads, so I was a step ahead of them thanks to the streets. Since I showed the streets love, the streets always showed love back, especially when out-of-towners were trying to take over.

I had called BU and told him to meet me over at Peekview Park off Old Forest Road at 7pm. I was dressed in all black, so it was obvious what I was about to do. It started getting dark around five, so by seven, I was invisible to the naked eye.

He called to see which side of the park I was on.

"Yo, ma, where you at?"

"By the basketball court." I'd been there an entire hour early because that was how I rolled.

"Damn, you out here in the pitch black dark with black on?" he asked when he finally noticed me.

Just knowing that his life was about to end put a smile on my face. But deep down inside, I was mad because I was not the one doing it.

"Black keeps me warm 'cause I'm always cold." The look on his face says he was confused.

Fuck it, he would figure it all out soon enough.

"Damn, home-boy," Clap said from behind him.

I saw fear settle into the lines of BU's face. I was wondering if he knew or remembered Clap's voice?

"Mane, it wasn't supposed to be like this, huh?" Clap asked him as he stepped in front of him.

BU was not even strapped. What the fuck?

BU was in such a deep state of shock that he couldn't even speak. That was why it was good to always keep your laundry clean. That was one body I would not add to my belt because I knew Clap wanted to handle it himself.

I walked away and left him to his business.

Bop. Bop. Bop.

I hoped that they were straight head shots. That was the only thing that would keep a nigga from speaking.

***

Time waits for no man. Fuck giving those Philly niggas forty-eight hours to leave my city. I gave them an option and enough time, but they refused to follow orders. So I had to show them just who the *boss* really was.

1927 Lakeside Drive. It was a trailer park out in the cut, all the way in the back. I was given a heads up by one of Ced's people that the Philly crew liked to keep a member posted in the car as a lookout. It was good to know.

He didn't see or hear me coming. Who would at three in the morning when they were already sleeping? The window was down. His seat was leaned back and one of his feet was hanging out the window.

Bop. Bop.

Straight to the dome. I was not there to play games, or even watch the after effects. That night I was carrying my P89 with an extra 17-shot extender clip. I turned the knob on the mobile home's door. Bing. It was unlocked. As I put my head inside, I saw a nigga on the sofa fast asleep with his forearm over his eyes.

Bop. Bop. Bop.

Straight fucking head shots. The fitted hat he had on flew off. Two down.

I moved my way around the place like I'd been living there. Fuck it, I might as well. I heard the muffled sounds of someone singing and water running. At three in the morning, one of these niggas is showering. What the fuck? The door was cracked so I gently pushed it open some more. The shower curtain was clear and gave me a good view. He had his head soaped up.

Bop. Bop.

Head shots. His body dropped. I walked over and yanked the curtain open just to make sure I hit. I let two more go into his body.

Bop. Bop.

Where the fuck was the other nigga at? He couldn't be far. He was not in the kitchen, so I kept moving. I opened the first door to my left real slowly, and there he was. I watched him for a second before I shot the lamp off the nightstand to wake him up. He sat straight up in bed. He tried to let his hand slide under his pillow but I stopped him by shooting him in the upper body.

He hollered out in pain. Bullets could make the hardest nigga scream like a bitch giving birth.

"All I asked you to do was to leave my town, but you refused." A hard head makes a bloody mess.

"Shawty, my forty-eight hours isn't up."

Who the fuck did he think he was talking to? "On my clock it is." Niggas played way too many games. "And by the way, I don't need to be sittin' in front of no TV, especially when I have a job to do."

There was no need to hear his comment. He should have listened to me from the start.

Bop. Bop. Bop. Bop.

All those niggas had to do was take their asses back to Philly, but naw. The so-called *boss* refused to listen to a bitch like me. That was a mistake he wouldn't make twice.

Jamaica

Chapter 44
I'm Just Too Nice

Ced woke me up with the high ass volume on the TV. I rubbed my eyes, adjusting them to the light from the screen.

"Neighbors this morning found bloody water in their driveway when they went to get their paper. The police were called to the scene, and they found three males inside of 1927 shot to death. There was another male in the car that sat in the driveway, also shot to death. No witnesses have yet to come forward, nor family members to claim their loved ones. This is a very sad story," the anchor lady reported.

"No niggas or bitches are gonna disrespect my man and think I ain't gonna check them. I'm just so nice when it comes to you, Mr. Cedrick Williams," I told him before rolling over and going back to sleep. Sleep may be for the weak, but I needed my beauty rest.

***

Everything was going well for us. The money practically counted itself, and we were just living. Traymon and I were beefing hard because half the day that nigga was high on boat, and the other half he was trying to track it down so he could get high again.

So instead of Beauty staying with him, I'd been letting her spend time with her grandmother, Bella. She enjoyed being over there because Bella had her other grandkids there. When I needed a babysitter for Beauty, Bella's door was always open.

Traymon called to check on her, but only every so often because he had found a new baby. Now the love of his life was *boat*.

That shit smelled just like death. He was dipping his weed and cigarettes and then smoking it while it was wet. Sooner or later, his ass was gonna be smoking crack. I knew for a fact that nigga wasn't getting shit else from me for free. He had money to buy boat, he better have money to buy work and whatever else he needed. I was gonna treat his ass just like any other nigga from here on out.

Chapter 45
Time Stopped
Nine months later...

Ced and his dad were on okay terms. They were trying to make their relationship work, and I was super proud of them both. I was a full-time mom, and I was loving it because I was the queen of my kingdom. Just don't push me because the killer in me was only sleeping.

Steven invited us over to his place so Ced could meet his stepbrother. I was excited for them because, truth be told, I didn't want to kill anyone in their family. Ced dropped his kids off at their mother's house, and I dropped Beauty off at Bella's for the night.

***

I was dressed in all-black, but no, killing was not on my mind. Once we arrived at Steven's house, I told Ced to go on in because I wanted to check on Beauty before she went to sleep.

"Don't make me come look for you."

"Just make sure you leave the door unlocked for me, Ced."

"You know I will."

He kissed me and got out of the car. I called Bella's phone and talked to Beauty for a few minutes. Just hearing her voice put me at ease. I knew I had to get out of this lifestyle because Beauty was my world, and I wanted to see her live a beautiful life.

As I opened the door and walked into the house, everything sounded peaceful and it seemed like everyone was getting along. I was so glad to hear them all talking. I closed the door and headed to where they were.

Time stopped when I saw Jay's face.

I heard the explosion first, then the pain in my chest. It felt like my heart had stopped beating and it scared me. Everything went black, but I heard Ced's voice.

"No. Baby, no."

I couldn't even open my eyes.

"Welcome to Street Heaven, Sweets," said a loud booming voice.

No. This can't be happening to me. I'm tripping. I am tripping really hard.

Beep. Beep. Beep.

Damn.

Beauty. Beauty. Her face was fading in and out.

Beep. Beep.

No, I am not ready.

Beep.

To Be Continued...
Lay It Down 2
Coming Soon

Coming Soon From Lock Down Publications

RESTRAINING ORDER

By **CA$H & COFFEE**

GANGSTA SHYT

By **CATO**

GANGSTA CITY **II**

By **Teddy Duke**

BLOOD OF A BOSS **III**

By **Askari**

SHE DON'T DESERVE THE DICK

SILVER PLATTER HOE **III**

By **Reds Johnson**

BROOKLYN ON LOCK **III**

By **Sonovia Alexander**

THE STREETS BLEED MURDER **III**

By **Jerry Jackson**

CONFESSIONS OF A DOPEMAN'S DAUGHTER **III**

By **Rasstrina**

NEVER LOVE AGAIN **II**

WHAT ABOUT US **III**

By **Kim Kaye**

A GANGSTER'S REVENGE **III**

By **Aryanna**

GIVE ME THE REASON **II**

By **Coco Amoure**

LAY IT DOWN **II**

By **Jamaica**

<u>Available Now</u>

LOVE KNOWS NO BOUNDARIES **I II & III**

By **Coffee**

SILVER PLATTER HOE **I & II**

HONEY DIPP **I & II**

CLOSED LEGS DON'T GET FED **I & II**

A BITCH NAMED KOCAINE

NEVER TRUST A RATCHET BITCH **I & II**

By **Reds Johnson**

A DANGEROUS LOVE **I, II, III, IV, V, VI, VII**

By **J Peach**

CUM FOR ME

An **LDP Erotica Collaboration**

A GANGSTER'S REVENGE **I & II**

By **Aryanna**

WHAT ABOUT US **I & II**

NEVER LOVE AGAIN

By **Kim Kaye**

THE KING CARTEL **I, II & III**

By **Frank Gresham**

BLOOD OF A BOSS **I & II**

By **Askari**

THE DEVIL WEARS TIMBS **I, II & III**

BURY ME A G **I II & III**

By **Tranay Adams**

THESE NIGGAS AIN'T LOYAL **I, II & III**

By **Nikki Tee**

THE STREETS BLEED MURDER **I & II**

By **Jerry Jackson**

DIRTY LICKS

By **Peter Mack**

THE ULTIMATE BETRAYAL

By **Phoenix**

BROOKLYN ON LOCK **I & II**

By **Sonovia Alexander**

DON'T FU#K WITH MY HEART **I & II**

By **Linnea**

BOSS'N UP **I & II**

By **Royal Nicole**

LOYALTY IS BLIND

By **Kenneth Chisholm**

I LOVE YOU TO DEATH **II**

By Destiny J

<u>BOOKS BY LDP'S CEO, CA$H</u>

TRUST NO MAN

TRUST NO MAN 2

TRUST NO MAN 3

BONDED BY BLOOD

SHORTY GOT A THUG

A DIRTY SOUTH LOVE

THUGS CRY

THUGS CRY 2

TRUST NO BITCH

TRUST NO BITCH 2

TRUST NO BITCH 3

TIL MY CASKET DROPS

Coming Soon

TRUST NO BITCH (KIAM EYEZ' STORY)

THUGS CRY 3

BONDED BY BLOOD 2

RESTRANING ORDER